Christine Anderson grew up in Northern Ireland but has spent many years living in Warwickshire, the Southwest of England and now resides in the Northwest. She spends her time either ensconced in a book, walking miles every day along the coastline or marvelling at the beauty of the Lake District. When she is not enjoying time with her family and beloved grandchildren, she likes nothing better than to while away the hours with a blank canvas and her paintbrushes.

I Remember You...

Christine Anderson

I Remember You...

Vanguard Press

VANGUARD PAPERBACK

© Copyright 2024
Christine Anderson

The right of Christine Anderson to be identified as author of this work has been asserted by her in accordance with the Copyright, Designs and Patents Act 1988.

All Rights Reserved

No reproduction, copy or transmission of this publication may be made without written permission.
No paragraph of this publication may be reproduced, copied or transmitted save with the written permission of the publisher, or in accordance with the provisions of the Copyright Act 1956 (as amended).

Any person who commits any unauthorised act in relation to this publication may be liable to criminal prosecution and civil claims for damages.

A CIP catalogue record for this title is available from the British Library.

ISBN 978 1 80016 980 7

This is a work of fiction. Names, characters, businesses, places, events and incidents are either the product of the author's imagination or used in a fictitious manner. Any resemblance to actual persons, living or dead, or actual events is purely coincidental.

*Vanguard Press is an imprint of
Pegasus Elliot Mackenzie Publishers Ltd.*
www.pegasuspublishers.com

First Published in 2024

**Vanguard Press
Sheraton House Castle Park
Cambridge England**

Printed & Bound in Great Britain

To my family for their love and support and for those much-loved family members who are no longer with us.

My grateful thanks to my family and friends who have bolstered my confidence in my ability to write this story, especially my sister Jacqueline and my niece Holly, who encouraged me in the early stages, reading through endless drafts and giving me such positive feedback. My thanks also, to my sons, Grant and Edward, for their continued technical help, without you this would never have come together, and to my daughters-in-law, Vicky and Kate, for your support and feedback. Thanks also to Pegasus for publishing this book and for their advice and guidance along the way.

Chapter One

Cornwall

Caroline was giving her neighbour, Edna, a lift back from town. Edna was eighty-six years old and normally a very fit woman, who would think nothing of walking the three miles to St Mawdley and back again to her home near the beach, but the last couple of years her hip had been giving her trouble, and now she was waiting for a hip replacement.

"I'm so glad I caught you, dear. I didn't want to have to ring Bert. He keeps telling me not to do that walk any more, and he's probably right. This blasted hip is really giving me jip today," she said, rubbing her thigh, trying to ease the pain.

"No problem, Edna. It was lucky you spotted me and shouted. I'm usually in such a rush to get to the deli before it closes, that I whizz about in my own little world, oblivious to anyone," said Caroline, who was a 'seasonal and shop local' enthusiast.

As they drove up the steep hill away from the harbour, with a red setting sun, up ahead, Caroline dropped her visor down, squinting in the bright sun.

"Have you had a busy day, dear?" asked Edna, shading her eyes.

"Yes, very busy. We are getting ready for the new exhibition to open at the weekend. It's Jack Yeats, a nineteenth century Irish artist. Very bold, vibrant colours. I think you would love it. You and Bert must come out, as my guests."

"Thank you, dear, that would be lovely. Isn't he related to W.B. Yeats?"

"Yes — his brother," replied Caroline.

"Well, Bert will like the W.B. connection, and I will like the Irish one," said Edna.

Bert was a retired English teacher with a passion for poetry, and Edna was a farmer's daughter from Cork.

"I'm sorry to hear the hip is bad today, Edna," she said, glancing over at her neighbour, looking concerned.

"Aye, it's my own fault. I sat too long in Pat's pantry, and the cold chill got to me. I was grand on my way in — no problem at all — but then the bloomin' thing catches me out. Sooner I get the operation, the better, I suppose. But I'm not looking forward to it, or the lengthy recovery," she said, stretching her leg, trying to ease it.

"Well, you know I will help you. Don't forget, I was a nurse many moons ago," Caroline said, turning off the main road and onto the bumpy lane which led to their two cottages, before it came to a dead end at one of Cornwall's hidden beaches.

"Well, I'm very grateful. Oh Lord, there's Bert and Peggy! I'm not going to hear the end of this," she said, as Caroline slowed down and stopped outside their cottage.

Bert was just coming out of the gate with Peggy, their gorgeous Bernese Mountain Dog, who was straining on her lead, eager to get to the beach for her evening walk.

Bert, a tall, fine-looking, well-built man with a mop of dark, pepper and salt, curly hair, came over to open the car door for his wife. "You all right, dear?" he asked, helping her out.

Edna swung her legs round and tried her best to get out of the low car without wincing. "I'm fine, dear. Caroline insisted on giving me a lift. Hello, Peggy, old girl," she said, pulling herself up by using the grab handle, as Peggy made a fuss of her.

"I keep telling you that walk is too far now. Here, take my arm," he said, helping her stand up. "Take your time. Oh, you are such a stubborn woman!"

Edna bent down to blow Caroline a kiss. She was as tall and slim as her husband and didn't look anything like her eighty-six years, with her honey-gold, wavy hair which she was adamant she would continue to colour till the day she died.

"Thanks, dear, much appreciated. See you soon," she said with a wink, as she closed the car door and took Bert's arm as they walked back up their path.

Caroline could hear them quietly arguing before Bert gave his wife a friendly pat on her bottom and helped her inside. They were a wonderfully loving couple, and Caroline was very fond of them. Their friendship had bonded them from the moment they met, and they treated her like a much-loved daughter.

Caroline tooted her horn and continued down the lane, turning right into her driveway and parking her car under the cherry tree. Butterfly Cottage was her home by the sea, where she had relocated after her husband died seven years earlier. She had found the typical Cornish, thatched cottage by accident when she was exploring the hidden byways of Cornwall while on holiday. Following the signpost 'To the beach' from the main road, she had fallen in love with it instantly. It had reminded her of the type of house she had drawn as a child, and she especially loved the long garden at the back, which swept down towards some wood, with the sea beyond. There was something so appealing — quiet and peaceful, with the sound of the crashing waves. Despite its dilapidated state, it had been a labour of love for her renovating it and had helped her deal with her grief. 'Never underestimate the curative power of keeping busy,' as her mother used to say. She felt safe, and it had everything she needed — it was perfect.

Caroline was an attractive woman in her late fifties, a typical English rose with a peaches-and-cream complexion, deep-blue eyes and fiery, auburn, shoulder-length hair — still wavy but now streaked with silver. She was tall and willowy with long, slender legs and a natural beauty she wasn't really aware of. People warmed to her easily. Her kind, compassionate nature shone through, making it easy for her to make friends, even though she was incredibly shy.

She picked up her mail from her post-box on the porch and opened her front door, kicking off her shoes and going straight through to her kitchen to make a much-needed cup of tea. As she waited for the kettle to boil, she gazed out of the kitchen window, eager to get out and enjoy the last of the evening sunshine on her patio. There was a red tinge to the cloudless sky, casting a warm glow on the last remaining leaves that were clinging to the branches of the trees. Tonight, when the sky would darken, a carpet of stars would be revealed in a midnight-blue sky.

With her cup of tea in one hand and her mail in the other, she slipped on her crocs and went through the stable door to settle down in her wicker chair. The scent from the roses and herbs, which grew in sun-soaked terracotta pots at the edge of the patio, drifted up to her. Putting her sun hat on, she sipped her tea, gazing down the long, narrow garden towards the woods, with a glimpse of the sea in the distance. Part of her looked forward to winter when the trees will have lost their leaves and she would have a wonderful view of the cliffs again, standing defiantly against the crashing waves. Every season here in this coastal idyll was a joy. She knew she was incredibly lucky to live here and appreciated every day.

When she had moved to this little Cornish hamlet near St Mawdley, a few years after her husband Robert died, she had only herself to think of, as their children had left home. Their two sons, David and James, lived at either end of the country.

David was a professional drummer in a heavy metal band and spent a great deal of time travelling around the UK and Europe. His wife Veronica was a full-time district nurse, and along with their three children, ranging from three to sixteen, they had very busy lives up in the Lake District.

Her younger son, James, had been a professional rally driver, but when he married Katrina, an interior designer, they settled in Surrey where James set up his own business, restoring classic cars in a workshop at their home.

Caroline respected the lifestyles of her children and didn't want to intrude, now that they were adults with families of their own. She usually waited for them to contact her but was always willing to help out when needed. But now that she was on her own, she wanted to live her life to the fullest and not waste a second. Losing Robert when she was only fifty-one had made her realise how quickly life can change, and in a way, the move to Cornwall was an act of independence. She had a stronger sense of herself again and more self-confidence than she had had during the dark years following his death.

The move had invigorated her. She enjoyed her solitary walks on the beach every day, the smell of the sea, the rush of the tide. It never ceased to lift her mood when she felt low. Many times, she had sat on the rocks, watching the waves, their rhythm filling her head and soothing her, gently easing the terrible grief she had carried for so many years after her darling Robert died. She had known true loneliness but now at last she felt contentment in this idyllic spot. She knew Robert would always be with her wherever she went — always in her heart.

She had always, even as a little girl, been content in her own company. She didn't need people around all the time to make her happy. The reality was that, apart from her family, a few old friends, a few new friends, she was essentially alone, but she accepted it, believing that was her destiny. This was a new adventure and inspirational in so many ways, reigniting her love of painting. She could while away the hours quite happily, sitting in her beloved garden, reading, painting and trying to write comic verses which amused her if no one else.

She rested back in her chair, drinking in the tranquil scene. It was moments like these when she wished she had someone to share it with, as the last of the sun warmed her face. She pulled her hat a little further forward to protect her hair from the sun, the deep, rich auburn beginning to fade, a gentle reminder of the passing years. At fifty-one, she had been young to be widowed, and now seven years later, she sometimes wondered if she could live this solitary life for the next twenty or thirty years.

She occasionally missed male companionship to go out to dinner with or take in a show at the local theatre, but she wasn't sure she could make the necessary compromises to share her life with someone again. She had been lucky to have had the love of a good man like Robert, and she didn't think she would ever find another. She was very set in her ways now, slowly getting back on her feet. For years she had compartmentalized her life — husband, children and work — but now she only had herself to consider.

A seagull came to rest on the garden shed, looking at her with his beady eyes, probably wondering if there was anything tasty to eat. She waved her book at him before he flew off towards the sea. They were a pest at times, but she still loved to hear their cries as she walked along the beach.

She looked through her mail, mostly bills and junk, but one caught her eye when she recognised the writing. It was her old nursing colleague, Joleen. She quickly opened it to find an invite to a nurse' reunion in a couple of months' time. She remembered seeing a picture on Facebook a few weeks ago, of them all in their student nurses' uniforms back in the early '70s, so young and naive., There had been talk then of a reunion — she must remember to reply later.

Joleen had been her closest friend from her nursing days. Quite a few years older than Caroline, she had lived an exciting life prior to settling down in her nursing career. She was a jovial type, only just over five foot in height, with a petite figure. She was originally from Co. Galway in Ireland and was often teased about being a little Irish leprechaun, which she took in good humour. Her typical Celtic features — a pale complexion, blue eyes and jet-black, shoulder-length hair which she wore in plaits — only added to the mythical image. She would keep them amused in the nurses' home after a long day on the wards, telling them stories of her life on a kibbutz in Israel and her travels in India. She seemed so adventurous and exciting to them all; she was the most exciting person that Caroline ever met. Most of her friends had come straight from school to start their studies and had lived very sheltered lives compared to Joleen, who went on to have a very successful nursing career. When she retired, she returned to her love of travelling and met Terry, a retired British Army captain, in a bar in Istanbul. They were the best-suited couple Caroline had ever met, and they spent their lives exploring the world in their camper van, only returning to their home in Carlisle to regroup and plan the next trip or, as in this case, the next nurses' reunion. Caroline loved her and looked forward to seeing her again.

A cool wind suddenly blew up the garden, making Caroline shiver. She finished her cup of tea and gathered up her mail and book, tucking them under her arm. She really didn't feel like cooking — she rarely did these days. If she could get away with a salad or a bowl of homemade soup, she was happy with that. The thought of preparing a proper meal was far down her list of fun ways to spend her time, but it was probably more to do with the fact that she hated sitting down to a proper meal on her own.

Later that evening, after a light supper and her bracing walk along the beach, she went through to the little study at the back of the cottage. It had been a lean-to when she had moved in — very cold and draughty — but she had had it insulated and a new roof put on, and it was now a cosy little room with a lovely view of the garden, just big enough for Robert's old desk and captain's chair. She always felt close to him when she sat down in his chair to do her correspondence. There was a faint scent of him here; the old, worn leather arms of the chair where he used to rub his hands while he was thinking.

She turned on the lamp which cast a warm glow, and she opened up her laptop to reply to Joleen's invite, looking forward to seeing them all again. It had been ten years since the last get-together, when most of their group had attended, but she wondered how many would turn up this time. Many of them, like Caroline, had moved to different parts of the country, so it wasn't always easy for them all to travel back to Warwickshire, but hopefully there would be a good turnout. It would be a fun night of reminiscing and hilarity.

After she emailed Joleen, she logged onto Facebook to look at the old student-nurses' photograph again. As she was scrolling down, she noticed a picture on 'Friends you may know' at the top of the screen. She was sure it was the Freddie Harrison she knew from school, her very first boyfriend.

She clicked on the link, her curiosity getting the better of her. Yes, it was definitely him — she would recognise those green eyes and wide grin anywhere. It read that he was a writer, living in France. She remembered that he was half French, with family in Paris. She thought of him sometimes, wondering what had happened to him, and in a moment of madness, she sent him a message.

"Are you the Frederic Harrison who went to school in Warwickshire in the late '60s? If you are, you may not remember me, but we knew each other as teenagers. I have just stumbled upon your profile, so just catching up to say hello!'

She hoped he didn't think she was stalking him or anything like that. She was just curious to find out how life had turned out for him. She hesitated quite a while, her fingers hovering over the keyboard, and then she quickly clicked 'send'.

What have I done? she thought. *Never mind, it may not be him anyway, and if it is, he probably wants nothing to do with me, after the way we parted.*

She remembered that day like it was yesterday. Ending her relationship with him had been one of the most painful things she had done, but she was only nineteen and had become infatuated with a medical student at the hospital where she was training, while Freddie was away at university in Oxford. The relationship with the medical student had ended disastrously, breaking her heart and her spirit.

She sat staring at Freddie's profile picture for a long time. In some ways it seemed like yesterday since they had been together, and in others like a thousand years had passed since then, seeing him on-screen, still looking so very handsome, his blond hair now streaked with silver and a neat, well-trimmed, silver beard. His smiling, green eyes seemed to be looking straight at her, sending a little tingle down her spine. Age had given him gravitas, and he was obviously confident in the person he had become.

She sighed. Would it be so bad to reconnect with an old love, become just friends? She didn't want anything from him. She wondered if they were capable of just friendship after all this time, but she had a longing to reach back into her past. Maybe it was seeing the old photograph from her student days, or maybe it was a sign of age and time passing, but she felt a strange loneliness inside, and she couldn't understand the melancholy. Why, after all these years, was she wistfully looking back at the days of her youth?

She sat back in the old leather chair, rubbing the worn arms, looking at the silver-framed picture of Robert on the desk. "What am I to do, Robert? I miss you so much. You left me too soon. You were always so wise, and I am such an impetuous fool sometimes."

She touched the photograph tenderly. She would always be able to hold him in her heart and in her mind, but she would never be able to hold him again and feel his strong arms around her. She sighed heavily before closing down her laptop, sat quietly for a moment, turned off the desk lamp and climbed the twisting, narrow staircase to her pretty bedroom in the eaves.

The next morning, the sun came peeping in through her small window. She never closed her bedroom curtain, as she liked to watch the stars at night before she drifted off to sleep. With no light pollution from streetlamps, a cloudless night sky was always breathtaking, filling her with awe in its true sense. She detested the casual use of the word 'awesome' these days, but the star-studded sky was truly deserving of that description.

It looked like a beautiful day, not a cloud in the bright, blue sky. She stretched and leapt out of bed to open her window to breathe in the fresh sea air. Every morning felt like the beginning of an exciting day. Living by the sea had always been a dream, and sometimes she had to pinch herself that she was actually fulfilling that dream.

She dressed in jeans and a blue sweater, putting on her favourite sapphire earrings. Blue, in all its shades, was Caroline's favourite colour, although she usually complimented her colour scheme with vibrant accessories, especially in her shoes which were a bit of an addiction. This morning she chose her navy and pink tartan pair with a medium heel, as she would probably be on her feet all day. Her jewellery was elegant and mostly antiques, gifts from her beloved Robert, which she treasured.

She went downstairs to the small kitchen at the back of the cottage, so small that she could reach every worktop from one central point, but she loved its charm. She had kept the original good quality kitchen units, not seeing any need to replace them with new ones. She had painted them a cheery pale lemon with a blue trim and added a brand-new wooden worktop. She had found dainty, wooden doorknobs, in the shape of a sailing boat, in the old-fashioned hardware store in St Mawdley, and they added a fun seaside feel. The kitchen was small, but it was more than adequate for her on her own. Admittedly, it was a bit of a tight squeeze if she had visitors, but that wasn't very often.

She filled her percolator with her favourite ground coffee and set it on the hob to heat, the aroma awakening her senses, the best smell in the world. She stood looking down the garden through the tiny eight-paned window, daydreaming, and then she remembered about her Facebook message the night before. She went through to the study to open up her laptop to see if there was a reply. She was indeed surprised when she saw a message alert flashing on the top of her screen. She clicked on it, and when she read it, she felt energised, like she had been plugged into an electric socket.

Yeah, I remember you…

Paris, France

Sitting on the balcony of his apartment in the 16th Arrondissement, Frederic Harrison looked down at the bustling cobbled streets below. The cafe on the corner, with its bright-red awning draped with fairy lights, is busy with customers enjoying the warm, autumn evening, relaxing in the comfortable cane chairs with their glasses of wine, chatting loudly. The noise and the sound of someone playing a guitar drifted up to him on the third floor. The 'City of Light' was beginning to come to life. His old friend, Michelle, came out to clear some glasses from a table outside her bar opposite. She saw him and waved. He waved back, raising his glass to her, telling her that he will see her later.

He had known Michelle since they were children, and she had hardly changed in all those years. She was still slim, her hair still a raven-black bob, and she still looked like and had the energy of a teenager. Their friendship began when he would come to visit his Aunt Cecile and Uncle Claude during the school holidays and also when he studied at the Sorbonne for a year after he finished his degree at Oxford. There had never been any romantic involvement between them; they were more like brother and sister.

So, when Frederic returned to Paris ten years ago after his divorce, taking over his aunt and uncle's apartment when they moved to New York, he was delighted to see Michelle had taken over her father's bar. She had two failed marriages behind her and no children, much to her regret, but she adored Freddie's grandchildren and had taken on the role of their great-aunt, spoiling them terribly when they came to stay with their grandfather during the school holidays.

Freddie hoped that one day she would meet someone who would really appreciate her. Both her ex-husbands had treated her very badly. It wasn't unusual in France for men to have mistresses and women to have lovers, but Michelle's ex-husbands had pushed her to the limit of tolerance, both of them flaunting their lovers in the bars and cafes in the neighbouring arrondissements.

"I will never marry again!" she had told Freddie after her last divorce, as they sat on his balcony with a bottle of wine, drowning her sorrows.

"Maybe one day, Michelle. Give yourself time," he had told her.

"Never again! I am going to devote my life to making Papa's bar the best in all of Paris!" she said, laughing and raising her glass.

"Good for you, and I shall devote my life to becoming the finest writer I can be," he smiled, clinking his glass with hers.

That had been ten years ago, and both of them had devoted themselves to their work. It had been a brave move for him, giving up his career as a history teacher at an independent school in England to devote his time to his writing. Paris had always felt like his second home.

He spoke fluent French, and it was the perfect place to start over again after his divorce. He now had several historical books published, his first novel and was just beginning an anthology of his poetry, which had been his passion since he was a schoolboy.

He turned his attention back to his laptop and the surprising message he had received from Caroline earlier. He hadn't realised at first who it was. He hadn't known her married name, but when he read her message and looked again at the profile picture, he had felt a stab to his heart. It had taken him a moment to compose himself, remembering all too well the girl he had loved all those years ago, his mind drifting back to when they were teenagers…

Forty years earlier

He was waiting on the stairs as Caroline came out of the cafe onto the top-floor landing, hoisting her school bag onto her shoulder and straightening her short skirt. He was leaning up against the wall with one leg bent, smoking a cigarette, one hand in his pocket, trying to look cool, his heart beating faster as he looked up at her.

"Hi Caroline, how are you?" he asked, as he flicked his heavy, blond fringe back off his forehead and looked directly up at her.

"Hi, Freddie, I am fine, thanks. How are you?" she said, coming down the stairs towards him, her long mane of wavy, auburn hair bouncing on her shoulders with every step she took.

"I am OK, thanks. Would you like to come to the pictures with me on Saturday night? Midnight Cowboy is on," he said shyly.

"Oh, yes, I would like that. I hear its brilliant — love the music," she said, looking up at him demurely from under her long, dark eyelashes.

He noticed, though, that her cheeks had turned pink.

"Great. Shall I meet you here at seven o'clock?" he asked. I think it starts at seven thirty," he added, grinning and so relieved that she had said yes.

He had been trying to pluck up courage for weeks to ask her out. Every day after school he had tried to catch her eye up in the café, but she was always so engrossed with her friends that she never seemed to notice him, but today she had, thank goodness.

"Ok, see you at seven," she said, coming down the stairs to pass him.

It was an awkward moment as they came close. His heart was beating so fast that he feared it would bounce out of his chest. She looked up at him. At over 6 feet, he was just a little taller than her. He sensed an intensity that unnerved him as their eyes met, and a shiver of excitement as she stood there in front of him on the landing. He reached out, touched her arm tenderly and felt a rush of warmth that seemed to fill his heart.

"Look forward to it. See you Saturday, then?" he said, wanting to kiss her right there and then but managing to stay looking cool.

She looked up at him. "Yes, see you Saturday. Bye, Freddie," she said, as they heard the cafe door open, the sound of 'Honkey Tonk Women' by The Rolling Stones drifting down to them.

They both turned shyly away from each other, as her friend, Alice, came down towards them, winking at Caroline as she joined her on the landing.

"Are you walking home?" asked Alice, linking arms with her.

"Yeah, I'm ready," said Caroline, as they skipped down the stairs.

She had turned to wave to him before she stepped out into the afternoon sunshine, while continuing the deep conversation with her best friend. He remembered watching her and thinking he would never forget that moment. He had run up the stairs, two at a time, to rejoin his friends in the cafe to tell them he had a date.

Present day

Frederic sat back in his chair, running his hand through his hair, pushing back his fringe, lost in thought. The wave of nostalgia was almost overwhelming. Caroline had been the love of his life; not fighting for her had perhaps been his biggest mistake. He was torn from his thoughts when he heard Francois, the new woman in his life, calling to him from the street below, her long, dark, wavy hair, reminiscent of the '40s, hidden under the bright-red hood of her shiny raincoat.

She was the first woman who had lasted more than a few weeks. All the others, since his divorce, had only been very short-lived. He had never committed to a relationship until Francois had captivated him with her lively, bubbly personality, but she could be very volatile, a typical Gallic drama queen of the theatrical world.

He leant over the intricate wrought iron balcony railings, blowing her a kiss, and then he turned back to his laptop, typing a quick reply to Caroline. *What harm can it do?* he thought. He took a sip of wine and closed down the screen. He locked the balcony doors and closed the tall, wooden shutters, walking back into the elegant apartment, beautifully furnished with French antiques left by his aunt and uncle. He picked up his battered, corded, velvet jacket from the old leather couch and ran down the spiralling wrought iron staircase of the nineteenth century apartment block, to join Francois and his friends for a drink in Michelle's bar.

Chapter Two

Cornwall

Caroline was driving along the narrow, twisting lanes towards St Mawdley and the art gallery where she worked part time. Dire Straits, 'Sultan of Swing', was blasting out from her CD player. She felt particularly chirpy this morning, especially after receiving that reply from Freddie. She couldn't help thinking it was quite a coincidence — or was it a quirk of fate — that they were in touch the very week that the Jack Yeats exhibition was opening at the gallery. Was fate playing little games with her? The last time she had seen the Irish painter was in the art gallery in Oxford, over forty years ago when she had visited Freddie in his student flat. She smiled to herself, remembering that happy time, a plethora of memories flooding her mind.

40 years ago

Oxford

It had been the first weekend that Caroline had visited Freddie since he had started his degree and she had started her nursing course. They had both settled into their new lives, enjoying student life. Freddie's life as a history student at Oxford was very different to hers as a student nurse learning on the job. They missed each other terribly, so this was a very special weekend for them — the first time that they could be alone together, with no parental interference.

They had been cuddled up in Freddie's room in his shared student accommodation. The sun was beaming in through the small window, but there was still a touch of frost on the corners of the glass. The room was freezing cold, and they laughed as they watched their breath in the air.

Freddie got up to switch on the small electric heater. "It will warm up soon," he said, taking her in his arms. "I love you, Caroline. I've missed you so much," he added, holding her tight.

"I've missed you too. It's so hard being so far apart. I love you, Freddie," she said, breathing him in as he leaned over to kiss her.

A little while later they were disturbed by Freddie's housemates crashing about in the kitchen, which was next to Freddie's room on the ground floor.

"Oh God, what a racket. Shall we go into town?" he asked, rolling on his side, propped up on one elbow, looking down at her and playing with her long, wavy hair.

"Sounds like a good idea. We can't stay here all day," she said.

"Well, I don't know about that!" he said, starting to tickle her.

"Stop, stop!" she squealed, tears streaming down her cheeks as he tumbled her back onto the bed.

The room had warmed up by the time they were finally ready to go out. Freddie suggested they go to the Ashmolean Museum.

"It's a fabulous place — you'll love it. They have just opened a Jack Yeats exhibition; do you like him?" he asked, knowing that Caroline loved art.

"The Irish chap? Oh, I love him — those big, bold, thick paint strokes. He was a genius!" she said.

Caroline had studied A-level art and had wanted to go to Art College, but with the advice from her parents and teachers ringing in her ears, she had chosen what was thought to be the more structured and stable career path of nursing. She didn't regret it. She enjoyed it, and her compassionate nature lent itself to being a kind, caring nurse. She still indulged her love of art at every opportunity. So, she was super excited when they arrived later that day at the steps of the grand, pillared entrance to the museum.

The Yeats gallery on the top floor was long and wide, with dozens of his paintings of Irish country life, horses of the travelling people, Dublin scenes, and right before them as they entered the gallery was The Liffey Swim.

"It's incredible, isn't it? How does he do that?" she said, staring at the work of art. "I love this place, Freddie!" she said excitedly.

They had wandered up and down the gallery, Caroline delighting in every painting she came to, stopping longer at some, unwilling to tear herself away from her favourites.

The gallery was closing as they made their way down after a lovely afternoon. The gift shop on the ground floor was still open as they passed.

Caroline pulled Freddie by the hand towards it. "Before we go, I must see if they have a poster in the shop of the Prancing Horse — it would cheer up my room," she said, going over to the back wall where posters were displayed. "Oh, they do!" she exclaimed excitedly, gazing up at a vibrant yellow-and-green print of a prancing horse and rider. "I have to have it," she said, taking a rolled-up poster over to the till.

"Let me buy it for you; it will be a memento of this perfect weekend," he said, handing over some cash.

"Thank you! I will think of you every time I look at it," she said, tucking it under her arm as they made their way back through the busy, bustling streets of Oxford.

Present day

Caroline smiled to herself at the tender memory. She still had that poster, now framed and hanging in the study. Over the years, it had just become part of her surroundings. She had always loved it.

As she parked her Mini in the carpark of The Mansion Art Gallery, her friend, Fiona, was just getting out of her car — tall and slender, looking stunning, as always, in black jeans and a white, ruffled shirt. Her long, blond, silky hair held back by a black, velvet band was immaculate, not a hair out of place. Caroline often thought she would look good if she turned up in a bin bag. She looked more like a supermodel than a retired police detective.

"Hi, Caroline, ready for a busy day?" she called, coming over towards her.

"Indeed, I am, Fiona, there is a lot to do, but it's very exciting. I can't wait to do the tour and see it all. Did you know we are going to have a professional artist giving an art class this weekend?"

"No, I didn't. That sounds fun. I might sign up myself, if there are any spaces left."

"Me too!" said Caroline, linking arms with her as they walked up towards the restored Georgian mansion, which was now home to the contemporary art gallery.

"So how is life out in the sticks?" asked Fiona, who lived in the town and couldn't imagine living anywhere so remote and lonely. It had been a big enough shock for her when she had moved to St Mawdley, after her life in London.

"Lovely as ever. I like my peaceful quiet life; it restores my soul!" she said, spreading her arms dramatically, embracing the gentle wind that rustled through the leaves as they walked through the wood beside the lake.

The grounds of the mansion were as much an attraction to visitors as the art gallery. They had been created by Capability Brown back in the eighteenth century and were typical of his design, with beautifully manicured lawns sweeping down towards a serpentine lake. Majestic trees stood at strategic places, providing shade from the Cornish sun.

"I know it's lovely out there, but I do worry about you. Maybe you should get a dog?" said Fiona, as they crossed from the wood over to the long, sweeping drive.

"I can borrow Peggy when I want to. I don't want the tie of a dog. Anyway, don't worry. I'm fine on my own, and I'm not lonely... most of the time," she said, hesitating, wondering whether to tell Fiona about the Facebook message.

"I sense a 'but' coming," stated Fiona, stopping on the path, raising an eyebrow.

"Well, in a moment of madness last night, I contacted an old boyfriend on Facebook."

"What! Are you crazy? That can lead to a whole lot of trouble," said Fiona, continuing to walk.

"I know. It was probably a very stupid thing to do, but I was feeling very nostalgic, and then out of the blue, his profile picture popped up on the screen. Cookies have a lot to answer for if you ask me. Anyway, I sent him a message," she said sheepishly.

"Did he reply?"

"Yes. I got a reply to this morning to say that he remembers me, dot, dot, dot. Whatever that means?"

"Dot, dot, dot? Maybe he means he remembers you…broke… his… heart. Did you?" asked Fiona.

"We didn't break up on the best of terms. Anyway, it's no big deal. He lives in Paris now, and it's only Facebook!"

"Paris, eh? Well, at least it won't be easy to arrange a date, but just be careful. People change a lot over forty years. He might be a serial killer or a drug dealer!"

"Oh, Fiona, for heaven's sake. You are letting your old professional life colour your judgement."

"Caroline, dear, I have dealt with a lot of women who have suffered at the hands of men they hook up with online, during my time with the Met," Fiona said firmly.

"I'm not 'hooking up'. But I hear what you say. I will be careful, I promise," replied Caroline, feeling slightly foolish.

"Whatever!" replied Fiona, raising her eyes to the skies, swallowing down words of wisdom that rose up inside her.

She opened the staff-room door at the back of the mansion, allowing Caroline to walk in ahead of her.

Later that day, after the gallery staff had had their tour and briefing of the exhibition, they all spilled out onto the lawn for a picnic lunch under the shade of the cedar tree. The staff and volunteers took every opportunity they could to enjoy the grounds of the magnificent mansion, often having their lunch under the trees by the lake.

Tom, a retired headmaster from Scotland, was holding court, as usual, with his endless amusing anecdotes, keeping them all in stitches. He was the longest-serving member of the gallery team, having retired early at fifty-five after a lifetime dedicated to his primary-school pupils. Everybody loved him, including the visitors who would stand enthralled, listening to his soft, Scottish brogue as he told them about the artwork, throwing in witty comments alongside the serious information.

Caroline and Fiona were propped up against the trunk of the tree, listening to him and Philip — another retired teacher — having a friendly argument about the merits of Expressionism, when a smart, silver, vintage, sports car pulled up and parked in the courtyard by the main entrance. The gallery was closed to visitors, so they were all curious to know who it could be.

A tall, elegant man, slim and in good shape, got out of the car, looking up at the mansion before walking over to the main door. Finding it locked, he turned towards the lawn, pushing his sunglasses on top of his thick, wavy, steel-grey hair.

Tom waved him over. "Hello, can we help you?" he called.

"Hi, sorry to disturb you all, but I'm looking for the education department," he said, striding over towards them.

His crisp, white shirt, with the sleeves casually but perfectly rolled up, was open at the collar, revealing the top of a deeply tanned chest. His hair was immaculately trimmed, he had a smooth shave and all the trappings of a sophisticated, successful man. As he approached, his face broke into a smile, showing perfect, white teeth. Caroline and Fiona looked at each other in surprise, as Tom got up to greet him.

"You must be Lawrence, the artist? Francesca, the head of that department, told me you might call," said Tom, reaching out to shake his hand.

"Hi, yes, I am. This is a nice spot," he said in a deep, warm voice, looking across the lawn towards the lake, giving a little bow to everyone.

"Sorry, Lawrence, but Francesca left early," said Tom.

"Oh, that's a pity. I just wanted to have a look at the studio where I will be, to see what I need to bring with me. Never mind, I can come back another day," he said, turning to go.

"Do you have the keys for the studio, Caroline? Could you show Lawrence?" asked Tom, turning to her.

"I do, actually. Of course, no trouble at all," said Caroline, getting to her feet.

Lawrence turned towards her, giving her a smile. "If you are sure, that would be great," he said.

"Just give me a minute to get my things together," she said, bending down to pick up her lunch bag.

"Lucky old you," whispered Fiona. "He is quite a dish — looks like a movie star!"

"Sshh, Fiona!" said Caroline, blushing. "Right, I'm ready. This way, Lawrence," she said, setting off at a brisk pace across the lawn ahead of this mature Adonis, who did indeed look like a movie star. Richard Gere in Pretty Woman came to mind.

Lawrence turned to the others, nodded a goodbye and quickly followed Caroline.

"I'm sorry to have disturbed your picnic," he said, when he caught up with her.

"No problem, we had finished anyway. So, are you local?" she asked, trying not to look directly at him. He had the type of good looks that made her nervous.

"Yes, I have a very small studio in St Mawdley — been there for the last year," he said, walking close beside her.

"St Mawdley is a lovely village, great place for a studio. What style are your paintings?" she asked, as they reached the main entrance, fumbling in her large shoulder bag for the keys and beginning to panic slightly when she couldn't find them. "Thank goodness," she said, as she pulled them out from the bottom of the bag.

"Mostly seascapes. I suppose you might say they lean towards the Expressionist, in the style of Jack Yeats. So, being local, that's probably why they approached me for this exhibition," he said, standing back as Caroline unlocked the main door, pushing it open with great effort.

The old Georgian door was extremely heavy, and the electronic opening device was switched off, so Lawrence leaned forward and helped her push the door.

"Thank you," she said, as their hands touched on the door handle. "Follow me, the studio is down here," she continued, going down some stone steps to the original basement, passing the well-stocked, modern gift shop and ticket desk.

"This is a beautiful building," he said, admiring the contemporary glazed walkway which led to the art department. "I love the blend of the modern and Georgian, the use of glass, and the old stonework is very clever," he said, touching the walls.

"Yes, it's magnificent. Right, here we are," she said, unlocking the tall glass doors which led into a brightly lit studio.

"Oh, this is great. Where will I be, do you know?" he asked, looking around the large space with its old, oak floorboards.

Three huge windows, floor to ceiling, flooded the room with light. He noted, thankfully, that there were electric blinds on each one. Natural light was great, but direct sunlight was not so great. He noted that the windows fortunately faced north.

"As far as I'm aware, you will have use of the whole studio. We will be setting up a dozen easels for the students. I think nearly all the places have been taken, which is good."

"That's excellent. So, will you be here as well?" he asked, taking a peep in the storage area, opening and closing cupboard doors.

"I might be. I would like to, but visitors come first. I will have to wait to see if there are any spaces left," she said, propping herself up against the bench which ran around the other two walls, while he checked out the art materials available.

"So, you like to paint? Well, I hope you can get a place," he said, turning round and looking at her directly.

Caroline felt the colour rising in her cheeks, and she jumped down from the bench. It was the first time in many, many years that she had ever felt unnerved by a man. His gaze was intense, and he was almost too good-looking. He smiled at her, revealing those fabulous perfect teeth. Caroline wondered if he was aware of the effect, he had on her. She thought he probably was. *For goodness sake,* she thought to herself. *Get a grip. You are nearly sixty, not sixteen.*

"Thank you, Caroline. I think I've seen all I need to see," he said, coming over to her.

"Francesca is back in tomorrow. You can ring her for more information," she said, as she quickly made her way over to the door.

"Yes, I will do that," he said, following her out and back up the steps.

When they reached the courtyard, the others were just beginning to come back in.

"Seen everything you need, Lawrence?" asked Tom, stepping aside to let the others past.

"Yes, thank you, I have indeed. I'll be off now. Many thanks, and I will see you all at the weekend, I hope," he said, glancing over at Caroline.

"Indeed, you will. This is going to be a popular exhibition. Nice to meet you — bye now," said Tom, as Lawrence went over to his car and sped off, sunglasses on and the roof down.

Fiona caught up with Caroline as they were filing into the Lecture Room for their briefing from the art director and curator.

"So, madam, how did you get on with the dishy artist?" she asked, as they found two seats together near the front.

"He's very nice, very charming," she replied, opening her bag and taking out a jotter to take notes.

"He's drop-dead gorgeous! But you have to be careful with his type," she said, as the curator took to the podium.

On her way home, Caroline couldn't help thinking about Lawrence. He really was most attractive, but he was probably happily married. *Anyway, I'm not interested,* she told herself. Then her thoughts turned to the Facebook message from Freddie. *Two men occupying my thoughts. They are like bloomin' buses,* she laughed to herself, as she pulled onto her driveway, putting both of them to the back of her mind and going through for a nice cup of tea.

That evening, after her walk on the beach, she went through to her small study and opened her laptop, looking at the Facebook message again. She stared down at it, wondering how to reply. How do you start up a conversation on Facebook, with someone you haven't seen in over forty years? She hesitated before sitting down, then her eye caught the Jack Yeats poster hanging on the wall. She sat down in Robert's old chair and typed her reply.

'Good to hear from you. So, how are you? Where are you? X'

She clicked 'send' and rested back in the old leather chair. Looking at the screen, she glanced over at the silver-framed picture of Robert, sitting on the desk. His strong, determined jawline, his beaming smile and warm, kind eyes brought a deep sense of comfort to her. He had been such a handsome man — she would never find another like him.

Oh dear, what would you think of me getting in touch with an old boyfriend? Well, I have done it now. There's no going back, but what harm can it do? It's just friendship. I'm not after romance, after all!

She closed her laptop and went off to make some supper.

After supper, she poured herself a G&T, with plenty of ice and a slice of cucumber, and settled down in her favourite armchair in the cosy living room in front of the fire, with the curtains drawn against the dark, starry sky. She still had quite a few bits of antique furniture dotted around the cottage, but many pieces had had to be sold when she moved. They were just too big for the little cottage, and the family didn't want them either. She had enough of her favourite pieces, though, to make the place feel like home. She rested back in the chair, scanning the tv schedule, to find nothing of interest. So, she decided to fetch her laptop and see if there was anything interesting in the world of Facebook, and there, waiting for her, was Freddie's reply.

'I am fine. Been here in Paris for the last ten years. Nice to hear from you. X'

That was indeed nice to hear, she thought. She felt a little flutter of excitement as she read the message. She fidgeted in the chair, looking around the room, her mind wandering, and she noticed that the oak beams on the ceiling needed dusting. *Concentrate,* she told herself, trying to think of what to write. She remembered his young, handsome face from all those years ago.

She typed a reply. 'So glad you remember me — in a nice way, i hope. Do you think we could be friends again?'

There was an almost instant response. 'I could never forget you. The image of you coming down the stairs in the Castle Tea Rooms is burned in my brain forever. Yes, we can be friends. Freddie. X'

Crikey, she thought. She also remembered that moment on the stairs of the tearoom that all the sixth formers frequented after school. Freddie standing on the lower landing, looking up at her as she came out of the cafe, his shock of blonde hair swept back off his handsome face. He was leaning against the wall with one long leg bent, one hand in a pocket, looking casually cool, smoking a French cigarette. He had asked her to go to the pictures with him on Saturday night, and that had been the start of their teenage romance.

She typed a reply. 'I am so glad we can be friends. X'

She rested back in the chair again, thinking if the past was best left in the past. She stared at the screen and wondered if she was opening up Pandora's box.

Chapter Three

Cornwall

The Patrons Evening at the mansion was one of the top Cornish art events to be seen at. It celebrated the start of the new exhibition, and it was looking like it would be a roaring success and the best-attended on record. The courtyard by the entrance was full of very expensive cars, looking like a showroom for all the top dealerships in the country. Fairy lights were strung along the branches of the trees by the lake, it would look magical when darkness fell. Hundreds of wealthy supporters were milling around the galleries, which were looking splendid, the chandeliers in the foyer gleaming, their light reflected on the ancient oak floors which had been waxed and buffed. It was a glittering, black-tie event. The expensively dressed women were covered in fabulous jewels, and so were some of the men too. There was a fair share of local celebrities, TV personalities and politicians, all keen to be seen photographed with the great and the good of the Cornish art world, with the backdrop of the beautiful art on display in the elegant galleries.

Waiters walked the galleries with silver trays of champagne and exquisite canapes, supplied by a local celebrity chef. Caroline and her colleagues were mixing with the guests, their name badges identifying them as staff. Their role was to socialise, but chiefly they were there to keep an eye that none of the visitors were getting too close to the valuable works of art with their glasses of champagne and sticky fingers, and the more the champagne flowed, the more difficult that became to do.

Caroline was thoroughly enjoying the evening. The galleries, usually so quiet, were buzzing with chatter and laughter. She was wearing her favourite midnight-blue, velvet dress, with its deep V neckline showing off a simple diamond-and-sapphire pendant and matching earrings. The full skirt, cut on the bias, just touched her knee, and scarlet high heels showed off her long legs. With her hair piled up into a loose chignon, she felt very sophisticated and as confident as she could be at these types of occasions. She normally avoided attending big events on her own. She missed having Robert by her side and felt even more alone amongst a crowd. But it was different here, as she had a role to play, and she was enjoying the performance.

She was just explaining — for the umpteenth time that evening — to a local businessman and his wife that Jack Yeats was indeed the brother of W.B. Yeats, when she saw Lawrence approaching, looking devastatingly handsome in a deep-purple, velvet jacket, with dark trousers, dress shirt and a brightly coloured, paisley-patterned bow tie.

"Good evening. Would you mind if I stole this lady for a moment?" he said to the businessman and his wife.

He took Caroline by the arm, steering her over towards the heavily laden buffet table which was set up in the foyer.

"You looked like you needed rescuing," he said, as he took two glasses of champagne from the silver tray on the table.

"Thank you. They were not really interested in the art — just here to be seen, I think," she said, feeling a little guilty and taking a small sip of champagne.

"One can always tell the art lovers from the socialites at these sorts of events, but it's a necessary evil if places like this are to survive. Art, at any level, has always needed the support of wealthy patrons. Anyway, it's nice to see you again — you look lovely, by the way," he said, raising his glass to hers. "Cheers!"

"Cheers and thank you. Not my usual attire — I spend most of my life in cropped jeans and T-shirts, but I've really enjoyed this evening. Have you just arrived?" she asked, as Lawrence led her over to the buffet table, which was laden with mouth-watering canapes, smoked salmon, fresh anchovies, blinis loaded with crème fraiche and caviar. There was a display of apricot and strawberry tartlets, topped with yellow and purple edible flowers, they looked like works of art in their own right. Lawrence picked one up and popped it straight into his mouth, giving Caroline a cheeky grin just as a very tall platinum blonde woman, her hair falling in waves over her bare shoulders, pushed her way to the table, giving Caroline a chilling look. She was dressed in gold lame, heavily made up and dripping in diamonds. She piled her plate with food, gave Lawrence a wink before returning to join a group of equally glittering attired women.

"She's definitely not here for the art," whispered Lawrence, grinning and moving away from the table.

Do you know her? asked Caroline.

"She owns a night club in Penzance, can't remember her name though" he said, taking Caroline by the arm and leading her over to look at one of the dazzling Caravaggio paintings.

Breathtaking, isn't it?" he said, leaning closer to look at the impossibly small figures on the boats in the Bay of Naples.

"Exquisite" replied Caroline, "So, when did you arrive?"

"I've been here a little while. Francesca was introducing me to a few of the team — nice bunch of people," He held her gaze with eyes the colour of aquamarine, and Caroline felt fixated and was almost lost for words for a moment.

"Yes, they all are really nice and friendly people. I love coming here," she replied.

"So, how long have you worked here?" he asked, taking a canape from a passing waitress.

"Oh, I started as a volunteer when I moved down here from the Cotswolds, after I retired a few years ago. Now I help Francesca one day in the studio and work in the galleries on my other day. It's great and gives me an interest, and I've made a good bunch of friends," she said enthusiastically.

"You look too young to be retired. What did you use to do?" he asked, cocking his right eyebrow in a very alluring way.

"My late husband and I had an antique business, but I sold up a couple of years after he died. Neither of my sons were interested in carrying on with the business — they preferred a more exciting way of life. A few years after that, I took the plunge, sold up our family home and moved down here"

"Oh, I'm sorry to hear you lost your husband. You are very young to be a widow. That was a very brave decision to move so far," he said, putting his hand lightly on her arm.

"Brave or foolhardy, I'm not sure which, but so far, so good. This place has given me a purpose again and rekindled my love of art. It also keeps my brain active, trying to retain all the information about the collections. It's wonderful to be a part of it all," she said, just as she caught the eye of one of the directors. "Excuse me, Lawrence. Much as I would love to stay here drinking champagne, I really should go and mix; I'm supposed to be working," she said, glancing back into the packed gallery.

"Very well, if you must. Will you be here at the weekend for my art class?" he asked, looking around the foyer.

"Your class is fully subscribed, so I won't, unfortunately, but good luck with it all," she said, as she put down her half-full glass of champagne on a nearby table. She knew it wasn't the alcohol that was making her feel slightly giddy.

"Well, I'm glad I have a full class but sorry you won't be there. Off you go then, I won't keep you any longer," he said, reaching down to give her a peck on the cheek, a subtle, expensive, male fragrance filling the air between them.

Caroline felt herself blush. She looked up into his mesmerising blue eyes and backed away, giving him a shy little wave as she reluctantly left him, returning to mix with the guests. As she was walking back through the gallery, she glanced round to see him in deep conversation with a group of women, including the platinum blond, laughing and joking. He was obviously very much at ease, attracting people to him like a magnet. She had noticed earlier the way women looked at him — she could tell he was used to being the star wherever he went. Fiona caught up with her as she came into the adjacent gallery.

"Did I see you drinking champagne with our dishy artist friend?" she whispered, giving her a playful nudge.

"Nothing gets past you. Yes, I felt very guilty, kept thinking I would be told to get back to work. He's a lovely man, though, very charming."

"I bet he is. You be careful. He's a man who loves women as much as he loves art. I know the type — believe me," she said, moving over to join a group looking at 'The Liffey Swimmers', the most famous painting in the collection.

Caroline woke the next morning, still feeling exhausted. Her legs and feet ached from all the standing around the night before. She wasn't used to wearing high heels and talking all evening, but she had enjoyed it all, nevertheless. She was glad she had the next few days off, though.

She lay back on her large, white pillows. Looking out through the window, she noticed a little touch of frost on the trees — autumn was definitely here. She snuggled further down under the duvet, reluctant to get up, her mind wandering back to the night before and all the lovely people she had met. Her life was so different now, compared to those dark, lonely times after Robert had died.

She was sure she had done the right thing in moving down to Cornwall, but it was a long way from the family. She missed them so much, but they were busy with their lives, and this was a lovely place for them to come visit. Plus, she loved being by the sea — it had always been her dream.

She could hear the waves now, crashing on the beach. It was a windy day but sunny, so with a dramatic throw back of the duvet, she was up and over to the window, opening it to breathe in the fresh sea air. "Time for coffee," she said to herself, making her way downstairs.

Later that afternoon, she was in St Mawdley to collect some acrylic paints she had ordered from the art suppliers, a wonderful little shop just off the seafront, packed to the ceiling with everything a budding artist or crafter would need. Marion, the owner, with her shocking-pink and purple hair tied in a long plait which hung down her back, was always very helpful and ready to chat, but sometimes it was hard to get away from her. She was born and bred in St Mawdley and knew everyone and everything there was to know, so she was a great source for local knowledge.

It was she who had told Caroline about the mansion when she first arrived, suggesting she volunteered. "Good way to make new friends, my dear," she had said. "Mind you, it's very posh up there, but it's been good for the town and brings lots of visitors."

Caroline was now sitting outside the cafe by the harbour, having a coffee and chatting to her sister on the phone. Her older sister, Elizabeth, and her husband Gregory had recently moved to the Ayrshire coast, so with five hundred miles between them, they kept in touch with a daily phone or video call. Caroline was telling her about the Patrons Evening and all the glamorous people and celebrities she had seen.

"It really was a spectacular event. I wish you could have seen it," she said.

"Sounds fabulous. I'm so glad you enjoyed it. You need to get out more to things like that. Did you meet anyone interesting? We do worry about you stuck out there in the middle of nowhere, all alone," said Elizabeth, who was always hoping her sister would find someone to share her life with.

"It's not the middle of nowhere. I'm only three miles out of St Mawdley, and I like being 'all alone'. Anyway, I must go, the line is breaking up. I'll catch you tomorrow. Take care, love to everyone. Bye bye," she said, disconnecting the call, pretending to have lost phone signal.

She really didn't want to get into discussing Lawrence or, heaven forbid, let it slip about Freddie Harrison. Elizabeth would only worry if she thought she had done what she did on Facebook, and telling her sister not to worry was like telling a fish not to swim.

She sat back in her chair. The sun was warm on her face, competing with the cold wind that blew onto the patio every now and again, but Caroline always liked to be outside whenever she could. The unique smell from the harbour — a mixture of fish, seaweed and salty air — brought back powerful memories of childhood holidays. It took her right back to those happy times, walking hand in hand along the shore with her father, playing tennis and cricket with him on the beach and rock pooling. The trips to the coast were always very special, happy times with her parents and her two sisters, but especially with her father, who she had adored. The sounds and smells of the sea always evoked wonderful memories of being happy and safe in his loving care.

Her father had died many years ago, about the age Caroline was now. Her mother had lived over thirty years on her own after he died, dedicating her time to her daughters and their families. She liked nothing better than spoiling her grandchildren, especially through her love of baking. She had been the matriarch of the family until the day she died, at the grand old age of ninety.

Caroline and her sisters missed their parents terribly, but life was busy raising families, and the years rolled by. The three girls all remained close, despite the physical distance between them. Elizabeth and her family were in Scotland; Katharine and hers living in the States. They did their best to all get together at least once a year and keep the family united, especially for the sake of the cousins who always enjoyed their time with each other. Caroline looked forward to their next reunion, hopefully next summer here in Cornwall before it got too busy.

St Mawdley was at its best, now that the height of the tourist season was over, but it would soon be half-term, so she had to make the most of the next few weeks before the narrow streets were once again packed with visitors.

She was just finishing her coffee when she thought she saw Lawrence heading towards her, head bent against the wind, a purple, woolly hat on his head and a college scarf wrapped around his neck. He was wearing a well-worn duffle coat. He was walking quickly and didn't see her as he pushed open the door to the cafe. A few minutes later, he came out with a takeaway coffee.

"Hello, Lawrence," she said, when she was sure it was him.

"Caroline! Hi, sorry, I didn't see you there," he said, looking surprised. "Just popped in for my afternoon treat. They do great pastries here, and I'm addicted," he said, holding up a brown paper bag.

"Yes, I know, I've just had one myself. So, is this near to your gallery?" she asked curiously.

"I'm just around the corner; a very narrow lane, looks more like an entryway. Blink and you will miss me, but I was lucky to get it. Call in and see me sometime. It's called The Wainwright Gallery. I've just closed up for the day, and I'm off to deliver a painting to a client in Truro, but please pop in. But I will only be open at weekends after half-term."

"OK, I will do that. Enjoy your pastry, and I will see you one of these days," she said, raising her coffee cup to him.

"Good, I will look forward to that. Well, I had better be off. You take care. Bye," he said, taking a slurp from his coffee cup and hurrying off down the road.

It was a couple of weeks until she was back in St Mawdley. Her days off from the gallery had been taken up helping Bert look after Edna, who had finally undergone her hip replacement. Bert had been very grateful to Caroline for helping care for her, but as she said, she was happy to put her old nursing skills to good use. Edna was the perfect patient and followed instructions to the letter, doing her daily exercises and regaining her mobility very quickly, which was no mean feat at eighty-six. She was now making good progress, no longer needing the crutches and managing very well with a stick and desperate to get out for a walk, but Bert was confining her to the house and garden path until she was steadier.

"He's being a right old fusspot," Edna told Caroline, when she came round to keep her company while Bert took Peggy for a walk.

"You just have to be patient, Edna. You can't risk a fall, for heaven's sake. Another few weeks, if it doesn't get too cold, and then you can go out for a gentle stroll," said Caroline, patting her on the knee as they sat by the fire.

"A few weeks! Oh dear… It's no fun getting old, dear, but it's better than the alternative! You keep active and young, whatever you do," she said with a grin.

"I will do my best, Edna," she said, just as Peggy came bounding back in.

Her thick, black-and-tan coat felt cold and damp from the sea spray. No matter how much Bert tried to deter her, she loved dashing in and barking at the waves.

"Peggy! Get into the kitchen before you soak us all," scolded Edna, as Peggy sheepishly retreated to the kitchen where Bert was just taking off his boots.

"I will be off now. I'm going into St Mawdley tomorrow, so give me a call if you need anything," said Caroline as she left, waving goodbye to Bert and Peggy on her way out through the front door.

The next day, Caroline took a trip into town before the half-term invasion. St Mawdley had a magic all of its own — not just the incredible light that attracted artists from far and wide, but the beautiful harbour, beach and quaint cottages that were dotted haphazardly among the narrow, twisting, cobbled streets. It was all so charming and reminiscent of days gone by. However, unlike the past, the quaint fishermen's cottages were now mostly second homes and priced well out of reach of the local people. Although Caroline enjoyed the peace and quiet of the town out of season, it was sad to see the heart and soul of what a working fishing port had once been, slowly disappear, but times change, and tourism had replaced the fishing industry in so many coastal towns. St Mawdley was lucky though, as more and more people were coming to live in the town and set up businesses to cater for the tourists and locals alike.

She parked her car at the edge of town and walked down the steep hill towards the harbour, where one of the few remaining fishing boats was making its way in, followed by a host of seagulls, squawking loudly, hoping for some scraps. Caroline stopped and watched, breathing in the magnificent smell of the harbour, watching the fishermen unload their catches.

It was a beautiful, autumn day, cold but sunny, with clear, blue skies. She was wrapped up warmly in a long, red, woollen coat and warm boots. Her head was uncovered as she enjoyed the feel of the wind blowing in her hair, although the damp atmosphere made her hair curl, especially the wispy bits of grey around her face.

She visited the bookstore owned by Sophia and her husband Mark, a young, friendly couple from London, who passionately believed there was still room on the high street for an independent bookstore, despite the trend of eBooks and Amazon. They had been proved right, as the locals as well as the tourists loved to browse the bookshelves that were stacked with best sellers, as well as giving space to local authors. There were comfy old armchairs in a back room for customers to sit a while and get a feel for a book in peace and quiet. The resident black cat, Guinness, would sometimes deign to hop on the back of the chair, looking over the shoulder of the reader, purring loudly. It was a comfortable place to be and take your time, and they had made the bookstore a 'go-to' destination in town and were very much part of the community now.

Caroline entered via a half-glazed door with the name 'The Book Worm' etched on the glass. A little bell on the door tinkled, alerting Sophia.

'Hi Caroline, how are you?' she said with a beaming smile.

She was a petite girl, with strawberry-blonde hair cut in a very short elfin style, which made her brown eyes stand out like two big saucers.

"I'm good thanks, Sophia, and you?" she replied, rubbing her hands together to warm them up.

"All good with us. Getting ready for half-term. We got that new crime thriller in that you asked about — it looks good. Let me show you where it is," she said, coming out from behind the counter, dressed in baggy, denim dungarees and sneakers.

She fetched the book from the middle shelf of the crime section.

"Oh, it's a whopper, isn't it? That will keep me occupied for a week or two. Thank you for getting it in," she said, scanning the front cover of the very thick book.

"No problem; anytime. So, what are you up to today?" asked Sophia, propping herself back up on her stool behind the counter.

"Just mooching around. Having a look to see what's going on. By the way, may I ask if you know The Wainwright Gallery?" she asked, tucking the book under her arm.

"Yes, it's just up from the harbour, Guillemot Street. It's a very narrow street — you could easily miss it. Turn right at the post-box, and it's halfway up that hill. Really nice stuff — expensive though. But watch out for dishy Lawrence — he's a real ladies' man," she said grinning.

"Yes, I can imagine that. I met him up at the mansion a while ago. I'm just curious to see his gallery. I will see if I can find it. Right-ho, let me pay you for this," she said, putting the book in her capricious bag and taking out her credit card from her pocket.

"Enjoy the book. Take care of yourself. See you soon," said Sophia, as Caroline left, waving goodbye.

She made her way along the front, looking out for the pillar box, and started to climb up the steep, cobbled lane until she saw the wooden sign hanging out from the wall: 'The Wainwright Gallery'. Behind the bow-fronted window with bullseye-glass panes were two impressive, striking seascapes. Caroline noticed they had impressive four-figure price tags too, but she loved the style, bold brushstrokes and vibrant colours.

She opened the door. Another tinkling bell announced her arrival, and she entered a small gallery with a beamed ceiling and a flagstone floor, all original features of what would have been a fisherman's cottage in days gone by. Its walls displayed an array of vibrant, dramatic paintings, mostly seascapes and secluded coves, with a few delightful paintings of St Mawdley harbour. Caroline imagined they would be particularly popular with the tourists, as would be the racks of limited-edition prints dotted around the gallery.

There was a small, marble-topped desk at the far end, in front of a very old, studded, wooden door. It was half open, and Caroline could hear a kettle boiling. She coughed and waited.

A few seconds later, a young girl in a very short miniskirt, with long, bright, titian hair cascading in tight curls around a pretty face, appeared with a coffee cup in her hand. "Oh, I'm sorry, I didn't hear you come in. Can I help you or are you happy to browse?" she asked with a huge smile, setting her cup out of sight on the desk behind a very elaborate Art Deco lamp.

"I was wondering if Lawrence was here?" Caroline asked, trying not to stare at this pretty young girl.

She looked like one of the subjects of a Rosetti painting, with her porcelain complexion and dancing, green eyes.

"Mr Wainwright is up in his studio. I can give him a ring. Who shall I say is calling?" she asked, reaching for her phone.

"I don't want to disturb him if he is busy. Just tell him Caroline called," she said, smiling at her, captivated by her looks.

"He won't mind. Let me call him and see if he can come down," she replied.

A few minutes later, Lawrence appeared from a back room, looking very much the working artist in paint-splattered jeans and a loose, billowing, blue shirt, wiping his hands on a cloth.

"Caroline, how nice to see you. So, you found me in my hideaway location," he said, brushing his wavy hair back from his face, leaving a smudge of paint on his forehead and smiling broadly.

"It's a lovely location — very quaint little street. I love your paintings — very impressive — and this is such a charming gallery," she said, glancing around.

"Thank you. Come up to the studio; I could do with a coffee break. Everything all right here, Mandy?" he asked, looking over at her.

"Yes, fine, Mr Wainwright. It's very quiet this afternoon," she said, smiling sweetly and sitting down behind the desk.

"Well, give me a call if you need me. Sorry, Caroline, this is Mandy. She is doing A-level art at college and helps me out a few afternoons and at holiday times. OK then, we will be up in the studio. This way, Caroline," he said, leading the way through a dark, cluttered back office and up what could only be described as a glorified ladder, to a loft room studio with huge skylights.

"Wow! This is everything I ever imagined an artist studio to be," she said, stepping up into the loft space, mesmerized by what she saw as she looked around the room.

There were various-sized canvases leaning up against the walls, a huge canvas on an easel with a sheet over it and pots of paint and artist material strewn all over the floor. There was an old, red, velvet couch in the corner, with a woollen throw draped across the back of it.

"Let me take your coat," he said, helping her out of it and throwing it over the sofa. He then cleared a well-worn leather armchair for her to sit on. "Sorry, it's a bit messy up here. Coffee OK for you? Milk, sugar?" he asked, flicking on a kettle which was sitting next to a pine mug tree with hand-crafted, brightly glazed mugs, on top of a paint-splattered fridge.

"Just a dash of milk, if you have it," she said, trying to take in the chaotic surroundings. "So, how long have you been here?"

"In this studio, just a year. I rented a cottage out of town when I moved from London five years ago, and then this came on the market. It's perfect for me, and I live in the small, attached cottage next door, so not much of a commute," he laughed.

"Sounds a perfect setup. So, what brought you to St Mawdley?" she asked, taking the mug of coffee from him, his hand brushing hers as he passed it to her.

"Always loved the place. Used to come here for holidays as a child, and then when I got divorced, I decided to give up the London rat race and do what I always wanted to do — paint," he said, picking up his stool from behind the easel and setting it down facing her. He propped himself on the edge, stretching his long, slender legs out in front.

"What did you do in London?" she asked, sipping her coffee and looking up at him.

"I was a frustrated architect, in a very busy practice, working alongside my ex-wife, so..."

"Ahh, I see. Well, you seem to have found a niche here. You really do have a beautiful style of painting," she said, looking at a stunning painting of the harbour, with a rough, stormy sea under a dark, menacing sky.

"Thank you, I'm glad you like them. I am very influenced by the Expressionists. It seems a natural way for me to paint, and thankfully, people seem to like them, although I sell more at exhibitions in London and online than I do here. But that suits me just fine — I don't intend to make a fortune; just enough to live on," he said, smiling at her, all the time watching her with those intense, blue eyes.

"A good attitude, and I couldn't agree more," she said, sipping her coffee, feeling a little self-conscious at the way he looked at her. She stood up and went over to look out of the skylights. "Quite a view from here, over the rooftops. I can see the sea too," she said.

Lawrence came over and stood very close to her, coffee cup in hand. "I like to open the windows, when the weather allows, and listen to the seagulls. It reminds me how lucky I am to be here."

"I know what you mean. The sound of the sea is so uplifting."

She turned to him for a moment, and her eyes locked into his before she turned back to the window. He reached across her and opened it, the screech from the seagulls drifting up from the harbour.

"See what I mean? Always on cue," he grinned, before closing the window again.

Caroline stepped away and looked at some of the canvases stacked against the wall. "These are fabulous — so dramatic. Where did you learn to paint?"

"Oh, I'm not trained. I have always dabbled, but when I came here, I found my style. There is great support and camaraderie among the artist community here. We all help each other out, and it's so inspirational down here. the famous Cornish light is truly breathtaking at times."

"So, you don't miss the London life?" she asked, turning back to face him.

"Sometimes I do. I go up to London now and again, for exhibitions, but I always love coming back. What about you? Do you miss your previous busy lifestyle?"

"I miss my family, the grandchildren and my old friends, but I had had enough of the antique world. I love it down here, and I have made lots of new friends. Do you have family?"

"No, we never had children. Claudia was not the maternal type — very career-minded — and I am a bit of a workaholic. I spent a lot of time with clients all over the UK and in Europe. Claudia kept the practice going in London, which she thrived on, but it wasn't conducive to a happy marriage. We were married for twenty years, but we were more like business partners for most of that time. I had affairs, and she did too. Sometimes you just steal a little bit of happiness here and there — it works for a time. Eventually she met someone she wanted to settle down with — one of our competitors — so we decided to go our separate ways. She and her new partner bought me out of the business, and we sold our home in Chelsea, which gave me the means to come down here to see if I could make a living doing what I love to do."

There was an awkward silence. Caroline thought his wife probably hadn't been too happy either. There were two sides to every story.

"I'm sorry to hear that. It must have been tough giving that all up."

"It was, but she's happy now, and so am I, and it gave me the funds and opportunity to do this," he said, waving his hand around the studio. "You have had a much tougher time, losing your husband." He reached down and brushed a loose strand of her hair from her cheek. "You have lovely hair — fabulous, rich colour, and the silver threads catch the light so beautifully. I rarely paint portraits; maybe you would let me try to paint you one day?" he said, studying her, with his head to one side.

"Ha! Before too long, there will be more than silver threads, but hey-ho. Anyway, I mustn't keep you from your work. Thanks for the coffee," she said, setting her cup on a table by the sofa.

"Thank you for calling. Maybe after half-term we could go out for a drink?" he asked, taking her hand in his and looking intently in her eyes.

"That would be lovely. I am off up to Warwickshire for a nurses' reunion next week, so when I come back, that would be great," she said, looking up at him, slowly releasing her hand and turning to the chair to pick up her coat and handbag.

"So, you were a nurse before you were an antiques dealer?" he said, helping her put on her coat.

"Yes, back in the '70s — a long time ago — but we all still keep in touch," she said, following him as he went over towards the stairs.

As she stepped off the last narrow tread, her foot slipped, and she stumbled. Lawrence held her gently by the elbow to steady her, but she was so quick to pull herself free that she nearly went over again.

"OK there?" he asked with a cheeky grin, putting his hand out again.

"Fine, thank you," she said, letting go of his hand, feeling her heart beating a little bit faster.

"Well, have a nice time at your reunion. It's good to keep in touch with old friends. Speaking of keeping in touch, may I have your phone number?" he asked.

"Of course. I will write it down for you," she said, looking around for something to write on.

He went over to a cluttered desk and picked up a notepad and pen, handing them to her to scribble down her mobile number. She was very aware of his closeness to her, and his cologne, which she thought was Dior, was very alluring, just like him.

"Great, thank you. I will give you a ring after next week," he said, bending to kiss her on the cheek.

She held his gaze for a moment before going through to the shop, where Mandy was engrossed in a magazine.

"Bye, Mandy, nice to meet you," she said, as Mandy quickly put the magazine under the desk.

"Bye, nice to meet you too," she said, standing up and wriggling her pert bottom, as she straightened her tight miniskirt.

"See you soon. Have fun and take care," said Lawrence, as she opened the door, the bell gently tinkling.

"Bye, Lawrence," she said, giving him a wave as she stepped out onto the street.

"Ooohh, she's nice, Mr Wainwright," said Mandy, winking at him, as he stood in the office doorway, watching Caroline walk away.

"Get back to your 'revision', Mandy," he laughed, going through to the office and back up to his studio, with a spring in his step, feeling optimistic about the lovely Caroline.

He stood looking out through the open Velux window, smoking a cigarette and thinking about her. He suspected she was older than she looked, unless she had been a teenage bride. She was certainly older than the women he usually dated, but he liked her style and elegance.

He sat down on his stool and lifted the sheet off his current piece of work, admiring it. He was pleased with how it had turned out. It had taken longer than usual, but it was worth his patience with his novice sitter. He loved the challenge of figure painting, a change from his usual seascapes. Variety was the spice of life, as they said. He turned his attention back to the canvas, carefully scrutinizing every detail. He sat back, satisfied, blowing cigarette smoke towards the open window before stubbing it out in a miniature, novelty fire bucket filled with sand.

Chapter Four

The following week, Caroline was preparing for her trip up to Warwickshire. She wasn't looking forward to the long drive and hoped that if she timed it right by leaving early the next morning, she would avoid the half-term traffic. Her bag was packed and everything ready, so there was nothing more to do than pour a nice glass of wine, put on her favourite classical-guitar CD and relax by the fire, before having an early night.

She settled down and picked up her laptop to check that there were no last-minute messages from Joleen, and thankfully there weren't. She hated it when carefully laid plans were altered. She was scrolling quickly through her Facebook page when she saw that Freddie had posted a current picture of himself and his daughter and grandchildren, with Warwick Castle in the background.

Blimey, I don't believe it, she thought to herself. He had made a comment about quality family time.

Over the last couple of months, since they had linked up, they had 'liked' and shared posts on Facebook and occasionally commented on them, but she had no idea that he was coming over to England. She quickly sent him a message.

'Great pic. Looks like you're having a fun time in the old stomping ground. You never know — we might bump into each other if you're staying in CastleAvon!"

She looked again at the picture. He looked well and happy. Apart from the grey hair and neatly trimmed beard, he hadn't changed a bit. *Wouldn't it be funny to bump into him?* she thought.

She set her laptop on the floor beside her and took a sip of wine. *It would be nice to see him again, for old times' sake,* she thought. If only they had known they would both be in Warwickshire at the same time, they could maybe have arranged to meet. *Ah well, not meant to be,* she thought, as she leaned back, closed her eyes and listened to the soothing sounds of a Spanish guitar. Before long, she had nodded off.

The fire embers were dying in the grate when she woke up, and the music had finished playing. She was annoyed at herself for dropping off to sleep. She straightened herself up in the chair, looking at the antique clock on the mantlepiece, feeling groggy. She finished off her glass of wine and picked up her laptop to switch it off. She noticed a message alert and hoped it wasn't Joleen to say the reunion was cancelled, or something awful. She clicked on it and saw a message from Freddie.

'You home too? I'm over to spend half-term with the grandkids. How long are you up for?'

Caroline noticed the message had been sent over an hour ago. It was eleven o'clock now. Was it too late to reply? she wondered, but she decided too anyway.

'Just for the weekend (nurses reunion Sat night.) I come back down on Sunday.'

A few minutes later, there was a reply: 'Shall we meet up for a coffee on Sunday morning?'

Caroline was surprised and excited at the thought. She replied: 'OK. Eleven suit you? The old Castle Tea Rooms?'

A reply from Freddie came straight back: 'Perfect, see you there.'

Well, well, well! I wasn't expecting that. This is going to be an eventful weekend indeed, she thought, as she put the guard in front of the fire, switched off the lamp and climbed the stairs to bed, not sure if she would be able to sleep with the butterflies jumping in her tummy.

Warwickshire

On Sunday morning, Freddie was having second thoughts about meeting Caroline. *Why do I act so impulsively?* he thought, as he dressed in jeans and a pale-lemon polo neck. He was just putting on tan brogues, when his six-year-old granddaughter came bouncing in.

"You look very nice, Grandpapa. Are you going out? Can I come with you?" she said, throwing her arms around his neck and kissing him on the nose.

"Not this morning, my poppet. I'm going to meet a very old friend, but I will be back this afternoon," he said, picking her up for a cuddle.

"Then can we go out?" she pleaded, hugging him tight, her long, blond hair cascading down her back in curls.

"Of course. We can go to the park and feed the ducks. Now, let's go downstairs and get me a cup of coffee before I go," he said, setting her down and picking up his wallet from the dressing table.

"OK, Grandpapa. Daddy is making pancakes, so you can have some too, but we had better hurry, before my brother eats them all," she said, taking his hand and pulling him along the landing, as she skipped happily in front of him.

Caroline was having second thoughts, too, about her impulsive decision to meet up with Freddie. She was sitting having breakfast in the hotel dining room with the last few remaining colleagues from the night before. They were all slightly subdued after a night of hilarity and catching up — not to mention a little too much wine — but it had been a great night, and now everyone was going back to their homes in all parts of the UK. Eventually, by ten o'clock, it was just Joleen sitting with her, finishing off the pot of strong coffee.

"What time are you heading off?" asked Joleen, looking at her watch and tucking her hair behind her ear.

She kept her hair in a short bob these days, but Caroline wasn't surprised that she still kept the jet-black colour, and she couldn't imagine her ever letting it go grey. Joleen would be a vibrant, action-filled woman until the day she died.

"This afternoon. I'm meeting an old friend later this morning. What about you?"

"Terry is picking me up in half an hour. He stayed the night with an old friend in Coventry. It's a long drive back to Carlisle, so I hope he is fit to drive! So, who is this mysterious old friend you are meeting, may I ask?" she said, raising an eyebrow.

"Freddie Harrison."

"What! Freddie Harrison, your old boyfriend that you cruelly dumped for what's-his-name — God's gift to womankind?"

Caroline laughed. "I'm surprised you remember. Yes, that Freddie."

"How could I forget all the drama when you ditched him for what's-his-name — the medical student; the self-indulgent, spoilt b*****d. I never liked him. Well, don't go getting all dewy-eyed over Freddie. How did you get back in touch anyway?"

"Facebook, of course. I just wanted to catch up and see what had become of him," said Caroline, sheepishly.

"For goodness' sake! I hope you're not looking to rekindle your old love. Well, I suppose you know what you're doing. Just take it easy — people can change a lot in forty-odd years. You had a good man in Robert — his shoes will be hard to fill," she said, patting her old friend's hand.

"Indeed, they are, but we are just meeting up for coffee — no big deal. It was a pure coincidence that we were both in town this weekend," she replied.

"Well, be careful, but have fun, my dear. You deserve a bit of that. It's been great seeing you and keep in touch. Hopefully see you long before the next reunion. Come up and stay with us when we get back from Italy in the spring, if you can tear yourself away from your coastal idyll."

"I will, and there is always a bed for you if you make it down to Cornwall," said Caroline, getting up to give Joleen a hug.

"I'm off, before I start blubbering. You take care of yourself," said Joleen, waving as she made her way out to the foyer, leaving Caroline the last one in the dining room.

She sat looking out through the window, sipping her coffee. She had been surprised that Joleen had remembered that time when she went out with Jason. Joleen had never liked him. She had known he was not right for her, and she had been cross with her for breaking up with Freddie the way she had. But she had always been there for her when things went wrong with Jason, which they did every few weeks. She was right when she said he was spoilt. The only son of wealthy parents, he had everything he ever wished for, and he used her like one of his playthings to take out when he felt like it, breaking her heart so many times. It had taken Caroline two years to realise her infatuation for him was destroying her, sapping her confidence and slowly killing her spirit, breaking her apart. Thankfully, Joleen had been there to help her pick up the pieces, until Robert had come along and saved her completely. He and Freddie had been the only two men she had ever truly been in love with, in her life.

The waiters were beginning to start clearing the breakfast tables, shaking her from her thoughts. She finished her coffee, folded the crisp, white napkin neatly on the table and made her way to the lift to get ready to meet up with Freddie. She hoped she could have his friendship once again.

As she arrived at the front of the Castle Tea Rooms, Freddie stepped forward, smiling. His silvery-blonde hair swept back off his tanned face and a neatly trimmed beard were the only differences from the person she remembered, who use to stand there, waiting for her after school. That memory was so vivid, it took her breath away. He was wearing a smart, full-length, navy wool coat over jeans and beautiful, tan leather shoes. He looked well-groomed and very elegant. He looked at her with the twinkling, green eyes she remembered so well, his wide, generous mouth breaking into a bigger smile.

"Hello, Caroline, good to see you," he said, reaching forward to kiss her lightly on the cheek.

"Hello, Freddie, nice to see you again," she said, looking up at him as he opened the door for her.

He had matured well; so very different from the last time she had seen him as a scruffy student on the steps of the nurses' home when they broke up.

"This old place has hardly changed," she said, as they walked past the cake shop on the ground floor.

The wooden floorboards still creaked as they walked across towards the stairs, shining with centuries of polish.

"Yeah, I'm pleased to see it hasn't been modernised. After all, it's been here since Shakespeare's day," he said, stopping briefly on the first landing.

He looked up towards the doors leading into the tearoom, a flashing image in his mind of Caroline coming down towards him all those years ago. He let her pass him as they made their way up to the top landing. They stopped together. It was like stepping back in time, as he held the door for her.

"After you," he said.

Not surprisingly though, it looked very different. The old Formica-topped tables that they remembered had been replaced by round tables with crisp, white, linen tablecloths and a little vase of flowers on each table. It was very much the typical English tearoom that the tourists expected nowadays in such an historic town, and this morning they had the place to themselves.

"I bet sixth formers don't come here any more — no juke box!" he said, grinning.

A smartly dressed waitress in a short, black dress and frilly, white apron, her dark hair tucked up under a little white cap, came over to them, smiling broadly. "Good morning, sir, madam. Sit anywhere you like, and I will be over to take your order in a few minutes. Shall I take your coats?"

"Thank you," they said in unison.

They unbuttoned their warm coats, handing them to the young girl. They made their way over to the table by the leaded window which overlooked the street below. The warm, honey-coloured stone of the castle walls and the ancient gateway to the town shone in the morning sunlight. Caroline sat down, while Freddie held her chair.

"These chairs are a lot more comfortable than the ones from back in the day," she said, as Freddie sat down opposite her.

"Yeah, the wooden chairs with the plastic seats. We used to tip back in them to see how far we could get before toppling on the floor. Nellie the waitress use to clip us boys round the ear, as we scrambled back on our feet!" laughed Freddie, relaxing a little.

The waitress came over just then. "We have just finished serving breakfast, but I could do a toasted teacake or croissant, if that would suit? Lunch starts at midday."

"Just coffee for me — I've already had a full English at the hotel," said Caroline, looking at Freddie.

"Coffee for me too, but I will have a croissant as well, thank you," said Freddie, smiling up at the young girl, who blushed as she hurried away.

"So... you are looking well, Caroline. Are you keeping well?" he asked, resting his hands on the table.

He smiled as he gazed at her, thinking how lovely she looked in the soft shade of blue she was wearing. He noticed the delicate, sapphire, flower stud earrings which matched her eyes perfectly, as she brushed her hair back behind her ears.

"I am fine, thank you. You are looking well, too. Enjoying being with your family, I'm sure?" she said, her eyes drawn to his.

"Lovely time, thanks, but its hectic with the grandchildren. Did you have a nice time at your reunion?" he asked.

"A real trip down memory lane. We had a lot of fun — a little worse for wear this morning," she smiled, mimicking a yawn.

"Well, you look as fresh as a daisy. Are you still nursing?" he asked, leaning forward slightly.

Caroline didn't put many personal details on her Facebook page, so he wasn't sure.

"I retired from nursing many years ago. My late husband and I were in the antique business in the Cotswolds, but for the last few years I have been enjoying the art world, working part time at a large gallery/museum near St Mawdley in Cornwall. I just love it," she said enthusiastically.

"Sounds like you have found a niche. I remember you enjoyed your art. I'm sorry to hear you lost your husband," he said, as they smiled awkwardly at each other, and a heavy silence fell between them.

"What about you? Are you enjoying life in Paris?" asked Caroline, as the waitress brought over pretty China cups and saucers, decorated with delicate flowers, setting them down in front of them.

"Very much so. I moved over after my divorce ten years ago. My aunt and uncle let me 'house-sit' their apartment when they retired and moved out to New York, so it gave me the opportunity to concentrate on my writing, which earns me a living, thankfully. I miss the family, of course, but I come back as often as I can."

"That's sounds exciting — you were always good with words. I remember the poems you used to write. I'm very glad you have been able to make a career from it," she said, feeling genuinely pleased for him.

"I'm actually working on a collection of poems at the moment, which I hope will get published next year — fingers crossed. So, what about you? What do you do apart from the art gallery?"

"Oh, this and that. I don't know where the time goes. I paint a little bit, write silly, topical rhymes a little bit, walk on the beach a lot and generally fill my days. I miss my family though, but they moved to opposite ends of the country when they got married, so I followed my dream to live by the sea. I try and visit them when I can, but Cornwall is a long way from anywhere. But it's a great place for them to come visit me when they get the time, which isn't often, unfortunately!"

Freddie smiled a smile that took Caroline back forty years. She leaned back in her chair, looking out of the window at the street below. Her eye caught the little ancient alleyway that was a shortcut back to school. She remembered how they used to kiss, leaning against the ancient stone wall, before heading back to class. She blushed slightly at the memory. She noticed that Freddie was looking in that direction too and wondered if he had been thinking the same thing. She turned to him, sadness in her eyes. It was so lovely to see him sitting there. This had always been their table, all those years ago — so many memories.

"Penny for your thoughts," he said, tilting his head to one side, the way he used to do.

"Thinking back — getting a bit too nostalgic," she said, just as the young waitress brought over a cafetiere of coffee and a croissant, the smell of freshly made coffee and warm croissant drifting between them. "That looks nice. I wonder if it will be up to French standards?"

"I'm sure it will," he said, breaking a bit off the end of the croissant and offering it to her, just the way they had always shared tasty treats.

"Thank you. Hmmm, it's good," she said, wiping a crumb from her mouth. "Shall I pour?"

Freddie nodded and pushed his cup closer to her, as she poured the coffee. "So, this is quite a coincidence, isn't it?" he asked.

"Certainly is. I was very surprised when I saw your Facebook post with the castle in the background. Your family look lovely. You have one daughter?"

"Yes, just one — Alison. She is married to Ben, and they have two children — a boy and a girl. I love them very much. What about you?" he asked.

"Two sons, David and James. Both married, with five children between them — all adorable," she said, sipping her coffee.

He was quiet for a moment, leaning back in his chair, staring at her, wondering again why he had come. It was like sticking a knife in an old wound.

His voice was full of emotion when he spoke. "I nearly changed my mind about coming this morning. I wasn't sure I could handle seeing you again."

"Oh, Freddie… And how are you handling it?" she asked nervously, hoping he didn't bear a grudge for the way she had broken up their relationship.

He didn't say anything for a moment, exploring his feelings gingerly, and then he straightened up, his eyes watery. "Not that well, to be honest," he said, looking down at his hands resting on the table.

Caroline didn't know what to say. She hadn't thought the emotions could run this high after all this time. Seeing him sitting there, exactly where he used to sit over forty years ago, it was as if the years just rolled away, the edges of the memory no longer blurred.

"Oh, Freddie. It was a long time ago. So much has happened since then. I am so sorry I hurt you all those years ago." She paused. "Im not proud of how I behaved but we were just kids. I bitterly regret the way we parted. The image of you walking away from me has never left me," she said sadly, biting her lip.

"I remember that day too, on the steps of the nurses' home. It's one of those moments that stick in the back of your mind," he said sadly.

They both sat quietly, both with that same image in their minds, of Caroline in her nurse's uniform, with her cape wrapped tightly around her, like some sort of emotional shield, protecting her from the hurt she knew she was inflicting but carried on doing it anyway in such a selfish way, standing on the top steps, looking down at Freddie but not looking him in the eye, telling him that it was over.

Caroline looked over at him now and saw the hurt in his eyes for the very first time.

"I just want us to be friends again, if we can," she said. "After Robert died, I was devastated and spent a lot of time looking down a deep, black hole. I remembered mistakes I had made in my life — one of them was ending it with you so cruelly. Some things you can't fix, but some you can try to make better. Over the years I have often wondered how you were, what you were doing. When I saw you on Facebook, I decided that was my chance to try to put things right between us. I am so sorry," she said, turning back to look out of the window, tears forming in her eyes.

Freddie didn't say anything for a while. He watched her from the far side of the table, the girl he had loved with all his heart, all those years ago. He felt a deep pang of sorrow for her, as he cleared his throat and took her hand in is. "Oh, Caroline, I am sorry you lost your husband. That must have been tough," he said, stroking her hand.

She felt the same warm thrill that she had felt all those years ago. "Yes, it was. He was a good man, a good husband and father. I loved him very much," she said quietly, almost in a whisper.

"You were lucky," he sighed.

She looked up at him. "I know, I was. I am sorry your marriage didn't work out."

"That's life. We got married while we were both students; she was pregnant with Alison," he said, holding her gaze.

Caroline realised they must have got together not long after she and Freddie had split up.

"Everything was fine for a while. We both adored our baby, but we were a mismatch, really. We moved to Paris, while I did my PhD at the Sorbonne, but she hated living there, so we came back and I took up teaching, which I hated. We stayed together until Alison started secondary school, but then things got too rocky, and we eventually divorced, quite amicably. She lives in a commune in Ireland now and is very happy with her new life and her new man." He hesitated, and their eyes met." I also have a new woman in my life, Francois. We have been together for a few months," he said, finishing off the croissant and wiping his mouth with the linen napkin.

"Oh! Does she know you are meeting me today?" she asked.

"Not yet," he said, looking her directly in the eye.

"I hope you can find happiness with her," she said, suddenly feeling a rush of something she recognised as jealously.

"We shall see," he said, sitting quietly. "What about you? Do you think you will ever marry again?"

She shook her head slightly. "No, I don't think so. But who knows? It would be nice to have someone to share interests with, go out to dinner with occasionally, walks on the beach, have coffee with — that kind of thing," she said.

"You are still a beautiful woman and still young — don't forget that," he said, taking her hand again.

"Too many grey hairs," she laughed, flicking her hair back from her face.

"Ha! Indeed, don't we all," he said, running his hand through his thick, silvery hair.

"You are still a handsome man, Freddie," she said, looking deep into his eyes. "We had that special first love, didn't we? The kind that one never forgets."

"We did. You will always have a part of my heart, Caroline," he said, kissing her hand, remembering she had been the love of his life and he would probably never find another love like it.

The forty years had slipped away the moment he saw her. It was like looking at the eighteen-year-old girl he had loved so much. Feelings like that just didn't vanish into mid-air, but it was hard to untangle them for what he should be feeling today. He felt guilty for thinking like this. He was with Francois now — he was not the type of man to cheat. This was just an old friendship, what he felt was just an echo from another time. Their lives were so different now, and it would be impossible to go back to what they once had, but they could be friends — there was no harm in that.

"Friends forever?" she asked, holding his gaze.

"Friends forever," he replied, patting the back of her hand.

They relaxed little by little after that and started chatting as easily as they had all those years ago. She was reminded of what a good sense of humour he had and how funny he could be. He was just as kind and gentle as he had been as a teenager. Seeing him was a trip back in time, the years slipping away in a mist, and she felt the same attraction to him as she had back then. She quickly reminded herself that she must consider him a friend and not a romance, but she couldn't take her eyes off him. It was as though he was some kind of mirage.

The tearoom began to get busy, with people coming in for lunch. They realised that the morning had flown by in a most enjoyable way. Each of them felt they had tidied up the past and what they had once was probably best left in the past.

Back out in the street, Freddie took her hands in his and kissed her on the cheek. "You take care of yourself, Caroline. I hope things work out the way you want them to — you deserve that."

"Ditto for you," she said, looking up into his eyes, then bending her head so that he couldn't see her eyes moisten with unused tears.

He put his hand under her chin, tilting her head to look at him and kissed her on the cheek again. "Bye, Caroline, it's been lovely to see you again. Take care, and keep in touch," he said, mimicking tapping a keyboard.

As he walked away, he turned and waved. He hadn't done that all those years ago when they had ended their teenage romance. Caroline watched as he walked on down the street towards the stone-arched gateway, his coat billowing out in the wind, just like it did when he was a student. A wave of sadness almost drowned her, but it had been so good to see him again. She pulled her coat collar up, wiped a tear away and wandered back to her car, thinking that this might well be the last time she made this trip. She had no family here now, her parents long dead. She doubted she would ever see Freddie again.

She turned off the main street, the beautiful church of St Anne's ahead of her, towering over the ancient, cobbled streets. She passed shops that had been so familiar to her as she was growing up. The old hardware store was still there, with its chaotic, crowded aisles, selling everything from loose nails to lawnmowers, presumably still doing well, she supposed old Mr Jackson would be long since gone. She wondered who in the family was carrying on, and then she noticed the sign proudly proclaiming, 'Jackson & Daughter' above the door. She remembered Eleanor Jackson from school. *Good for her,* she thought.

She passed the old pub, with its colourful tiles decorating the entrance. She had never set foot in the place. Pubs were different back then — drinking dens for wastrels, as her mother used to say. Caroline remembered walking past with her school friends, giggling and pretending to be drunk from the fumes that drifted onto the street when the swing door opened, and an old drunk stumbled out.

Turning the corner, she came to the square where she had parked, ornamental trees lining the parking bays, with the Cenotaph still standing in the centre. More memories flooded back, of standing with her father on wet, rainy Remembrance Sundays. The raindrops were beginning to fall again now, as she took one last look around her childhood town and got into her car. As she turned on the ignition, the wipers came on, slicing away at the heavy raindrops that streaked across the windscreen and bounced upon the roof. She settled herself, switched on her CD and set off for the motorway and the long drive back to the Southwest. Tears streamed down her cheeks, to match the raindrops.

Freddie walked back to his daughter's house, along the quiet streets of CastleAvon, tears stinging his eyes too. He thought how little Caroline had changed. The moment she looked at him with her big, blue eyes, the years just fell away, tugging at his heart. He had been worried that might happen, and sure enough, it had. He felt the same attraction that he had felt as a teenager, which was crazy — they were just old friends reconnecting. He had Francois now, and his life in Paris. Caroline would find love again one day. A lovely woman like her should not be on her own — it was only a matter of time. She had been brave and determined to start a new life after she lost her husband, and when she was ready, she would find the right man. He wiped the tears away as he got close to his daughter's home. Sometimes fate could be cruel, teasing with a glimpse of what could be and then snatching it away again. He and Caroline had memories that were part of them, memories that had made them the people they became, and he would always cherish that.

Chapter Five

Cornwall

The wind had been howling through the night, a storm blowing in from the Atlantic. Rain was now lashing against the windowpanes, the trees bending, branches breaking off. Caroline lay listening, snuggling back under the duvet, warm and cosy, thinking about her trip the previous days.

They say one should never go back. Nowhere or no one is as good as you remember. To return to places and people that you hadn't seen for decades was a risky thing to do — the rose-tinted memory could be devastatingly broken so easily.

But that hadn't happened yesterday. When she saw Freddie standing at the entrance to the tearoom, the years slipped away, and in her mind, she was back to her eighteen-year-old self. She was sure he had felt the same. But life had moved on since the last time he had stood in that doorway. Her memory of him hadn't been shattered though; he was still the same kind, sweet person she had loved all those years ago, and she was glad they had met again.

The rain was easing slightly, just the pitter-patter of raindrops on the windowpanes, but the wind was blowing fiercely. She threw back the duvet and went over to look out at the garden, just as her phone started to ring. She pulled on her dressing down and picked it up, but she didn't recognise the number. *A bit early on a Monday morning for nuisance calls,* she thought. She was just about to delete it when she had second thoughts and answered the call.

"Morning, Caroline, it's Lawrence. Are you back safe and sound to the wild, windy Southwest?"

"Hi, Lawrence. Yes, I got back yesterday before the storm blew in, thank goodness. It's wild out here!" she said, sitting down on the edge of the bed.

"Wild here too. The boats in the harbour are being tossed about like corks in a jacuzzi. I'm glad to hear you are back safely." He hesitated a moment before he carried on. "So, can we arrange to meet for a drink after the storms blows through?"

"I would like that," she said, clutching her tummy as butterflies began to dance about.

"How about next Saturday at the Harbour Inn? We could have a bite to eat if you like?"

"That would be lovely — I look forward to it."

She thought she could hear a cigarette being lit, and she was surprised. She didn't take him for a smoker.

"Great. I will book a table for seven, if that suits you?" he said.

"Perfect, I will see you there."

"Look forward to it, Caroline, see you on Saturday. Meanwhile, take care if you go out, there's been a lot of damage to trees. Bye for now."

"Bye, Lawrence, you take care too," she said, and the line went dead.

Well, well, well, good job I answered, she thought, as she stared at the phone. Then, with a smile on her face, she decided to add the number to her list of contacts.

The storm raged for the rest of the week. She hadn't been able to get to the gallery, as a tree had blocked the lane, and as it was not a public highway, it was low on the list of jobs for the authorities. But luckily, she had enough food to keep her going, and thankfully the power lines were still intact. She had been worried about her neighbours, Bert and Edna, but when she battled her way in the wind to check on them, she found they had adapted the wartime spirit and were managing very well.

It was Friday before the storm abated and Caroline got out for a walk on the beach. The waves were still crashing in loud and strong, which she found very exhilarating, but a lot of debris had been brought in on the tide, including huge tree trunks and a worrying amount of plastic.

She met Bert and Edna coming back from their walk, Peggy bounding along in front. Edna was walking with just a stick for support, on the rough ground.

"Hi, you two. Good to be out again, isn't it?" she said, as Peggy nuzzled in close to her.

"It's grand. We've been cooped up enough these last few weeks," said Edna, waving her stick in the air.

"Well, look at you now, striding along as good as new. I don't suppose you know if the tree has been cleared off the lane yet?"

"Not yet, Caroline, it might well be Monday. Do you need to get out, is there anything we can help you with?" asked Bert.

His cap flew off, leaving his thick, black, curly hair blowing wildly in the wind. Peggy ran after it, bringing it back to him.

"No, it's OK. I was hoping to go into town tomorrow, but I guess I will have to cancel."

"That's a shame. Was it important?" asked Edna, looking concerned.

"Believe it or not, it was a dinner date, but hey-ho, it can be rearranged, I'm sure," she said, looking slightly embarrassed. It had felt awkward saying she was going out with someone.

"A dinner date! Oh, that sounds nice! It's about time you got out and had a bit of male company. Bert and I are always saying it's a shame for you to be on your own. Bert is there nothing we can do to get this girl into town for her date?" asked Edna, with determination.

Bert scratched his head and put his cap back on. "I will give young Nigel a call and see if he can come and shift the tree to the side with his tractor, and then I could give you a lift in the Land Rover. Your little car wouldn't make it, but the Landy might."

"Oh, Bert, I couldn't put you to all that trouble."

"Nonsense. I can't promise, mind you, but we will give it a damn good try," he said, pulling his cap down tighter on his head and giving her a wink.

"We shall get you to your date, have no fear," said Edna with a beaming smile, sounding like a fairy godmother.

Caroline had spent a great part of Saturday preparing for her date. She felt more like a teenager than a woman in her late fifties. Her sister had told her on the phone earlier, during their hour-long conversation, to try and relax.

"It's only dinner," she had said. "No big deal," but she had been as excited as Caroline when she had told her. It was Gregory who had told her to tell Caroline to calm down and play it cool.

She had just finished blow-drying her hair, which was always a disaster due to the stubborn nature of her thick, wavy hair, but she eventually managed to tame it into a sleekish bob, which she knew as soon as she hit the sea air, would bounce back into its natural wavy way.

She had selected her outfit several times but finally settled on designer jeans and a lavender-coloured, cashmere, cowl-neck sweater. She had had the jeans for years, but they were comfy and still smart, and thankfully, at size twelve, they still fitted her. Slipping on her favourite mock lizard-skin, tan, high-heeled ankle boots, she took a look in the full-length mirror. "You'll do," she said, as she hurried downstairs, putting on a beautifully tailored, pale-blue, three-quarter-length cashmere coat. She picked up her handbag which matched her boots and set off for Bert and Edna's house at the bottom of the lane.

"Oh my, oh my, you look lovely dear. Bert! Caroline is here, and you'd better grab a blanket for that dusty old car seat — she's got a lovely coat on," called Edna, when she answered the door.

"Thank you, Edna. It feels a bit surreal to be going out on a date."

"Well, just relax. He is a lucky chap to have you as his dinner date," she said, just as Bert appeared.

Zipping up his wax jacket and holding a tartan car rug under his arm, he said, "Right-ho, let's get going, young lady," he said, running over to the Land Rover to open the door for her, as Edna waved goodbye.

It was a very bumpy ride up the lane towards the main road. Lots of debris and fallen branches were scattered about — perfect for puncturing tyres, except for those on a 4x4. But it wasn't long until Bert dropped her off outside the Harbour Inn, with the offer to come and pick her up.

"Thanks, Bert. Can I ring you a bit later when I know what time?"

"Of course, my dear. I don't go to bed before midnight. You have a lovely time. Bye bye, dear," he said, as she jumped down and watched him drive off.

She stood at the bottom of the steps of the pub she knew so well, the fairy lights under the sign swinging in the wind, but tonight it felt like an alien place to her. There were some lads drinking and smoking on the terrace, under the heat lamps. They watched her as she came up the steps, then one of them stepped across and opened the door for her. She smiled and thanked him, and he gave her a wink. Did he know she was on a date, or was she getting paranoid?

She was really hoping Lawrence was already there. It was just after seven as she walked up towards the bar, when she heard him call her name. She looked over, and there he was, as handsome as ever in jeans, a navy, V-neck sweater and a pale-blue shirt which matched his eyes perfectly.

"Hi, you look lovely," he said, as he came over to her, kissing her on the cheek, helping her off with her coat and setting it on the spare chair at their table.

"Thank you. You have got us my favourite table by the fire," she said, settling down in the chair.

"Good, I'm glad. This sounds like a corny line, but do you come here often?" he said, grinning.

Caroline laughed. "Ha, not really, but when I come with friends or family, we always try to get this table. It's quite busy tonight, isn't it?"

"What can I get you to drink?" he asked, as the waiter came over with the menu and the wine list.

"Just a glass of red," she answered, looking up at the waiter.

Lawrence looked at the wine list and ordered a bottle of their best red. "Is that OK for you? Neither of us are driving, so we might as well have a bottle. I noticed you were dropped off by someone?" he said.

"Perfect, thank you. Yes, I got a lift in with my neighbour, Bert. It's a long story, but we had a tree come down during the storm, which blocked the lane, so Bert managed to get through in his 4x4. It would have been impassable in my little car."

"My goodness, have you been trapped all week? You poor thing. Well, I can give you a lift back if you want?"

"If you have a 4x4, that would be great — save me calling Bert out."

"I have a beaten-up old jeep that I use for collecting supplies and stuff. It's a real boneshaker, but it will get you home," he said, just as the waiter brought over the wine.

"Thank you, that's very kind. I will give Bert a ring later and tell him he doesn't need to come back for me."

"Cheers. That colour really suits you, by the way," he said, raising his glass to her and looking intently into her deep-blue eyes.

"Cheers," she replied, taking a sip from her glass, unable to take her eyes off him.

Caroline was surprised how quickly she relaxed with him. The food arrived, and they chatted about the storm.

Lawrence told her how bad the town had been battered. "I was glad I was up a side street. The shops on the front got flooded by the very high tide, but all the shopkeepers rallied round with sandbags, to protect as much as they could. Sophie was lucky in the bookstore and escaped any damage, but Pat's cafe patio tables ended up in the harbour."

"Oh, my goodness, poor Pat! It was a dreadful storm," she said, as she told him about the tree trunks and the huge amounts of plastic washed up on the beach, but she was lucky that her cottage was spared. "The tree on the lane was the most disruption I had," she said.

"You should have called me, I could have come out to help," he said, looking at her with interest.

"Oh, I couldn't have done that, we've only just met. I can't start calling in favours!" she laughed.

"Well, I hope you don't hesitate in the future, now that we're friends," he said, raising his glass to her again and giving her a cheeky wink.

The conversation flowed as easily as the wine, helping her to relax. She laughed while listening to Lawrence's amusing stories about his life as an architect, travelling around the country to some very remote locations, helping to create grand designs for his super-rich clients. He said he had always felt guilty creating luxurious homes for people who would only ever use them as holiday homes once or twice a year. Before he had retired from it all, he had started a project — building affordable, eco-friendly, timber homes, which he was very proud of, especially as it had set a trend with many of his like-minded architects in London. Other similar projects were now being built around the country. He had even encouraged one of his former colleagues to get involved with the local planning department here, to put forward a plan to develop some derelict farm buildings into eco-homes for young, local families.

Caroline was delighted when she heard that, knowing that it was what young people needed to encourage them to stay in the community and bring up their children in this wonderful location. She listened to his lovely, warm voice, captivated by it. She had forgotten how nice it was to share time with an intelligent, attractive man. She was beginning to realise that maybe she had locked herself away long enough. She would only stay young if she kept doing the things she loved to do, and she loved doing this.

A folk band was setting up in the corner by the window, and the bar was filling up and getting noisier. They were a typical sea shanty group of bearded men wearing spotted neckerchiefs and big boots, singing their hearts out and encouraging everyone to join in. Caroline and Lawrence had finished their meal and quite a bit of the wine, but Lawrence had switched to water as he would now be driving, so Caroline was feeling very mellow, warmed by the fire and very comfortable in this lovely man's company. Lawrence moved his chair round beside hers, as they relaxed and listened to the folk group, and when he took her hand in his, it felt the most natural thing in the world.

By eleven, the music was coming to an end. The punters were making their way home, and the waiter had brought over the bill.

"Time to get you home, I suppose," he said, taking her hand and kissing it gently, gazing at her with an intimacy in his eyes.

"Thank you, it's been a lovely evening," she said, as he helped her with her coat.

They walked out onto the steps, with a view of the harbour in front of them and stood listening to the eerie whistle of the boat masts as they rocked gently in the wind, with the moon shining brightly on the rippling water. It was a magical scene.

Lawrence put his arm around her as she gave a little shiver. He turned her towards him, kissing her lightly on the lips. "I have been wanting to do that all evening," he said, his eyes fixed intently on hers.

Caroline wasn't sure how to react. No one other than Robert had kissed her on the lips for over thirty years.

"I'm sorry, I shouldn't have done that. Please forgive me," he said, seeing the look of surprise on her face.

"No need to apologise, it was very nice," she said, touching his face, the wine making her feel quite brazen. She was sure she must have consumed most of the bottle. This man made her feel good and wanted. For so many years she had felt like a voyeur of life, and now she felt she was living it again.

He smiled down at her, cupping her face in his hands. "May I try again then?"

"You may indeed," she said, as their lips met again, this time for a little bit longer.

A couple of lads came out of the pub and whistled as they walked past, making Caroline and Lawrence break apart.

"Come on, let's go and pick up my jeep before I destroy your reputation," he said, pulling her in close to him, his arm draped across her shoulder as they walked along the harbour towards Guillemot Street.

The ride back to her cottage was indeed bumpy in the 1950s jeep, and they laughed and giggled as they bumped along the lane. Caroline hadn't been so relaxed and happy in a very long time, and she was sure she was a little bit tipsy. As they got closer to her home, she was getting nervous about whether to ask Lawrence in for a nightcap.

They pulled into her driveway, and Lawrence switched off the engine. He reached across to kiss her again, this time a little more passionately. He pulled back, looking at her. "Come on, let's get you in safely," he said, jumping out and running round to help her out. He lifted her down, kissing her quickly before setting her on the ground.

They walked up the path, his arm across her shoulder. "One more kiss?" he asked.

His voice was soft and warm, his blue eyes dropping to her mouth as they stood under the canopy of the porch. Caroline looked into his eyes and felt herself melt in his arms, as he kissed her long and tenderly.

"Thank you for a lovely evening," she said, breaking away breathlessly.

She unlocked the door, stepping inside. Lawrence stood with his hand on the doorjamb, looking at her with a grin on his face.

"Thank you... I enjoyed it," he said, reaching over for another kiss.

Caroline pulled back. "Good night, Lawrence," she said quietly.

"Good night, Caroline. I will call you in the morning. Sleep well," he said, as he turned and walked back to the jeep.

Caroline closed the door behind her, leaning against it and wondering what might have happened if she had been brave enough to ask him in. She wasn't sure she was ready for a man like Lawrence Wainwright.

Lawrence climbed into the jeep, reaching for his cigarettes under his seat, lighting up as he drove down the bumpy lane. He thought how close she had come to asking him in. Pity, he thought, pulling deeply on his cigarette. She was a very attractive woman, but she was also very fragile. He would need to take it slowly and gently with the lovely Caroline.

Chapter Six

Paris

Freddie was preparing to leave his daughter and son-in-law's Victorian home in CastleAvon, for Paris, just after breakfast. The half-term had flown by, every day being a day of adventure with the children: trips to the park, visiting the castle to watch the knights joisting, the jesters performing tricks and a trip down the river in a rowing boat. They had loved it all, and they had loved having him to stay. He was going to miss them all.

Alison and Ben were good together. They had a strong family unit, but with their jobs, Alison a full-time teacher and Ben an IT consultant for a multinational firm, their lives were very busy, trying to juggle childcare and raise their family. They had no family support. He was in Paris, Alison's mother was on her hippie commune in the West of Ireland, and Ben's parents lived up in Orkney, so it was tough for them, but they managed, as so many young families had to do these days with the exorbitant cost of childcare. It was breaking his heart to leave them and wished he could do more to help.

"We are fine, Dad, don't worry. Just make sure you come back as often as you can," said Alison, as she sat alone with her father up in his bedroom while he packed his bags.

"I will, darling, and if you need me, you only have to call me," he said, taking her in his arms for a final quiet hug.

The two of them had always been very close. Alison's mother had not been around much as she grew up. She had always been off on eco campaigns around the country, Greenpeace demonstrations and camping at Greenham Common, often staying away for weeks at a time. So, Alison and her father had a very strong bond. It wasn't until she and Ben got together at university, marrying as soon as they graduated, that Freddie felt he could take the opportunity to follow his dream and move to Paris, where he could begin his writing career in earnest.

"Come on, let's get breakfast," said Allison, picking up her father's travel bag. "Ben's been making pancakes, and the children have made an extra-big one for you," she said, taking her father's hand as they walked along the landing.

After breakfast, the children were fussing round him in the narrow hall as he gathered his things together. He picked them both up, hugging them tight and kissing them.

"Be good children for Mummy and Daddy. I love you both," he said, setting them down before turning to his daughter.

"Take care, Dad, we are going to miss you. Come back soon, won't you?" she said. Allison was tall and slim like her father, with the same green eyes, which were now brimming with tears.

"I will be back for Christmas, which won't be long. I love you," he said, brushing her long, blonde hair back from her face, kissing her on the forehead. He slung his bag over his shoulder, kissing her one more time before turning to his son-in-law who was standing beside her.

"Goodbye, sir, take care of yourself," said Ben, shaking his hand firmly.

Ben was a kind and caring husband and father, and Freddie loved him dearly. At six-foot-four, with a stocky build, he was considerably bigger than Freddie, a real gentle giant with a mop of dark, curly hair.

Freddie stretched his arms round Ben's large frame and hugged him tightly. "Bye, Ben. You take care too."

They all stood in the porch in a group hug, the children clinging to his legs. Then with a final wave, he walked down the path to the waiting taxi. He waved goodbye again as they turned the corner of the Victorian Street, heading for the train station and the long journey back to Paris.

Later that evening, after an uneventful journey, he put his book back in his bag, just as Eurostar was coming into Platform 6 at the Gare du Nord. He took out his phone to let Francois know that he was back in Paris. He had texted her earlier to tell her he was on his way. He had been very remiss in contacting her over the last week, but he knew she was busy anyway, rehearsing for the new play. He just hoped she wouldn't be huffing, which she did if she felt neglected. She could behave like a spoilt child sometimes. She was fifteen years younger than him and had never been married or had children, so she was used to getting things her own way.

He had met her in the bar a few months ago at Michelle's sixtieth birthday party. Freddie had been attracted to her instantly. She was so full of life and vitality. Up until then, he had steered well clear of getting involved with a woman. When he had arrived back in Paris after his divorce, casual relationships had been all he was interested in. He had given up his career to concentrate on his writing, and he didn't want any complicated relationship to get in the way. But when he and Francois met, they had hit it off right away and had spent the whole evening in the corner of the bar, talking, before going across the road to his apartment where she spent the rest of the weekend with him.

The train had stopped, all the passengers making a beeline for the exit. He wondered if Francois had come to meet him. When he climbed the stairs to the main entrance, he was pleased to see the petite figure waving to him, her hair scraped back tightly in a ponytail, and she was dressed all in black, as usual. The only colour was her bright-red lipstick.

"*Cherie!*" she called, running over to him, flinging her arms around him and kissing him, as other passengers pushed past them.

Freddie set his bag down and took her in his arms. "Good to see you. I've missed you," he said, looking down at her and stroking her cheek. "Come on, let's go. I'm exhausted, starving and desperate for a drink," he said picking up his bag.

They walked out of the station, arm in arm, and stood waiting for a taxi. It was cold, wet and gloomy, which matched his mood. He didn't know why, but he hadn't felt the usual buzz of excitement as the train had neared its destination. He had spent a lot of the journey thinking about his family, missing them.

He also had been thinking about Caroline, even though he had been pushing her to the back of his mind since they had met less than a week ago at the cafe. The past was swirling around in his mind, images of her pushing rational thoughts aside. Seeing and touching her had brought back so many emotions that had lain deep for decades, but those feelings had been so intense all those years ago, it wasn't surprising that they had been resurrected.

He had managed to bury them though, while he was with the family and playing with the children, but alone on the train, they had inched their way into his thoughts again. He was annoyed at himself for agreeing to meet up with her. He should have known it would have brought back those feelings — a love like that never really dies.

Francois cuddled in close to him as they stood in the taxi rank. She looked up at him with her lovely, big, brown eyes, melting his heart. He reached down to kiss her lightly on the lips, just as a taxi pulled in to take them back to the apartment.

Freddie watched all the familiar sights flash by. He loved this city, and he loved his life here, but he couldn't shake the feeling of melancholy. He looked down at Francois nestled in against him and kissed the top of her head. She looked up at him, her big, brown eyes sparkling from the passing streetlights, and kissed him on the lips.

"I've missed you, Frederic," she said, just as the taxi pulled up outside Freddie's apartment.

It was raining heavily now as they got out, the cobbled streets shining with the fresh rainwater.

"Let's go over to Michelle's for a drink and something to eat," he said, taking her hand in his.

"Oh, I forgot to tell you. Michelle has a new man — Alain, a pastry chef from Marseille. He is very handsome. They seem besotted with each other!" she said, as they waited for the traffic to pass.

"That's a bit quick. When did this happen?" he asked.

"I think it has been going on for a while. He worked for the catering company that did her birthday party, so he has been her secret lover since then, but he moved in last weekend. His pastries are delicious!" she said, grinning.

"Well, I look forward to meeting him," said Freddie, as they opened the door to the bar.

The bar was already packed. Sunday night was a popular night, the local theatre company enjoying their one night off, so lots of Francois' friends were already there and already quite drunk. They welcomed Freddie back in their usual effusive manner, a large glass of wine thrust into his hand. Francois was quickly enveloped into their midst.

Michelle appeared from the kitchen when she heard the sounds of a welcome and came round from behind the bar, holding the hand of a handsome, young man; tall, athletic-looking, with blond, sun-streaked hair and a deep, Mediterranean tan.

"Welcome home, *Cherie*. We have missed you," she said, kissing him on both cheeks. "Frederic, I want you to meet Alain, my new pastry chef and my new love," she said, putting her arm around the young man, gazing up at his face.

"*Bonsoir,* Frederic. I am delighted to meet you," he said, with a beaming smile.

Freddie was very surprised. He had no idea that Michelle was seeing anyone, let alone this boy. He thought he couldn't be more than twenty-five. He knew now what Francois had meant when she said they were besotted with each other. Michelle was gazing at him adoringly. The alarm bells in Freddie's head were deafening.

"*Bonsoir,* Alain, nice to meet you," he said, shaking his hand.

Alain reached forward and kissed him on both cheeks. "Oh, you British are so formal," he laughed, slapping Freddie on the back.

"You look tired. Are you hungry? What can I get you to eat?" Michelle asked Freddie, as she leaned in closer to Alain. She could see how surprised Freddie was and thought she would talk to him later, when he had rested after a good meal.

"I am tired — it's been a long day," he said, taking off his coat and hanging it on the back of a chair.

"Well, sit down, and I will get you your favourite cassoulet. How were the family? I bet those little grandchildren of yours have grown. Oh, they are so very adorable! I hope they come back to visit soon," she said, kissing him again and escaping back through to the kitchen with Alain.

Francois glanced over at him, giving him a wink and beckoning him over to the bar, but he shook his head and picked up his glass of wine.

She sauntered over to him, stroking his hair before sitting on his knee. "Told you he was handsome," she said, grinning.

"You didn't tell me he was a boy!" said Freddie.

"She is like a new woman, so in love. Maybe I should get myself a toy boy," she laughed, trying to kiss him.

Freddie turned his head away. The shock of seeing Alain had not improved his mood.

"Poor, poor Freddie. You are in bad mood. You too tired for some fun? Come on over to the bar," Francois said, standing up.

Freddie kissed her lightly on the lips. "I'm going to have something to eat first. Are you going to join me?" he asked, as she shook her head and went back to the bar. "You go ahead then — don't mind me," he said to himself, watching her throw her arms round one of her many friends. He was feeling absolutely deflated, and he took some more wine, hoping it would revive him.

Later, after he had eaten some of Michelle's delicious pork cassoulet and drank another glass of wine, he began to feel more relaxed.

Michelle came over on her own, with some apricot tart on a plate. "A little treat for you. Alain is a superb pastry chef. You must try some," she said, sitting down beside him. "You are shocked, Frederic, I can tell. I'm sorry I didn't tell you about him before. We have been seeing each other since my birthday — he made the cake for me. He looks much younger than he is. I'm not completely mad, but I have fallen madly in love with him."

"I am surprised. So how old is he if I may ask?" he asked nervously.

"Thirty-nine, so not much younger than Francois," she replied.

"Touché! He seems very nice, and he is indeed a very good pastry chef," he said, taking a bite from the delicious apricot tart, catching some crumbs in his hand.

"Be happy for me. I never thought I could fall in love again, but I have, and I trust him. Maybe it will be third time lucky for me, eh?"

"Of course, I'm happy for you. I'm just nervous for you," he replied, finishing off the tart.

"Don't be. I have told him if he ever cheats on me, I will kill him — a crime of passion, *non*?" she laughed.

"If he ever cheats on you, I will kill him for you!" he said, grinning, as she kissed him on the cheek and went back to the kitchen.

The bar was filling up and getting very noisy, but somehow, he just couldn't get into the swing of things. The shock of meeting Alain had passed, but he truly hoped Michelle was not making a terrible mistake. He would certainly keep an eye on them, especially Alain, and if he put one foot wrong, he would sort him out in double-quick time.

"You, OK?" asked Francois, coming back over to him, bending down and kissing him longingly on the lips.

"Haven't you missed me? You are very quiet," she said, sitting on his knee again and playing with his hair.

"I'm tired. It's been a long day, I'm sorry," he said, pulling back from her and looking at her pretty heart-shaped face with its pale complexion.

She had beautiful, deep-brown eyes with thick, dark, arched eyebrows. She was very sexy and very alluring, as she sat there draped across him, her arms around his neck.

She sat looking at him, studying his face. "What's the matter, Frederic? Are you cross about Alain?"

"No, not cross — just cautious about him," he replied, as she stroked his forehead.

"He is very nice. I have got to know him this week. I think he really does love her. They are always kissing and cuddling, and his pastries are amazing!" she laughed.

"Hmmm, we shall see," he replied thoughtfully.

"Has something happened over in UK? You seem far away. Your mind is somewhere else — do you want to tell me?" she asked, tilting his face up to hers.

"No, nothing happened. I'm just tired. It was really busy, especially with the kids," he replied, stroking her long, dark, silky hair, which she had just shaken loose from the band that held it back.

"I think you are not telling me something," she said, raising an inquisitive, perfect eyebrow.

"No, of course not. I'm just whacked. I need to get some sleep. Come on, let's go, I've missed you," he said, attempting to kiss her, but this time she pulled her head away.

"I don't want to go yet. I will stay on here for a while. You go. Good night, Frederic," she said petulantly, unfolding herself from him, getting up and making her way back over to the bar.

No one could ever hide anything from her; she always picked up on vibes. Her friends jokingly teased her that if she wasn't a witch, she was definitely psychic.

Freddie picked up his bag and waved goodbye to Michelle and Alain, who were wrapped up in each other's arms by the kitchen door.

Francois didn't bother to turn round as he left.

It was a week later that Francois turned up at his apartment. She hadn't answered his calls all week, and eventually he gave up, assuming she was huffing. So, when she arrived late on Friday night, he was surprised.

"Hi," he said, as he opened the front door.

She walked straight past him, taking off her black cape and throwing it dramatically on the chair in the hall. He followed her into the living room where she was standing by the fireplace, looking incredibly sexy in a short, black, silk dress and very high-heeled, black, suede shoes. He went over to her and tried to take her in his arms.

"*Non!* Not until you tell me what you got up to in England that you are so guilty about."

"Nothing. I'm sorry. I was just tired when I got back on Sunday and shocked about Michelle and her toy boy. Come here and let me kiss you. You look gorgeous," he said, reaching out to her again.

"*Non,* Frederic! Something happened, and I want to know," she said, stamping her foot on the parquet floor.

Freddie walked over to the drinks cabinet, an elaborate Burr Walnut antique left behind by his aunt and uncle. "Do you want a drink? I'm having one," he said, pouring himself a large brandy. He held it up to her, but she shook her head, tossing her black, shiny hair back off her face.

He sat down on the large leather sofa facing the fire, patting the seat beside him, but she remained standing. He took a sip of brandy, letting it slowly go down. "OK, you are right. Something did happen, but it's no big deal."

"I knew it! What happened?" she exclaimed, her eyes wide and staring at him.

"I just met up with an old friend for a coffee, that's all."

"What old friend?"

"Just someone I knew from school. It just brought back old memories. I won't be seeing her again."

"*Her? Mon Dieu!*" bellowed Francois, striding across the floor and slapping him on the cheek, making him spill some brandy on his trousers.

"Francois! What the hell…" he said, mopping his trousers with his handkerchief.

She marched out into the hall, picking up her cape and opening the door. Freddie got to her before she went out, catching her by the arm.

"Wait, let me explain. It was nothing for you to worry about."

"Hmmph! Nothing? You come back all moody and quiet. You call that nothing. I had missed you. You didn't call me from England, and then you didn't even want me when you come back. It's over, Frederic!"

Freddie pulled her back inside and held her close to him. "I'm sorry, I should have told you, but it really was just a very old friend who happened to be in town at the same time. We were just catching up over a coffee, nothing more than that — I promise you. You know I'm not the type to cheat on you. Please, come on, take your coat off. Let me get you a drink, and we can do some catching up."

Francois looked up at him, her big eyes brimming with tears. "I love you, Frederic, but I don't think you love me. Maybe you didn't cheat on me, but maybe you thought about it!" she said, as a single tear rolled down her cheek.

He bent down, kissed her lips and held her tight. He then picked her up, slammed the front door closed with his foot and carried her into his bedroom.

Chapter Seven

Cornwall

Caroline woke up to bright sunshine pouring through her window, not a cloud in the sky. She stretched and smiled, remembering the night before at the Harbour Inn. It had taken her a long time to get to sleep after Lawrence had left, but she was glad she hadn't asked him in. The chemistry between them was so intense, heaven knows what might have happened. She hadn't felt that way for a very long time.

At the insistence of friends, she had tried internet dating a couple of years ago, but after spending a few boring evenings with men she never wanted to see again — not to mention the risks — she had stopped trying to meet anyone. But Lawrence was different. Apart from his classic good looks, he was a charming gentleman, intelligent, gifted and shared her sense of humour. She propped herself up on her pillows, looking out of the window, just as her phone rang.

"Good morning, Caroline, I hope you slept well."

"Good morning, Lawrence. Yes, I did sleep well... eventually."

"Me too, but it also took me a long, long time to stop thinking about you. It was a lovely evening, and it ended too soon, but it was probably for the best. Anyway, what are you doing today? It's a beautiful day; would you like to come for a drive with me along the coast to Godrevy?"

"That would be lovely," she said, leaning forward and pulling back the duvet, thinking how nice it was to have a man take her out for the day.

"Great! I will pick you up at ten — is that OK? By the way, I won't be in the jeep, you will be pleased to hear, so I will park the car on the road and walk down the lane for you."

"Ten is fine for me, see you then," she said, jumping out of bed and heading for the shower.

An hour later, Lawrence was on her doorstep, dressed casually but effortlessly stylish in jeans and a chunky-knit, pale-blue jumper, with a beautiful bunch of flowers.

"To thank you for coming out with me," he said, handing them to her and kissing her on the cheek.

"Oh my, they are lovely. Come in while I pop them in water," she said, holding the door open for him to follow her to the kitchen.

"This is very quaint. I didn't realise last night that it was thatched. It's a fabulous setting," he said, as he looked out of the kitchen window and down towards the woods, with the cliffs now visible in the distance.

"I just stumbled upon it while I was on holiday and knew it was for me, so luckily the owner was willing to wait till I sold our old home. She was a friend of my neighbours, Bert and Edna, and none of them wanted it to be bought by a holiday-let investor. It's very small, as you can see, but it suits me fine," she said, brushing close to him as she reached for a vase.

"Here, let me get that for you," he said, lifting the vase down from the shelf and setting it on the bench.

Their hands touched, sending little shock waves up her arm.

"These are lovely. I will arrange them properly later, but this will do for now," she said, filling the vase with water and dropping the flowers in. "Thank you so much," she said, just as he reached forward and kissed her, holding her close, looking at her in a way that made her feel flustered.

"My pleasure. I like giving beautiful flowers to a beautiful woman," he said, gazing down at her.

"Well, thank you again. Shall we go?" she said, easing herself out of his embrace.

"Ready when you are," he said, smiling as he followed her out into the hall, helping her on with her coat.

They walked up the lane and met Bert and Edna coming back from their early morning walk with Peggy.

"Morning, you two. What a fabulous day. Lawrence, these are my neighbours, Bert and Edna. Lawrence has just called to take me out for the day," she explained, anxious that they didn't think he had stayed overnight.

"Good morning," said Lawrence, shaking their hands then reaching down to pat Peggy.

"Well, have a lovely day. We wondered who the car on the road belonged to — very nice it is too," said Bert.

"Yeah, that's mine. Couldn't risk my tyres down the lane. I used my old jeep last night, when I dropped Caroline back."

"Nice to meet you, Lawrence. Have a lovely day. We are off up to Exeter this afternoon, to visit Kenny for a few days, so we will see you when we get back, Caroline," said Edna, dragging Bert away before he started talking about cars.

"Have a nice time and safe journey. I will keep an eye on the house," said Caroline, waving goodbye as she and Lawrence set off down the lane.

"They're a nice couple. I hope we both put them right about last night. Couldn't have them thinking I stayed over, eh?" he laughed, as he opened the door to a gleaming, silver sports car.

"Indeed," she grinned, swinging her legs onto the red leather seat. "This is rather nice," she said, stroking the walnut dashboard. "What is it?"

"An E-type Jag — 1965 Series 1. She goes like the wind. My 'divorce present' to myself, and my pride and joy," he said, getting in beside her. He grinned as he started her up, the engine rumbling under the bonnet.

Winking at her, they took off down the road, both enjoying the thrill of the big V8 engine.

By the time they got to Godrevy, the weather had changed, and a heavy mist was beginning to roll in off the sea on a stiff wind. They parked by the cafe after the thrilling drive along the coast road, and as they opened the car doors, the cold wind took their breath away. Caroline's hair was flying around her wildly as she reached into the car to grab her multi-coloured, mohair scarf and attempted to wrap it around her head.

"Glad I brought this," she called to Lawrence, as he stood with his back to the wind, trying to zip up his vintage, leather flying jacket.

"Its wild up here today," he said, coming round to help her with her scarf.

Scarf secured and both wrapped up well against the wind, they set off across the field, following the trail towards the top of the hill, for a good view of Godrevy Lighthouse. Lawrence put his arm around her and pulled her in close to him, as they battled against the wind. They had talked non-stop during the drive over and laughed a lot. She felt very easy and comfortable with him. He was very good company and had an easy, friendly style and a similar taste in music, which she discovered when he asked her to select a CD from his collection of Rock and Classical in the glove box.

The view over to the lighthouse was dramatic, despite the mist, with the huge waves crashing on the rocks, seagulls ducking, diving and squawking. With

Lawrence's binoculars, they could just about make out the seals on the island, sheltering from the wind, looking totally unperturbed. The wind was so fierce on the headland that they decided to retreat to the safety of the cafe and hope that the weather would calm down later.

They hurried back over along the path towards the cafe and were not surprised to see it was quite busy. They were not the only people to chicken out of a bracing walk. They found a table by the fire, which had just been vacated. Lawrence held the chair for her while she sat down, unwrapping her scarf and taking off her coat, hanging it over the back of the chair.

"What can I get you?" he asked, unzipping his coat.

"Just a flat white, please," she said, rubbing her hands together near the fire to warm them, as he went over to the counter to order.

When he came back, he reached over and touched her cheek. "You have lovely, rosy cheeks after all that fresh air."

Caroline touched her face and found it was freezing. "I hope I don't have a lovely, rosy, red nose — that's not a good look," she laughed.

"You look beautiful — the epitome of good health," he said, sitting down opposite her just as the waitress brought over their coffee.

"Aah, that's lovely — just what I needed," she said, taking a sip of coffee.

Lawrence sat looking at her over the brim of his cup. "Yeah, it's good coffee," he said, setting his cup down. "I really enjoyed last night with you, Caroline. But I can't for the life of me understand why you are still living alone, and someone has not whisked you away."

"I thought I was content the way I am. I can do what I want when I want to. I have my work at the mansion and a nice bunch of friends. I tried internet dating, and it wasn't for me, so here I am. I get lonely now and again, but on the whole, I am just fine. I don't want drama in my life or a broken heart."

"Internet dating is a disaster, if you ask me — very risky for a woman — so I'm glad you stayed clear. So there has been no one in your life since your husband? That's a long time and a terrible waste of a good-looking, fun woman like yourself. You said you thought you were content — does that mean something has changed?"

Caroline felt her cheeks blush. She knew it was because of last night that she realised she wasn't content to be on her own so much. "I enjoyed last night too," she said shyly, looking up at him.

He reached forward and took her hand. "Good, I'm glad," he said, as the door opened and another couple came in, letting in a blast of cold air. "Shall we just stay here for lunch? It looks too cold for a walk. Maybe we can go down onto the beach later, if the wind dies down, or do you want to go somewhere else?"

"Let's stay here. We have a nice table by the fire, and everywhere will be busy today, with people being fooled by the blue skies and sunshine."

"Great, suits me," he said, catching the waitress' eye, for a menu.

It was after two o'clock before they ventured out after a delicious lunch. They walked over to the car, hand in hand, Lawrence opening the door for her.

"Fancy a quick walk on one of the best beaches in Cornwall? I'll drive down," he asked, holding the door open.

"Lovely idea — walk off that delicious pudding," she said, as he bent down to kiss her before closing the door.

They spent another hour walking along the beach, with their arms around each other, the waves crashing onto the sand. They took pictures of each other, with the lighthouse in the distance. Every so often he would stop and turn her towards him, kissing her. He was being very bold, but she liked it.

"I love being with you, Caroline, you are bewitching me," he said, holding her tight as they watched the waves crashing onto the beach.

No one has ever said that to me, she thought, as they quickly dodged a wave.

By the time they got back to the car, the light was beginning to fade, and by the time they got back to Butterfly Cottage, it was dark. Lawrence parked his car on the road, tucking it in as much as he could.

"Are you happy leaving your car here in the dark? I can walk down the lane on my own," said Caroline, as Lawrence opened the door for her.

"No way am I letting you walk down there on your own. There are branches, twigs and debris all over the place. The car will be fine. It's well tucked in," he said, taking her hand and using his phone to light the way.

They had nearly reached the cottage when Caroline went over on her ankle, after stepping in a pothole. She cried out in pain and fell against Lawrence, grabbing his arm.

"My God are you OK?" he asked.

"It's my ankle. Oh Lord, it really hurts. How stupid am I?" she cried, tears running down her cheeks.

"Let me take your weight; it's not far," said Lawrence, holding her up and half carrying her to the front door.

Caroline fumbled in her pocket for the keys, handing them to him. He got her into the hall, closing the door with his foot, and half carried her to the kitchen. He set her down on a chair by the table.

"Do you think it's broken? Shall I try to get your boot off?" he asked.

"I don't think it's broken, probably just a bad sprain."

"OK. I'm going to try and ease your boot off. If it hurts too much, just scream."

"Don't worry, I will?" she said, as he undid the zip and slowly eased the boot off. Caroline moaned and groaned but didn't scream. But when the boot came off, her ankle swelled up like a balloon and started throbbing.

"Got any ice packs?" he asked, looking very concerned.

"No, but there are frozen peas in the freezer — they will do," she replied.

Lawrence propped her leg up on the other chair, with a cushion underneath, and fetched the peas, placing them around the swelling. "That looks nasty, you poor thing. Maybe I should get you to hospital for an x-ray?"

"No, I'm sure it's just sprained. It will be fine in an hour or two."

Lawrence stood looking at her. She was very pale. "Well, I need to get you somewhere more comfortable. How about a nice cup of tea as well?"

"That's a good idea. If you could help me into the sitting room, I can lie in the sofa. A cup of tea would be lovely."

A little later, Lawrence had her ensconced on the sofa, well propped up with her leg elevated, the bag of frozen peas resting against her ankle and a couple of painkillers inside her. The swelling had gone down a little, but she knew she couldn't put any weight on it. Lawrence had lit the fire, which was now roaring away, and he settled down in the chair beside it.

"Well, this is a fine end to our lovely day," he said, grinning at her.

"I'm so sorry — it's been a fabulous day. I can't believe how stupid I've been," she said, looking utterly miserable.

"Don't be silly; it's not your fault. Are you sure it's just a sprain?" he asked, coming over to kneel beside her.

"I'm sure, but it will be a while till I can put any weight on it. I may have to sleep here tonight."

"Nonsense. I will get you up to your bed, but first I will get you something to eat. What would you like? I can go and get a takeaway?" he said, coming over to kneel beside her.

"I'm not hungry — that was a huge lunch. Are you hungry?"

"No, not really. Shall I make us an omelette? Have you got eggs?"

"That would be perfect. There are some eggs on the bench and some salad in the fridge.

"Right. Prepare to be impressed by my culinary expertise," he said, kissing her before getting up off his knees and heading for the kitchen.

Caroline could hear him whistling as he opened cupboard doors, looking for the saucepan and crockery.

She lay back on the cushions, looking at her ankle which was the size of two. She was sure it wasn't broken, but if the swelling hadn't gone down by the morning, she would get it x-rayed. She felt utterly miserable and annoyed with herself, especially as she had been aware of that particular pothole and had meant to get it filled in for weeks. She sighed and shook her head, looking up at the ceiling, disgusted with herself. Thank God Lawrence had walked her up the lane. If she had done that on her own, she could have been there for ages, waiting for one of her friends to answer her call for help, as she knew Bert and Edna were away.

Lawrence was a true gem, so kind and thoughtful. What a way to begin a possible relationship, which she was hoping it would turn out to be. She hoped it wouldn't spoil things.

A moment later, Lawrence popped his head around the sitting room door. "You, OK? Won't be long — I've found everything."

Caroline smiled at him. "That's the good thing about having a small kitchen — not many cupboards to search."

He laughed and disappeared, whistling again.

A little later, after a delicious cheese omelette, Lawrence threw another log on the fire and rested back in the winged chair, their tea trays on the floor beside them.

"That was delicious, thank you so much. You have exceptional culinary expertise, me thinks," said Caroline, raising herself up on the sofa, carefully trying not to annoy her ankle and wincing with the pain.

"Omelettes are my speciality, I must confess. I don't cook much for myself. If I get engrossed up in the studio, I can often forget the time and end up ordering a takeaway when I realise, I'm starving, or go round to the pub, which of course, is very handy. But I do enjoy cooking; just not much incentive to spend time in the kitchen cooking for one. What about you? Are you a secret Delia Smith?"

Caroline laughed. "Ha! If only. A very plain cook when I have to, but like you, I can't usually be bothered to cook much of a meal for just me. I live on 'one-pot-wonders' or salads and pasta."

"The joys of living alone, eh? Can I get you anything else? A coffee?"

"Not for me, thanks. The painkillers are making me drowsy, so hopefully I will get a good night's sleep, but go ahead and make yourself one," she said, trying again to get comfortable but wincing every time she moved her leg.

"Shall I get you some more pain relief, and then when that kicks in, I will help get you upstairs?"

"That's a good idea. I am so sorry to put you to all this trouble," she said, reaching her hand over towards him.

He leaned forward and took her hand, kissing it. "No trouble at all. I'm just glad I was with you when it happened. Right, I will go get you some more painkillers and make myself a coffee," he said, bending down to pick up the trays and taking them into the kitchen.

An hour later, as a CD of Van Morrison came to an end, Lawrence came over and sat on the edge of the sofa, looking down on Caroline as she lay back on the cushions with her eyes closed. He leant forward and kissed her on the lips.

She opened her eyes, smiling up at him. "Sorry, I must have dozed off."

"You have been asleep for the last few tracks. I think it's time I helped you up those stairs and see how you cope. I am happy to stay the night if you need me. I don't mind the sofa."

"Thank you, that's very kind of you. Let's see how I manage the stairs. They are very narrow, so it's probably best if I go up on my bottom, if you can hold my leg up."

"I can do that. Right, up you get. Lean on me and try to hop out to the hall."

With great effort, Caroline swung her legs round, keeping her right foot off the ground. Lawrence put his arms around her and lifted her up, while she held him tight. After very slow progress up the stairs, she was very grateful when she made it over to her bed. She sat on the edge, looking very pale. Lawrence sat down beside her, and she rested her head on his shoulder.

His arm around her, he kissed her on the top of the head and said, "I'm not happy about leaving you on your own. Let me stay. I promise I will not take advantage of a lady in distress," he said, grinning at her as she looked up at him.

"Let me rest a moment, and then let's see how I manage over to the bathroom. I don't want to impose on your good nature."

A few minutes later, Caroline, with great determination, hopped her way to the bathroom and back to the bed, where Lawrence sat watching her.

"I think I will manage. I don't like you leaving your car out on the road overnight, and what about your gallery? If you could bring me up a jug of water and more painkillers, I will be all right for the night."

"The car will be fine, and the gallery is closed during the week over the winter, anyway. I will go downstairs, while you get yourself into bed, and bring up what you need, and then we can decide what's best."

Caroline watched him go and then managed to get undressed and get into bed. She lay back on the pillows, exhausted by the effort but determined not to impose on Lawrence any longer. She was fiercely independent and had become accustomed, over the last few years, to coping with things on her own, but she was very tempted to let him stay.

However, she was concerned about his car out on the main road. It was a classic sports car, and she imagined it was worth a lot of money. If anything happened to it or it was stolen, she knew Lawrence would be devastated. So, with that thought, she decided she would insist that he went home.

A few minutes later he appeared at the door, knocking softly before coming in with a tray set with a carafe of water, a glass, painkillers, a packet of biscuits and a few of the flowers he had given her, in a small bud vase.

"Here we are. I brought biscuits in case you got peckish in the night," he said, setting the tray on her bedside table.

"Thank you. That's lovely, and the flowers are, too," she said, smiling. "You are a very kind man."

"All part of the service for a damsel in distress. Now, how did you manage getting into bed?"

"Quite well, actually. Really, I will be fine. There is no need for you to stay."

"Are you quite sure? I won't force my company on you, but I will be back in the morning and bring some crutches that I have in my attic, that I used when I broke my leg a few years ago. I think you are going to need to keep your weight off that ankle for a few days."

"Thank you, that would be great. There is a spare front-door key hanging up in the hall cupboard. It's the one with the lighthouse on the keyring. You can let yourself in if I don't manage to get downstairs."

"Will do, but don't attempt to come downstairs on your own! I really hate leaving you. I will ring you first thing in the morning before I come in case you think of anything else you might need, but if you need me during the night, just call me, promise?" he said, pleadingly.

"I promise," she said, as he bent down to kiss her.

"I had better go, before I break my promise to not take advantage of you," he laughed, backing away and giving her a little wave as he closed the bedroom door behind him.

A few moments later, she heard him shout 'goodnight', and then the front door banged shut.

She reached over and filled a glass with water, taking a sip before she turned off her bedside lamp. She looked out of her window at the dark, night sky studded with stars, and she found herself wishing she hadn't asked him to go.

Next morning, after an anxious phone call to check Caroline had survived the night without falling and injuring herself even more, Lawrence arrived. He knocked on her bedroom door, bearing two cups of gourmet coffee and two croissants from the bakery around the corner from his studio.

Caroline was back in bed, resting, after having nervously made the journey to the bathroom by hopping and leaning on furniture. It had exhausted her, but she was glad to get her teeth and hair brushed before Lawrence arrived, and she was relieved to see the swelling in her ankle had gone down, but it was now beginning to turn fifty shades of purple.

"Good morning. You are looking chirpy this morning. Brought us some coffee and my favourite croissants," he said, setting the coffee on the tray and handing her the croissant and butter on a plate, with a napkin.

"Oh, I love these. They look like the ones from Pat's Pantry?"

"The very ones — best in the Southwest! I am so glad to see you looking brighter. I hardly slept last night, imagining you lying in a heap after falling with a broken ankle and unable to reach your phone. I should have stayed — it would have been easier," he said, pulling over the dressing table stool to sit on beside her.

"I admit I was nervous going to the bathroom first thing this morning, in case I fell, but I actually slept really well, probably thanks to the painkillers. I think the swelling has gone down, so I'm sure now that it's just a bad sprain," she said, sticking her ankle out from under the duvet for him to see.

"Blimey, look at the colour of that! I've brought the crutches. They are out in the jeep, so as soon as I get you downstairs, I will fetch them. By the way, there was a tree surgeon in the lane when I arrived, dealing with the fallen tree, so at least it will be passable again. I'm going to fetch some gravel to fill that pothole, by the way."

"Oh, you don't need to do that."

"Nonsense. I'm being selfish actually, cos I don't want to buckle a wheel on the Jag the next time I come out in her."

"You are far too kind, thank you. I should have done it ages ago, but I just kept driving around the damn thing. This is really good coffee," she said, taking a sip.

"Yeah, I'm a regular at Pat's for my morning coffee — an essential before I lift a paintbrush. So how do feel about getting up and coming downstairs?"

"Absolutely fine. I don't want to be stuck up here. If you can help me down, that would be marvellous."

"No problem. As soon as we finish this, I will leave you to dress and help you when you're ready," he said, finishing his croissant and taking his coffee over to the window, to look down at the garden. "This is a lovely view of the cliffs. It's a cracking location," he said, sipping his coffee.

"I know. I appreciate it every morning when I wake, even if it is a bit remote. It's at times like this that I can see the benefit of living in a community. It was one of things my sons were concerned about, but I managed to convince them I would be fine, but maybe they were right."

Lawrence came back over to sit on the bed beside her. "You've got years yet to worry about living out here. Anyway, look at your neighbours. Did you say they were in their eighties?"

"Yes, both of them are eighty-six! However, they are not living alone — they have each other. Sorry, sounds like I'm feeling sorry for myself. I'm just a bit shook up by being immobilized."

"Understandable. When these sorts of things happen, you begin to realise you're not indestructible. When I broke my leg, I thought my world had collapsed. It's awful being dependant on others."

"How, where and when did you have your accident?" she asked.

"Austria; skiing; nine years ago, when I was staying with my brother and his wife. I was in the unfortunate position of having to rely on my wife for help when I got back home. It was the final straw in our relationship. Although we still lived and worked together, we were leading separate lives. As soon as I was mobile, she moved in with her now-partner."

"Poor you, but at least she stuck around when you needed help."

"That's true, I suppose. Anyway, enough of all that. I'm going to take this tray down and leave you to dress, or do you need me to help?" He grinned mischievously, as Caroline raised an eyebrow. "Give me a shout when you're ready," he said, raising a hand in mock surrender.

"Thanks, I will. Oh, before you go, could you hand me the tracksuit from the bottom drawer of the chest? I don't think I can reach on one leg. It will be easy to put on."

Lawrence fetched the tracksuit, setting it on the bed beside her and kissing her before he left her to dress. Caroline wondered what she had done to deserve this gorgeous man in her life, and she hoped her damned ankle would heal quickly.

Over the next couple of days, Caroline improved and managed on her own to get up and down the stairs on her bottom. Lawrence insisted on coming out in the evenings, bringing a takeaway for their dinner. Her friends from the gallery, as soon as they heard why she wouldn't be in for work, had organised a rota to keep her company during the day, which greatly amused her.

On Tuesday, Fiona arrived with a lovely lunch from the deli. They sat in the kitchen, enjoying it with a glass of wine, watching the wind bend the trees in the woods. Caroline told her about her 'dates' with Lawrence and how kind he had been.

"I'm very jealous but also very pleased for you. He sounds a real gem but take it easy and be careful. Don't get too involved too soon. You don't know much about him," she said.

Caroline smiled. "He has been so kind and so very thoughtful. I never imagined him being so caring — he really is, Fiona," she said to reassure her.

"I'm sure he is, but don't let him rush you into anything till you know more about him, that's all I'm saying."

"I won't. Just relax. Take your suspicious 'cop hat' off. Anyway, I am a very lucky woman, apart from the time I fell in that darned pothole! And I am very lucky to have the support of you guys," she said, knowing how very grateful she was for their company and friendship, especially as Bert and Edna were still away at their son's home. It was lonely out at Butterfly Cottage without any neighbours.

On Wednesday, it was Tom and Philip on the rota. Tom had rung her that morning to say they would be with her later, and as the wind was dying down, they were going to walk out from their homes in St Mawdley.

"We are going to stop at the pub for lunch on the way, and providing I can drag Philip away from the bar, we will be there early afternoon," he said, chuckling.

Caroline could hear Philip in the background, shouting, "Other way round, Caroline, you know what Tom is like!"

Caroline laughed and told them she looked forward to seeing them, no matter how inebriated they were.

She had just settled herself on the sofa, after managing to get to the kitchen, on the crutches, to make herself some lunch. Everything was such an effort, and she was glad to get her ankle up on the stool and have a rest before the 'chuckle brothers' — as everyone called them — arrived. They even looked like a comedy duo. Tom was smaller than average build, with a thick head of jet-black hair and a swarthy complexion, whereas Philip was a big bear of a man, with a mop of white, curly hair. The rapport between the two men was also comedy gold.

She had left the front door unlocked, to save her having to get up to let them in. She rested her head back and closed her eyes, and before long, she had drifted off to sleep.

She was woken a little later, by a knock on the door. "Come on in, it's open," she called, assuming it was Tom and Philip.

She heard the door open, but no one spoke, so with great difficulty, she hobbled on the crutches and out into the hall where she saw a young man standing. He was dressed in torn jeans, a hoody and a baseball cap pulled down over his forehead, and he carried a large rucksack. Caroline was taken aback and felt very stupid to think she had just invited a stranger into her home.

"Hello, can I help you?" she asked nervously.

The young man glanced around the hall and then looked at Caroline. "I won't hurt you. Just give me the valuables," he said, looking at the antique silverware sitting on the hall table.

Caroline was shaking with fright. "What the hell... Get out of my house before I call the police," she said, shaking one of the crutches at him.

He grabbed hold of the crutch, unbalancing her, and she fell to the floor, crying out in pain as her ankle took the force of the fall.

"I told you I didn't want to hurt you. Just tell me where your jewellery is," he said, stepping past her to go into the sitting room. "F.......g hell, it's like an antique shop in here, Mrs," he said, starting to lift silver items off the tables and opening the display cabinet to take out a Georgian silver coffee pot and cream jug.

"Leave my stuff alone and get out!" she screamed at him, trying to get up.

But he had kicked the crutch out of her reach, and she realised she was helpless, as she watched him stuff her treasured possessions — all of them gifts from Robert — into his rucksack. Her heart sank when he grabbed the French Ormolu George 111 carriage clock.

"Please leave that. You won't be able to sell it — it's too distinctive. It was a present from my late husband. Please..." she cried, as he looked around for something to wrap it in.

"Me heart bleeds for you," he sneered, as he wrapped it up in a woollen scarf that Caroline had left on the sofa and unceremoniously stuffed it in the almost-full rucksack. "Right, Mrs, where's the jewellery? And don't tell me you haven't got any, cos I can see some fancy looking earrings, for a start," he said, approaching her.

Caroline tried to twist her diamond-and-sapphire ring around, hoping he wouldn't see it, but he did.

"Hand it over," he said menacingly.

She could sense the anger in him — no doubt, drug induced.

Caroline was terrified but managed to reach over for the other crutch. She tried to hit him with it, but he grabbed it and twisted it out of her hand.

"Get it off, or I'll pull it off for you!"

"It doesn't come off — my knuckle has swollen. I can't take it off. You won't be able to either," she cried, as he took hold of her hand and pulled at her antique, diamond-and-sapphire engagement ring.

"Get the bloody thing off, you stupid woman, or I'll cut your bloody finger off!" he screamed at her, looking around for something to help him prise it off. His eye caught sight of a letter opener on the hall table, and he went out to get it just as the front door opened and Tom walked in.

"What the hell is going on!" shouted Tom, when he saw Caroline lying on the floor and a young, thuggish-looking man standing in front of him, brandishing what looked like a paper knife, threatening him with it.

"Get out of my way, grandad!" he shouted, picking up his rucksack.

Just then, Philip appeared behind Tom, holding his hiking pole. The young lad took one look at the size of

Philip, who was blocking the light in the doorway, and tried to make a run for the back door. He shoved Tom up against the front door, winding him, and turned to run. Philip lifted his pole and whacked him behind the knees, sending him crashing to the floor, screaming. The two men then threw themselves on top of him as he kicked and screamed abuse at him. Caroline managed to crawl over to the sofa, and she grabbed her phone to call the police.

"Have you got any rope, Caroline?" shouted Tom, as he held onto the intruder's legs, while Philip lay sprawled across his torso, pinning him down.

"There's an old washing line hanging behind the door, in the hall cupboard!" she shouted, as Tom calculated in his mind if he could get to it.

"I've got him Tom, go for it!" shouted Philip, as Tom released the man's legs and grabbed the washing line from the hook behind the door.

With Philip's considerable weight, he managed to hold the lad down while Tom unwound the washing line. Within a few minutes, they had his hands tied behind his back and his legs tied together. The intruder was shouting insults at them and trying to kick free, as Tom and Philip stood over him.

"Not bad work for a couple of grandads," said Philip, breathing heavily from the exertion.

Tom went over to help Caroline up from the floor onto the sofa, leaving Philip on guard.

"My God, Caroline, are you hurt?" he asked, as she rested back against the cushions.

"No, I'm fine. Didn't do my ankle any good though," she said, feeling so relieved. "Thank God you arrived when you did. He threatened to cut my finger off!"

"What! You little swine!" said Tom, going over to give him a kick in the shins and another for good measure.

A little while later, they heard the police siren. Tom went over to open the door to let them in, the young officer doing a double take at the scene before him.

"Looks like you have all secured," he said, looking at the lad lying on the floor, trussed up like a chicken. "Lucky for you, we were just up the road — been an accident up by the B & B. Anyway, let's be having you," he said to the thief, as his colleague came in, also doing a double take.

Before long, they had him in handcuffs and were leading him away. They had taken a brief statement from Caroline, Tom and Philip and had listed and photographed the items that the burglar had attempted to steal. They said they would come back for them if they were needed as evidence, but as he was caught red-handed and there were three witnesses, they didn't think it would be necessary. They knew the criminal and told her they had a list of burglaries that they suspected he was involved in. They thanked Tom and Philip for their bravery but advised them not to tackle intruders themselves, in the future.

"You are lucky, gentlemen, that he didn't have a knife, or this could have ended very differently," said the police officer, as he left.

Philip poured them all a stiff brandy as the police car drove away. "Well, that was an exciting afternoon," he said, sitting down beside Caroline, who looked as white as a sheet.

"I can't thank you enough, guys. You are both superheroes," she said, trying to smile, but she was still shaking as she cradled the brandy goblet for comfort.

"Well, it's certainly going to give us something to talk about for a while, eh, Tom?"

"You can say that again," said Tom, sipping his brandy. "Thank God you are all right, Caroline, it was a terrible ordeal. Just sit back and try to relax. Would you like us to ring Fiona and ask her to stay the night with you?"

"Oh, that would be good. I'm just a bit shaky. If she can't, I'm sure Lawrence would stay," she replied.

Tom and Philip glanced at each other. Fiona had told them about Lawrence, and they were all a bit concerned about the dashing, sophisticated Lawrence. Fiona thought he was too good to be true.

"I'm sure she will. I'll give her a ring now," said Tom, taking his phone out of his pocket.

By the time Lawrence arrived, a couple of hours later with a takeaway dinner, Caroline was feeling better. The shock of the ordeal had left her very shaken, but the brandy and Tom and Philip's company had helped her realise that it could have ended so differently.

"It's a strange thing to say but thank God I hurt my knuckle when I fell the other day, otherwise he would have been able to get my ring off my finger and scarpered before Tom and Philip arrived," she said, recounting the events to Lawrence, who had listened in disbelief at the tale.

"You had a very lucky escape, all of you," said Lawrence to them all. "Thank God you guys arrived when you did."

"Well, now that you are here, Lawrence, we shall make tracks. Fiona will be out soon. I will just phone for a taxi — neither Philip nor I fancy walking home in the dark after a couple of large brandies," said Tom, just as there was a knock at the door.

Lawrence went to answer it. "Oh, hello, it's getting quite busy here all of a sudden," he said, holding the door open as Fiona came rushing in, acknowledging him with a nod.

"How is she? What a thing to happen," she said, hanging her coat in the cupboard, ignoring Lawrence and going straight through to the sitting room. "Caroline! Thank goodness you are OK."

"Fiona, thank you for coming; it's very kind of you," she said, reaching forward to give Fiona a hug.

"Nonsense, no trouble at all. I can stay as long as you need me," she said, kissing Tom and Philip on the cheek. "The heroes of the day, I hear."

"Ahhh, shucks! All part of the service," said Tom. "We will be going now — it's getting like Clapham Junction in here," he laughed, getting his phone out again, to ring for a taxi.

"Don't get a taxi — I'll give you a lift," said Lawrence.

"That's a good idea, Lawrence. I'm going to have an early night anyway, and as Fiona is staying, there is no need for you to come back," said Caroline, looking exhausted. She always knew that Butterfly Cottage was small, but with the three men and especially Philip's giant frame, and now Fiona as well, the sitting room felt positively Lilliputian.

"Oh, all right, if, you're sure. I left a fish pie in the kitchen, so you girls can have an early supper. Can you manage up the stairs without me?" he asked.

"I'm sure I can manage that," said Fiona. "Caroline and I can have a girlie night in, and I will get her up to bed, no problem, but only after you've told me all the details from your afternoon of catching criminals!" she said, grinning over at Caroline.

The men all hugged Caroline as they were leaving, making her promise to lock up well. Tom and Philip told her not to hesitate to ring them if she needed any undesirables dealt with, trying to ease the tension and make her smile. Lawrence said he would ring her in the morning, as usual.

"You can have the morning off, Lawrence, I'll be here," said Fiona, as she let them all out, locking the door firmly behind them. She turned to Caroline. "Right then, Mrs Reynolds I shall go put our supper in the oven, and then you can tell me all about your eventful afternoon," she said, peeping her head around the sitting room door, before going into the kitchen to attend to the fish pie and grab a bottle of wine and a couple of glasses.

The sun was shining the next morning when Fiona took Caroline a cup of tea.

"Morning, how are you feeling? Did you get a good sleep?" she asked, setting the cup on the bedside table, as Caroline eased herself up on the pillows.

"I got a few hours' sleep, but I kept waking up, thinking I could hear something or someone moving about outside. I know it was my imagination playing tricks on me. When I did manage to drift off, I had horrible dreams. Thank God you were here, Fiona. I think I might have gone crazy if I had been on my own."

"That's all quite a normal reaction to what has been a terrifying ordeal for you. You will soon be back to your old self. Now, drink up your tea, and then we can have a nice, long, leisurely breakfast, and if you're up to it, later you can come with me when I deliver some pots to the craft shop up near Carbis Bay."

"Oh, that would be lovely, I would love to do that!"

"Great. I'll go and get myself dressed and help you downstairs when you are ready. Just give me a shout," she said, patting Caroline's hand.

"Thank you, Fiona, you are an angel."

"I shall just flutter off then and brush up my wings," she laughed, as she closed the door behind her.

Later that morning, they drove off in Fiona's little sports car to deliver the order of porcelain pots to the craft shop. The drive along the coast road was spectacular in the winter sun.

"There is no finer view in all of Cornwall," said Caroline, when they pulled into a car park just above the beach.

"Yeah, it's spectacular, isn't it? Have you been to the beach cafe here? The food is amazing, and it's run by a lovely couple of guys — Timothy and Thomas. They call it 'The Two T's Bistro'."

"Sounds fun. Hope I will get down those steps," said Caroline, looking over at the rustic, wooden walkway down to the beach.

"There's a ramp to the side, so I'm sure you will manage. Just don't have too much wine with your lunch, or I might not get you back up again!"

After a delicious lunch of vegetable bourguignon, with herb dumplings for Caroline and stuffed potatoes cakes and pea curry for Fiona, washed down with a glass of perfectly chilled Chardonnay, the girls rested back in the comfortable chairs at their table by the window and watched the giant Atlantic waves roll onto the beach.

There were no surfers today, as it was much too rough, even for the dedicated of St Ives Bay.

"That was a fabulous lunch. It's so nice to come here out of season. Thank you for bringing me, Fiona. It's just what I needed to take my mind off yesterday's events. I still can't believe it actually happened."

"Well, try not to think about it too much. Thank God for Tom and Philip arriving when they did. Just look at it like a bit of a wake-up call, as regards to your security out there on your own," said Fiona, finishing her small glass of wine.

"I know what you mean. I've never worried about being on my own there. Usually, Bert and Edna are about. They rarely go away; it was just an unlucky set of circumstances, with me being incapacitated and them away. I will have to think seriously about making myself feel more secure — maybe get an alarm fitted."

"That would be a good start. I know how much you love it there, and it is truly idyllic, but it is a lonely spot. Maybe you should get a dog?"

"Maybe I will just borrow Peggy, if Bert and Edna go away again. I'm not sure I want the tie of a dog," she replied quietly.

"That might work. Anyway, have you got room for pudding?" asked Fiona, as the waiter came to take their plates away.

"I think I could manage a bit of that delicious-looking cheesecake," said Caroline, eyeing the sweet trolly.

By the time they got back to Butterfly Cottage, it was just beginning to get dark. They were both quite tired after the day's outing. Caroline flopped down on the sofa, while Fiona got the fire going.

"I had better send Lawrence a message. He said he would bring out a takeaway this evening. I don't know about you, but I couldn't eat another thing."

"Me neither. Bread and cheese will do for me this evening," said Fiona, putting a match to the kindling. "You and Lawrence getting along quite well?" she asked.

"He has been a real trooper these last few days. I'm very fond of him," she replied.

"Hmmm, well don't rush into anything — just take your time," said Fiona, as she took the log basket out to the back door to refill it from the log pile.

By Friday morning, after a good night's sleep, Caroline was feeling much better and more resilient, and even her ankle was beginning to look more normal. She had been so glad to have Fiona's company, but Bert and Edna were due back later this morning, so she insisted that Fiona got back to her own home.

"You have been a godsend, Fiona. Thank you so much for staying with me."

"No trouble at all — I enjoyed myself. If you are sure, you will be OK, I will get back and crack on with some more pots. Jennie at the craft shop wants another fifty by the end of the month, ready for Christmas trade. It's getting like a full-time job these days!"

"I'm so pleased for you. Off you go when you're ready. Bert will be over when they get back, and Lawrence said he would bring out dinner this evening, so I shall be fine."

"OK, I'll get off now. Make sure you lock up well, after I go," she said, grabbing her cape from the hall cupboard and giving Caroline a big hug.

Caroline watched her drive off, and she closed the door, turning the lock securely. She leaned against the door and felt her heart racing. She closed her eyes and took a deep breath. *Get a grip,* she said to herself, holding tightly to the crutches. The panic was beginning to rise, and she wished she hadn't put on such a brave face for Fiona, but she felt she couldn't impose on her dear friend's good nature any longer. Tears came to her eyes, and she tried to bite them back. She hated feeling like this. She knew she needed to get on top of this and put that incident out of her mind.

She went through to the kitchen and had just made herself a cup of tea and was sitting in the kitchen when she heard footsteps on the gravel. She leapt up, wincing slightly when she put too much weight on her ankle. She looked out of the window nervously, but when she saw it was Bert, she felt the tension slip away. *Thank God!* she said to herself, as Bert knocked on the door and she hobbled over to let him in.

"Caroline, my dear, whatever happened to you?" he said, looking shocked when he saw the crutches.

"Oh, Bert, it's been an awful week," she said and burst into tears, as Bert took her into his big, strong arms, comforting her.

"Drink that sweet tea, my dear. I'm just going to ring Edna," said Bert, after Caroline had told him what had happened.

Minutes later, Edna arrived with Peggy, looking very concerned.

"You poor girl. Of all the awful things to happen, and us miles away. I'm so sorry, Caroline, but thank the Lord that scumbag didn't hurt you. You will be all right, and your ankle will mend in no time. You need to get an alarm fitted, and so will we, Bert. Peggy isn't enough these days," she said, looking over at her husband.

"Aye, you're right. Mind you, these sorts of incidents are rare round here, but times are changing, I suppose. All down to drugs, of course. It's getting to be a bit of a problem down here, with so much unemployment out of season. He was probably just an opportunist though."

"Well, I certainly handed him an opportunity on a golden plate by leaving the door unlocked," said Caroline, patting Peggy who had decided to put her head on her lap. She was an intuitive soul and one of those dogs who could sense sorrow, and Caroline had never been more grateful for her company.

"You stay here, Edna, and I will go and find the number for that alarm company that Trevor used at their place. We will get this sorted as soon as we can. Meanwhile, I suggest Peggy stays here with you overnight. She's a grand guard dog, you know — she can hear a pin drop in the middle of the night."

"Thank you, Bert, it would be a great comfort," said Caroline, ruffling Peggy's coat.

"Or I can stay with you, if you want," suggested Edna.

"Peggy will be great, if you are sure you two are OK without her?" said Caroline.

"Don't you worry about us, dear. She snores a lot, mind you," laughed Bert, as he went out through the back door.

"Right then. What can I do for you, dear? What about a fresh cup of tea?" asked Edna, filling the kettle.

"That would be lovely, thank you," said Caroline, grateful to have her dear, sweet neighbours back.

Later that afternoon, Bert arrived over to take Peggy out for her walk. "I've brought over one of your sticks, Edna, for when Caroline thinks she can manage without the crutches."

"Good idea, Bert. Did you get hold of Trevor about the alarm?" asked Edna.

"Aye. Martin is calling out tomorrow to give us a quote. Are you coming for a walk with me and Peggy?"

"Will you be all right on your own for an hour, dear? I could do with a walk after that long car journey."

"Of course, I will, Edna. Off you go. Lawrence is coming out this evening with a takeaway, so I will just go through and put my feet up. Thank you so much for staying."

"If you are sure. Ring us if you need anything. Take it easy, dear. Everything will be OK," said Edna, giving her a hug.

"Come on, Peggy," said Bert, bending down and clipping her lead on, as she sat patiently, brushing the floor with her bushy tail.

"Bye bye. Bye, Peggy," Caroline called, as she waved them off, suddenly feeling very alone again as she locked the back door securely. *This is ridiculous! I can't believe I'm so dependent on having people around — this is not me!* she thought.

She propped the crutches against the wall and tried walking with the stick around the kitchen, managing to put some more weight on her ankle. So, with renewed determination, she decided to ditch the crutches. She hobbled through to the hall to double-check that the front door was locked, but when she looked at herself in the hall mirror, in her baggy tracksuit and not a trace of makeup, she was dismayed. She looked awful — pale and drawn, with dark shadows under her eyes. She felt like a victim, and she didn't like it one little bit. The woman who looked back at her from the mirror looked old, and her eyes looked tired.

"No wonder. No bloomin' sleep because of that little scumbag," she said to the reflection. She shook her head sadly, staring into her own eyes. "Pull yourself together, for heaven's sake," she said, as she hobbled into the sitting room.

She looked around the room, remembering the terror she had felt as the thief picked up her treasured items and then threatened her. Her heart began to beat faster as the memory came flooding back. She sat on the edge of the sofa, breaking into a cold sweat. *Breathe slowly, for God's sake,* she told herself, and slowly her heart rhythm returned to normal. She leaned her head back on the cushions and thankfully fell into a deep sleep.

It was dark when she was woken up, a couple of hours later, by the chiming of the clock. She rubbed her eyes, feeling very groggy. She reached across and switched on the table lamp. The fire that Edna had lit was slowly dying, so she pulled herself to her feet and threw on another couple of logs. She stood for a few minutes and watched the flames begin to dance up the chimney, and then she put the fire guard in place.

"Right, time to smarten yourself up," she said, and with a monumental effort, she got herself upstairs to have a shower and to change her clothes before Lawrence would arrive. She hadn't seen him since Wednesday, although he had phoned often to check that she and Fiona were coping OK. He had been so kind and thoughtful all week. She felt she wanted to try — not just for him, but for herself as well.

When he arrived a little later, he was very surprised to see her looking very glamourous in a sapphire-blue silk blouse over a pair of black, wide-legged palazzo pants, which hid the fact she was still wearing trainers. Her hair was swept up in a loose chignon, revealing her long, elegant neck adorned with her dazzling diamond-and-sapphire pendant and matching earrings.

"Wow! What a change in you since Wednesday! You look gorgeous!" he said, standing back and admiring her.

"I'm not going to be a victim, and I am fed up wearing baggy, old tracksuits" she said, with a huge smile.

"Good for you. You are quite a woman!" he said, setting the takeaway lasagne and a bottle of wine on the hall table and kissing her.

She kissed him back, grateful to have his strong arms around her, making her feel safe again. He picked her up and carried her into the sitting room, setting her down gently on the sofa and taking her in his arms again.

A few minutes later, her phone rang.

"Leave it," whispered Lawrence, as he kissed her throat.

"I can't — it might be important," said Caroline, struggling to sit up and reach for her phone, which was vibrating on the side table.

"Caroline, it's Bert. Do you still want your guard dog over to keep you company tonight? I see Lawrence's car is there."

"Hi, Bert, yes please, if that's OK with you?"

"Of course, it is, dear. I'll drop her over shortly. I will let her in through the kitchen door and won't disturb you. Bye, dear."

"Bye, Bert. Thank you."

Lawrence sat looking at her. "Did I hear right? I was kind of hoping I could keep you company tonight," he said, smiling.

Caroline raised her eyebrow. "Now that wouldn't do at all. What would Bert and Edna think of that, for heaven's sake?"

"Pity. We were just getting comfortable," he said, taking her face in his hands to kiss her, just as Peggy came bounding down the hall, her paws slipping on the parquet floor as she skidded into the sitting room door.

"Quick! Grab the lasagne off the hall table, or she will have that for her supper," said Caroline, as Lawrence leapt up to save their gourmet dinner from the jaws of a hungry Mountain Dog.

When he came back into the sitting room, holding the lasagne, Peggy was firmly ensconced at Caroline's feet.

"I see I have been ousted," said Lawrence, looking askance at Peggy. "I shall go and pop this in the oven to warm up."

"Lovely, thank you. Sorry about this, but she takes her duties very seriously — don't you, you gorgeous girl," said Caroline, ruffling Peggy's thick furry coat, as she rested her head on her lap.

Caroline was glad of the disruption. She was beginning to feel out of her depth with Lawrence's passionate kisses.

"You arrived just in the nick of time," she whispered in Peggy's ear, as Lawrence retreated to the kitchen, looking slightly annoyed, knowing that the evening of romance would be hard to rekindle.

Chapter Eight

Paris

Freddie was sitting at his desk which overlooked the street below, staring at his blank computer screen.

He leaned back in his chair, rubbing his hands through his hair in frustration. He got up, walking through to the large kitchen to make another coffee, leaning on the worktop and waiting for the bubbles to appear in the percolator. He still preferred his coffee made in this old-fashioned way, even though there was a fancy coffee machine sitting in the cupboard — a gift from his daughter. He rinsed his cup under the tap, shaking the excess water off, and poured the coffee, adding sugar but no milk, and then he went back through to the living room.

He stood by the French doors that led onto the balcony, drinking his coffee. There was a soft, pearl mist hanging over the rooftops, and down below, people were hurrying about with umbrellas, splashing in the puddles on the cobbled street. He loved it when he could sit on the balcony to write. The noise didn't distract him. Strangely, in fact, he felt it inspired him. Sitting at his desk in the silence of the apartment wasn't helping this morning, although he thought even the street noise out on the balcony wouldn't help him today.

Francois had left in a huff last night. She was so volatile and easily upset — a typical theatrical drama queen. She had been staying with him every weekend since he had come back from CastleAvon, and they were getting on well, enjoying being together. She had reluctantly forgiven him for meeting an old girlfriend, but now and again she brought it up, if she thought he was not being attentive enough.

Last night, while they were cuddled up on the sofa, Freddie was browsing on Facebook, when Francois saw a photo of Caroline standing on a cliff, with a lighthouse in the distance. "*Qui est-ce?*"

Freddie quickly scrolled on. "Just an old friend."

Francois sat up straight. "*Who* is that? Is it *her*? Why you got picture of her — you still in touch? *Mon Dieu!*"

Freddie set his laptop down on the marble coffee table and turned to her. "It's only Facebook. Don't be silly."

Francois pushed him away, stood up abruptly and glared down at him. "You still love her? Why you friends with her? I hate you, Frederic. I'm going!" she said, running out into the hall.

Freddie heard the front door bang and rested his head back on the sofa, exasperated. *God almighty, she is hard work.*" He knew she was extra stressed, as her new play was opening next weekend. She had a major role, and she was hoping it would lead to bigger parts, maybe even film or TV. He would let her calm down before he called her — he had found it was the best way to deal with her dramatics.

It had unnerved him though, seeing Caroline in that photo. He wondered who had taken the picture. She looked very happy. He wondered if she was seeing someone. Then he thought back to that day in CastleAvon, leaving her standing in the street with tears in her eyes. He had had tears in his eyes when he turned to wave to her, but he had done his best to put her to the back of his mind, where she had been for the last forty years.

He hadn't slept last night, and now this morning, despite the coffee, his mind was a fog, and the words just weren't coming. He decided to go out for a walk, even if it was raining. The wet streets of Paris would be relatively quiet, and he could think and hopefully get a word or a line to inspire him to write more. It wouldn't be the first time he had sat on a bench by the Seine, frantically scribbling in his notebook when an idea for a poem came to him, or standing on the gilded Alexandre 111 bridge, staring into the fast-flowing water below, hoping for inspiration.

It was nearly one o'clock by the time the rain had eased, and the streets were busy again, with Parisiennes coming out of their offices for their usual long lunches. The street cafes were filling up, people grabbing tables under the awnings. Freddie wasn't hungry, even though he had been walking for hours, trying to switch his mind off Caroline and back onto his work. He had argued silently with himself. What did it matter to him if some man had taken that photo of her? He had lots of photos taken with Francois. He wondered if Caroline felt the way he did when she saw their photographs on Facebook?

What did he feel? Was he just remembering a time of uncomplicated love, or was he jealous? How could he be? It had been years since they had meant anything to each other, and then they had only been kids. *Ahh but does anyone truly forget their first love?* he wondered.

He sat down on the steps by the river, watching a bateau-mouche cruise past, filled with tourists, even on this cold, wet, November day. Young lovers, with arms around each other, were taking in the sights, sounds and sheer beauty of the most romantic city in the world. It was a city he loved and felt at home in, after spending all his school holidays here with his mother's French family, followed by a year at the Sorbonne, when he became fluent in French.

But he had made his life in England where his daughter was brought up, and that was her family's home. He missed them terribly. He stood up, feeling a chill creep through his body from the cold steps. He took one last look at the people on the boat and turned to walk back to his apartment.

Later that evening, he tried to call Francois, but she didn't answer, which didn't surprise him. It would probably be the end of the week before she calmed down. He remembered, though, that Saturday was her opening night, so he would go round to her apartment on Friday to see her and wish her well.

He made himself some pasta, took it through to the living room and sat down on the sofa with a glass of wine, Simon & Garfunkel playing softly in the background. He hated sitting at the big kitchen table on his own, eating his supper, especially when he hadn't written a thing all day and was exhausted with the effort of trying.

When he finished his pasta, he set the plate on the floor and picked up his laptop to lazily browse through Facebook. Sure enough, there was another picture of Caroline, sitting on a sofa with her leg propped up and a pair of crutches beside her. Lots of her friends had sent her messages, wishing her a speedy recovery. He wondered what she had done to herself and also wondered who had taken the photograph, but he didn't make a comment or send an emoji reply. *This is ridiculous,* he thought, as he scrolled past it to see his other posts. He got fed up with it, finished his wine, switched off the CD and went to bed to try to get some sleep.

It was over a week before he looked at Facebook again. He had managed to write at last, and every waking moment that week was dedicated to his work. By Friday, he was pleased to have added another poem to his anthology and was able to relax.

The weekend had been a hive of activity. Francois had welcomed him as if nothing had happened between them when he called round on Friday to wish her well for the opening night. She was bubbling with excitement because she had heard a film producer was coming to see the show.

He had spent the whole weekend with her at her apartment. The party after the show on Saturday night had lasted well into Sunday morning, celebrating the great reviews. Francois, in particular, had been mentioned as one to watch, which thrilled her.

Her career had gone into decline when she entered her forties, even though she looked ten years younger, but there seemed to be fewer roles for older women these days. Everyone had to be young, gorgeous and vibrant, unlike the male actors who had a wealth of roles offered to them as elegant, silver-haired heroes, but now she was being recognised as a good character actor, elegant with striking feature and very attractive. She was delighted and hopeful of better opportunities ahead.

Freddie had returned to his apartment late on Sunday night, exhausted. He was getting too old to be partying all weekend, but he was glad that he and Francois were back on a good footing, at least for now, but he never knew with her. He did love her, but he wasn't sure that he was 'in love' with her. She didn't fill his mind the way that

Caroline did these days. He thought of her incessantly and couldn't get her out of his head.

He tumbled into bed, leaving his clothes in a heap on the floor, too tired to put them away. But sleep wouldn't come, and he eventually picked up his laptop from his bedside table to browse the internet. As usual, he stumbled onto Facebook.

There had been no more photographs from Caroline. He hoped she was OK and had recovered from whatever injury she had suffered. He should have wished her a speedy recovery and felt guilty that he had not. He scrolled back through the posts and found the one of her in her sitting room with her leg elevated. He typed a comment, hoping that she was better, and wished her well. He closed up his laptop, switched off the light and eventually fell into a deep, welcome sleep.

Chapter Nine

Cornwall

Caroline woke on Saturday morning to a bright-blue sky dotted with wispy clouds slowly passing across her window. She had slept really well for the first time that week. Peggy's reassuring snores at the bottom of the stairs had been very comforting. She could hear her now, padding about in the kitchen. Outside it was tranquil and peaceful. The only sound was the rolling and crashing of the waves on the beach beyond the woods, until her phone started ringing.

"Good morning, how are you this morning? Sleep well?" asked Lawrence, in his deep, husky voice.

"I'm very well, thank you, and I slept like a log."

"I assume Peggy was very reassuring. Would you like to go for a drive and a bit of a walk?"

"Oh! That would be nice, but I can't walk too far, as you know. Where shall we go?"

"There is a lovely, sheltered cove near the town, that not many people know about. I can park the car right by the beach, and we can have a gentle stroll and then come back to town for lunch. How does that sound?

"It sounds perfect. I will be ready when you are," she said.

"OK, I will be with you at eleven — is that OK?"

"Yes, that's fine. See you soon," she said, as she set about getting ready, feeling more like her old self.

She was sitting at the kitchen table, having a coffee with Bert who had come over to collect Peggy, when Lawrence opened the door with the spare key. Peggy bounced down the hall, nearly knocking him over.

"Peggy! Come back here!" shouted Bert. "Sorry about that, Lawrence. She is pleased to see you."

"No problem. She and I are old friends now," said Lawrence, patting Peggy before she ran back to Bert.

Caroline wondered if she detected a slight sarcastic tone to his comment about Peggy.

"Come on, old girl. Let's go for your walk and leave these people in peace. I will drop her back this evening, if you want me to?" asked Bert, putting Peggy's lead on.

"Thank you, Bert, that would be great. It's very reassuring to hear her snoring at the bottom of the stairs. I will miss her when I get the alarm fitted. Are you sure you don't mind letting Martin in to quote on fitting the alarm here?"

"Of course not. I will bring him over after he has done our quote. You go off and have a nice day out."

"Thanks, I'm being really spoiled these last few days. See you later. Bye, Bert," she said, as Bert closed and locked the kitchen door behind him.

"Are you ready to go?" Lawrence asked, coming through to the kitchen and bending down to kiss her. "By the way, I had better give you this key back, while I remember, now that you are mobile again," he said, leaving the key on the table.

"OK, thanks, and thanks for being such an attentive carer all week. I don't know what I would have done without you and Fiona."

"The pleasure was all mine, and I am very glad to see you almost back to your old self. Now, stand up and give me a hug, and then I will take you on a mystery tour," he said, pulling her up into his arms and kissing her.

Caroline eased herself back and looked up at him. "I don't know what I have done to deserve you, Lawrence Wainwright. You are my knight in shining armour," she said.

"Happily, at your service, madam. Now, let's go. I think you will love where I'm taking you."

Half an hour later they arrived at a small, secluded beach which was deserted. The sand was like white powder, and the sea was an azure blue, blending into an invisible horizon with the sky. It had a magical, eerie atmosphere, and Caroline was captivated.

"We could be on a Caribbean Island. It is so beautiful — paradise to have it to ourselves too," she said, holding her face to the winter sun as they sat down on a large rock, side by side, Lawrence's arm protectively around her shoulder.

He pulled her closer to him, kissing her. "Maybe we will go to the Caribbean one day. Would you like that? I have friends who have a glorified shack on Anguilla, near a place called Rendezvous Bay. It really is paradise, with soft, powder-white sand like this but even finer. It's heavenly — you would love it." he said.

"Sounds idyllic. I have never been to the Caribbean, but I would love to go. Especially with you," she added shyly.

"Let's do it after the New Year, if it's available. I can do some painting while we are there. If you don't mind, that is?"

"Oh, I'm sure I could pass the time quite happily while you paint," she said, smiling at him.

"I have painted down here quite often, but I never tell my clients exactly where it is. I usually title the painting 'A Cornish Cove', but I'm sure it will get discovered by the tourists one of these days, especially when you see books entitled 'Secret Beaches'. Sometimes, when I see them in the bookstore, I feel like buying them all up, but then Sophia would only order more," he said laughing, as they sat contentedly watching the waves roll in, white surf splashing on the sand.

Caroline shivered slightly. "Although this looks like the Caribbean, I imagine Rendezvous Bay is quite a bit warmer," she said, rubbing her hands together.

"It sure is. Come here and let me warm you," he said, holding her tight and rubbing her back to warm her up. "Come on, let's go back and I will make us some lunch. I want to show you my humble abode," he said, standing up and pulling her up by the hands.

Lawrence parked the Jag in the garage at the back of his cottage, and they walked round to the front door. The charming, stained-glass door was right at street level, and a narrow path separated it from the cobbled street. The door opened directly into a cosy living room, with a log burner glowing gently on top of a flagstone hearth.

It was a typical fisherman's cottage but furnished in a very contemporary, masculine style — very typical of Lawrence. A black leather Egg chair, by Arne Jacobsen, sat by the fire. Caroline recognised the sleek Danish designer, and although her own cottage was full of antiques, she admired the lines of the 60s designers. A smart but very worn, large, dark-green, leather Chesterfield sofa took up the entire back wall, with the bookshelves above filled with art books and stylish pieces of Troika and other Cornish pottery. There was even an elegant, smooth, white sculpture which looked very much like a Barbara Hepworth. The other walls displayed Lawrence's paintings.

"This is gorgeous, Lawrence," she said, following him through to the kitchen.

"It suits me just fine. I don't need to rattle around in a big house any more. I took my favourite pieces from our old place and left Claudia whatever else she wanted. Cup of coffee?" he asked, as they came into a surprisingly large, modern kitchen, flooded with light from three big Velux windows and French doors leading onto a small courtyard. "This is an extension that I added on when I moved in. The old kitchen was not much more than a cupboard, and as I'm not into gardening, I decided to use the space to build this."

Caroline stood over by the French doors, looking out to the small, neat and tidy courtyard, with the garage backing onto it. Lawrence came up behind her, as the coffee machine gurgled in the background. He put his arms around her, kissing the back of her neck. She leaned her head back, as he kissed her on the lips.

"Hmmm, you taste good and smell wonderful — I like that perfume you're wearing. Come with me and let me show you the rest of the cottage — coffee can wait," he said, taking her by the hand and leading her up to his bedroom up in the eaves.

"It's charming," she said, when she saw the small bedroom, simply furnished with a king-size bed, crisp white linen, a large oak dresser and a wardrobe built into the stairwell. A small window overlooked the courtyard. Caroline went over to it to look out.

"It's adequate. I don't need anything more," he said, coming up behind her, turning her around and kissing her. "Apart from you." His eyes burning into her, she looked away.

"What are you afraid of" he asked, turning her head to face him.

"You" she replied softly.

"You have no reason to be afraid of me. I would never do you any harm"

She held his gaze. "Then it's me I'm frightened of. Im not ready for this" she said, glancing over at the bed, standing there like an elephant in the room.

"You are driving me a little bit crazy, Caroline. I thought …."

"Im sorry Lawrence if I gave you that impression" she tore her eyes away from his and looked out through the window. "I think I just heard the coffee machine ping. I could do with a coffee" she said, easing herself away from him and going back downstairs.

"And I could do with a drink!" he muttered to himself and followed her.

It was a few minutes before Lawrence joined her in the kitchen. Caroline watched as he went over to the coffee machine. He was very quiet, and she sensed a change in his mood. He handed her a coffee, went through to the sitting room and sat down in his Egg chair. Caroline followed him through.

"What's wrong, Lawrence?" she asked, as if she didn't know. She thought she had extricated herself from that awkward moment up in the bedroom quite well. Surely, he didn't really expect her to give in to him.

Especially after the week she had had, not to mention the fact that they had only known each other a couple of weeks, but maybe that's the way the modern dating world worked. If he thought she was a prude, so be it.

"Nothing. Sit down and have your coffee," he said, nodding in the direction of the large sofa.

Caroline sipped her coffee, stubbornly refusing to be told to sit, and began to look at some of his paintings on the walls.

"These are beautiful, so atmospheric," she said, thinking she didn't much like the chilly atmosphere in the room.

"Thank you," he replied curtly, sitting back in his chair, one leg bent over the other, watching her.

She continued walking round the room, leaning on Edna's stick, looking at the paintings, but Lawrence remained silent. She could feel him looking at her, as she stood with her back to him. She eventually sat down on the sofa, clutching the coffee mug in her hands, looking across at him.

"So, what shall we do now?" he asked, smiling at her. "I could make us an omelette, or would you like to go out for lunch?"

"Let's go out — my treat. You have been treating me to takeaways all week," she replied, thankful that he seemed more like his old self.

"OK, that's a deal. Finish up your coffee, and I will take you somewhere I bet you haven't been before," he said, sounding quite chirpy again.

By the time they arrived at the mystery lunch destination, Lawrence had reverted to his usual charming self. Caroline was surprised and delighted when they parked the car by a converted railway carriage on a nearby beach.

"Wow, this looks interesting. I didn't know this place existed," she said, as they climbed aboard.

"Isn't it fun? The food is excellent, as well. I'm glad you like it," he said, as they followed the waiter through the glossy, wood-panelled carriage to a small table set with a white linen tablecloth, shining cutlery and a little Art Deco lamp by the window.

"It's like stepping back in time. It reminds me of the Orient Express, except for those," she said, sitting down on the sumptuous upholstery and looking out through the window at the waves crashing on the beach.

"Ahh, you've been on the Orient Express, to Venice?" he asked.

"We travelled from Paris to Istanbul. It was our silver wedding anniversary treat. It was wonderful," she replied quietly.

Lawrence raised his eyebrows, looking impressed, just as the waiter came over with the menus.

After a delicious leisurely lunch, they set off for the next part of Lawrence's mystery tour and ended up at the Tate in St Ives, where they spent the rest of the afternoon enthralled by the modern art and the magic of Barbara

Hepworth's sculpture garden. Lawrence took a selfie of them outside the gallery, laughing at the camera as he tried to get them both in focus.

On the drive back to St Mawdley, Lawrence took a diversion into what was locally known as a 'bucket & spade' resort.

"I bet you have never been anywhere like this either!" he said, as he parked his car by some steps in a rough and ready car park.

"I think I can honestly say that I have never been anywhere like this," said Caroline, as they walked slowly up to the steps of a karaoke bar.

The noise was deafening when they entered the crowded bar. Lawrence nodded over towards a booth in the corner, where there were a couple of spare chairs. "Sit yourself down, and I will go up to the bar," he shouted over the noise.

Caroline watched him push his way through the crowd towards the bar. He seemed to know quite a few of the people who came up to him, slapping him on the back. She also noticed some long-legged girls in frayed, skimpy shorts, sidling up to him at the bar and draping their slim, tanned arms across his shoulders. He seemed very much at home here, and that greatly surprised Caroline, she wondered if she really knew him at all.

A little later, although it seemed an age to Caroline, he came back with a beer for himself and a G&T for her.

"Cheers!" he said, as he sat down on the chair beside her. "So, what do you think?" he asked, speaking into her ear.

"It's quite unlike anything I've ever seen before. You seem to know a lot of the locals." she said, smiling at him.

"I come here every so often, they are a fun bunch, especially on Karaoke nights, speaking of which..." he said, setting his beer on the table and going over to a basket by the stage, pulling out a hat and a feather boa. He sauntered back over to her with a cheeky grin on his face. We're up next, by the way."

"What do you mean?"

"I've signed us up for a duet. Elton John and Kiki Dee — 'Don't go breaking my heart'," he said, laughing at the look of shock on Caroline's face.

"What! I can't sing! You won't get me up on that stage."

"Too late to back out now — we're on. Come on, it's time you let your hair down," he said, grabbing her by the hand and helping her up and over onto the stage.

"Lawrence, I can't do this!" she pleaded, as he plonked a straw cowboy hat on her head, a pink feather boa around his neck and slipped on a pair of star-shaped sunglasses.

He handed her a mike as the music started, the crowd cheering as he started belting out the well-known number. Caroline stared in disbelief as her turn came. It took her a moment before she timidly sang the words on the cue card. Lawrence laughed and wrapped his arm around her, as Caroline did her best to sing along.

The applause from the rowdy crowd was rapturous. Caroline thought they would have cheered at anything, as Lawrence took a bow and handed back the props.

"You did well!" he said, as he downed his beer when they got back to their seats.

"Don't ever do that to me again. I was mortified," she said, taking a large slurp of her G&T.

"You were great! Good to see you let your hair down. You need to live a little, Caroline. You've had a rotten week, but you mustn't dwell on it. Lighten up!" he laughed.

Caroline shook her head, still in a state of shock, as they sat and watched the next act perform a terrible rendition of Frank Sinatra's 'My Way', which received some more rapturous applause.

"Come on, Kiki, let's get you home," he said, finishing his beer and taking her hand, waving goodbye to the people at the table.

Caroline was a bit subdued on the journey home. She was exhausted, and her ankle was beginning to throb — it had been a long day. What disturbed her more was that she had seen a side of Lawrence at the karaoke that she never dreamt existed. It had just been such a shock, after the cultured afternoon they had just enjoyed at the Tate. She was beginning to realise that Lawrence Wainwright was a very complex individual.

"Didn't you enjoy the karaoke just a teeny bit?" he asked, as they neared Butterfly Cottage.

"Not really. It's not my scene, I'm afraid. But you were very good as Elton — a very polished performance — but I won't be in a hurry to go again."

"Well, I'm glad you had a go," he said, as he pulled onto her driveway. He reached across and kissed her, looking at her for a minute before he got out and ran round to open the car door for her.

"Aren't you coming in?" she asked, when they reached the porch, and he kissed her on the cheek.

"I have a commission piece to finish. Much as I would love to spend the rest of the evening with you, I need to get an early night and crack on with some work tomorrow."

"Goodnight, then. It's been a lovely day, full of surprises and a very interesting evening," she said, as he kissed her goodbye before walking briskly down the path, waving as he drove off.

She locked the door, double-checked it and went through to the kitchen, feeling exhausted and very alone again. She poured herself a glass of wine and sat down at the kitchen table, reflecting on the day. It had been lovely in so many ways, but she had seen a couple of sides of Lawrence that had surprised her, and she felt she had failed to please him in some way, which was something she hadn't felt since she was a child when she had misbehaved. She also got a feeling that the karaoke bar had been some sort of test, and she feared she had failed it too.

She had certainly never expected to see Lawrence, who was always so suave and sophisticated, behave in such an uncharacteristic way. If only he had given her some warning about the karaoke, but it probably wouldn't have made any difference. She was much too shy a person to be comfortable performing on the stage. She would have needed more than one large G&T to relax sufficiently. Apart from that, she was also uncomfortable with the young girls who all seemed to know him so well. They must have thought she was so old. She certainly felt old compared to them, even though she was dressed in what she thought was casually trendy jeans and her favourite mock-croc boots, which were now killing her, but thank goodness she had left the stick in the car, or they would have thought she was geriatric!

She sighed, staring out at the full moon peeping over the tops of the trees. This dating game was not an easy one to play, especially when it had been nearly forty years since she last played it, and she was beginning to wonder if she even wanted to. She finished her wine, made herself a hot chocolate and was just about to take it through to the sitting room, when she heard a knock on the kitchen door. She jumped nervously and then remembered it would be Bert with Peggy.

"It's only me, Caroline," called Bert, peering through the glass panel, putting his key in the lock.

"Hi, Bert, hello Peggy," she said, as Peggy came though, nuzzling at her legs.

"Just brought your guard dog round. I saw Lawrence drive off."

"Thanks, Bert. Yes, we both needed an early night — it's been a very busy day."

"Everything OK, dear? You seem a bit low. If you are still a bit nervous being on your own, Edna will come over."

"I'm fine, thanks, Bert. Just really tired — exhausted actually. Peggy is a great comfort, but I will be glad when I get the alarm fitted on Monday."

"I'll see you in the morning when I come over to take Peggy for her walk. Be a good girl, Peggy. Goodnight, Caroline."

"Goodnight, Bert," she said, cuddling Peggy and leading her into the hall where she settled down on her rug at the foot of the stairs. "Nite, nite, Peggy, sleep well. I hope I do," she said, deciding to go up to bed.

She climbed the stairs with her hot chocolate and a hundred and one thoughts buzzing around in her head.

When she woke the next morning, after a restless night of tossing and turning, she decided that she needed to take a more positive attitude. No more dwelling on what had happened, but as Lawrence said, she needed to lighten up a bit. She picked up her laptop from the floor beside her bed and logged into Facebook. She thought she would post the photograph that Lawrence had taken of them in front of the Tate Gallery in St Ives and share it with her friends and let them know she was seeing someone and get their reaction. She wasn't worried about her sons seeing it — they rarely checked out her Facebook page. She would tell them about Lawrence if and when the time came.

She noticed that Freddie had commented about the picture of her with her resting her leg, last week. It was nice of him to wish her well. She always felt a little flutter when he commented on her posts, and she always enjoyed seeing his. He seemed to live an exciting life in Paris, and his women, Francois, looked very chic and very French, like someone out of a 1940s wartime, French Resistance movie.

She uploaded her new picture without adding any comment and looked forward to what reaction, if any, that she might get from her Facebook friends. A few minutes later, comments started appearing about the photograph, lots of 'likes' and thumbs-up emojis, which pleased Caroline enormously.

So, with renewed vigour, she threw back the duvet and headed for the shower, ready to embrace what lay ahead.

Paris

Freddie was also in bed on Sunday morning, trying to catch up on his sleep after the opening-night party. He had slipped away in the early hours, leaving Francois who was on a high from the success of their first night and had no doubt continued partying until dawn.

He, too, was browsing Facebook, when the photograph of Caroline and her new man — presumably — popped up on his feed. He stared at the image of the two of them, faces touching, laughing at the camera. Caroline looked very happy — she had obviously recovered from her injury. He looked a bit suave and cocky, he thought, didn't seem her type. *Jesus Christ! Freddie Harrison are you jealous?* he said to himself.

He looked at the photograph again, but he couldn't bring himself to 'like' it or even leave a thumbs-up emoji. He switched off his laptop and flung it over onto the bottom of the bed in a fit of temper. *Damn it,* he thought, as he thumped his pillow in the hope of getting it into a more sleep-induced shape, before he hauled the duvet over his shoulder, squeezed his eyes shut, eventually drifting off to an uneasy sleep and unsettling dreams of Caroline and her new man.

Chapter Ten

Cornwall

Later that week, Caroline was in St Mawdley to do her shopping. She was keen to get back to normal now that her ankle was completely healed. She wasn't due back to work until Friday, so she thought she would call on Lawrence to see if he fancied a coffee at Pat's. He had been busy the last few days working on another commission piece, but she hoped he would have time for a walk down to the harbour on such a lovely frosty morning.

It took him a while to answer the door. She nearly walked away, thinking he was out, but when he did answer, he looked very surprised to see her.

"Good morning, this is a nice surprise," he said, kissing her on the cheek. "Come in, I'm busy packing. I'm off to Miami on Saturday," he said, going through to the kitchen.

"Miami? When did this come about? You never mentioned it," she said, following him into the kitchen which looked like a bomb had hit it.

"Didn't I? I'm sorry. I go every year to the International Arts Festival. It's way out of my league, but it's fun and good networking. It's been chaos this week, trying to get a commission piece finished, not to mention getting a selection of my best work taken up to London for an exhibition in Chelsea when I get back," he said, piling some dishes into the dishwasher.

"Oh, I see. I had no idea. It sounds very exciting. How long are you away for?" she asked, feeling very deflated, not quite sure how to react.

"Not sure. I'm so sorry I didn't mention it. Anyway, how are you? You look better," he said, looking round the kitchen for any dirty dishes.

"I'm fine, getting back to normal. I was going to ask if you had time for a coffee, but obviously not," she said, stepping out of the way as he grabbed some cups — one of them with a lipstick mark on the rim — from the bench behind her and put them in the dishwasher.

"Sorry, love, I'm up to my ears. Listen, I will try and get to see you on Friday before I go."

"I'm working Friday, and it's Bonfire Night in St Mawdley. A bunch of us from the mansion are getting together. I thought you might have joined us. Never mind, have a nice time, if I don't see you. Take care. I will be off now and let you crack on."

"Bugger it, I forgot it was Bonfire night — it's going to be heaving here. OK. You take care too," he said, kissing her on the cheek. "I will be in touch," he added, as he continued clearing up in the kitchen, whistling to himself.

She waited for him to see her out, but when it was obvious, he wasn't going to, she went through to the front room. She noticed a couple of the seascapes were missing from the walls, and she assumed they had gone up to Chelsea too. She shouted goodbye as she left, closing the door behind her.

She was annoyed with him and kept thinking he would call her name as she walked up Guillemot Street to where her car was parked, but he didn't. She felt like thumping him, she was so annoyed at him. She obviously wasn't important enough to him, to be included in his plans.

She didn't speak to him again until Friday, when he unexpectedly came out to the mansion to see the Giacometti exhibition and say goodbye. She was working, as she had told him, so it had been a surprise to see him. He had apologised profusely for not telling her about his trip, and despite the hurt and anger she had felt, she forgave him as soon as he took her in his arms and stole a kiss, as they went down in the lift to the cafe during her break, and once again, she was like putty in his hands.

"It's a fabulous exhibition. I'm sure it's been popular," he said, as they sat having a quick cup of coffee.

"Yes, it has. I will miss it when it packs up and goes back to its home."

"And I will miss you when I'm away. Will you have time for a bite to eat this evening, to wish me Bon voyage?" he said, taking her hand, gently stroking it and looking deeply into her eyes.

"I'm supposed to be going to the beach bonfire party with the others, but I suppose I could meet you for an early supper. What time were you thinking? I finish here in half an hour."

"That's perfect. An early supper at the pub down the road — would that suit?

"Yes, that's fine. Oh, my goodness, look at the time. I must get back to the gallery," she said, just as Fiona walked past on her way up to the staffroom for her break. Caroline called her over.

Caroline called her over. "Fiona, you remember Lawrence, don't you? Why don't you stay and have your break here and keep him company? I will be finished in half an hour," said Caroline, picking up her folder and tucking it under her arm.

"I would be delighted for you to join me, Fiona. Let me get you a tea or coffee?" he said, pointing to the empty chair.

"OK, a coffee, please," said Fiona, sitting down in Caroline's chair as Lawrence caught the waiter's eye.

"Super. I will see you shortly. Shall I meet you in the car park?" asked Caroline, kissing him goodbye on the cheek.

"I will go and pick up my car from the car park and meet you outside. We can leave your car here while we grab a bite to eat," he replied.

"You haven't forgotten about the beach party, have you?" asked Fiona, looking surprised when she heard them arranging a dinner date.

"No, of course I haven't. It's just a quick bite to eat with Lawrence before he flies off. I will come and join you all later," replied Caroline, rushing off.

Fiona raised her eyebrows and looked at Lawrence, just as the waiter set down a coffee in front of her.

As Caroline walked back along the corridor to the gallery, she was slightly annoyed with herself for falling for his charm so easily. She had been very hurt and upset that he still hadn't bothered to explain why he hadn't told her about Miami or about his Chelsea exhibition. Maybe she would hear more this evening. She also knew that Fiona was a bit miffed that she had changed her plans, but she would explain it all to her later, and she hoped that she and the others would understand.

Fiona picked up her coffee cup and looked at Lawrence across the table. He made her feel a little nervous as he sat watching her. She had only ever met him briefly a couple of times and hadn't particularly warmed to him. He was just too damned good-looking and had a very intense way of looking at you with eyes that were a very cold, icy blue. She had seen that trait before many times, especially in her ex-husband. He had captivated countless women with his good looks. She hoped, for Caroline's sake, that Lawrence wasn't a womanizer too.

"So, Fiona, what did you do before you came to volunteer here? Let me guess: a fashion designer or a model — something glamourous, I would say," he said, smiling at her.

"You are way off the mark, Lawrence. Believe it or not, I was in the police — a detective at the Met. I took early retirement," she replied, taking a sip of coffee.

"Really? My goodness, that is a surprise. You look nothing like any police officer I've ever met. Any particular reason for early retirement or is that too intrusive a question?" he asked, shifting his position.

"The stress of the job. I finally had enough of dealing with the thugs of London, after having a run-in with a particularly nasty piece of work. I came down here for a quiet life. I work here a couple of days a week, like Caroline. The rest of my time I spend learning to make pots."

"You're a potter? How interesting. Where is your studio?" he asked, leaning back in the chair.

"I wouldn't call it a studio. My kiln is in the garage, and my wheel is in the garden shed. I live just outside St Mawdley. You have a gallery in St Mawdley, don't you?" she asked.

"Yes, I do. I moved down from London, too. There are a lot of us city types down here — some of the locals say we are taking over," he said, grinning.

"It's so much better than London. I would never go back, would you?"

"No, I don't think so. This place suits me at the moment. I do go back occasionally though, to exhibit when I feel the need. Can't really depend on the tourists to make enough money," he said, finishing off his coffee. He sat quietly, watching her for a few minutes before he continued speaking. "I'm sorry, Fiona, but if you'll excuse me, I will need to set off to walk that long stretch down to the car park and get back in time for her," he said, calling for the bill.

"My break is nearly over anyway," she said, finishing her coffee, as he got up to kiss her on the cheek.

"Thanks for keeping me company, and maybe I will see you in St Mawdley one of these days. Come see my little gallery. Maybe we could do business with your pots?" he said, putting on his coat.

"Oh, I'm not sure they are good enough for an art gallery. Some of the craft shops stock them but thank you anyway. Bye, Lawrence, I must be off," she said, getting up and hurrying off as he paid the bill.

She hoped her instinct was wrong. The mood had altered when she mentioned she was an ex-cop. She just wasn't sure that the gorgeous Lawrence was all Caroline thought he was, and she really hoped she wasn't going to get hurt. She was also annoyed with her for changing her plans at a drop of a hat, to suit Lawrence.

By the time Fiona got up to the top floor for the last hour of the day, the visitors had all drifted away or gone down to the cafe for a delicious, Cornish cream tea before they headed for home. She loved this time of day, knowing she could find a quiet corner of the gallery to sit and reflect on the busy day, or maybe even read her book, but her thoughts kept wandering back to her meeting with Lawrence and she couldn't put her finger on what was niggling her about him.

She had met many men like him in her life, both professional and personal. He reminded her a bit of her ex-husband, which wasn't a good thing. She just didn't think he was Caroline's type. She wasn't really surprised when she had started going out with him. He was extremely attractive, but Fiona thought that Caroline, like herself, was content with her own company, she didn't think she had wanted to get into a relationship, but she imagined Lawrence Wainwright was hard to say no to, if he set his sights on you.

Fiona never intended to get involved with anyone again. She had wasted enough of her life on her lying, cheating, good-for-nothing ex-husband, and she wasn't going to waste any more time on anyone else. She was quite content with her work and friends at the gallery and was enjoying her newfound passion in pottery. She had no room in her life for a man.

But maybe it was different for Caroline. She had had a good marriage and the love of a good man. Maybe she wanted a little bit of that again. Fiona wasn't sure she would get that with Lawrence. She sighed. She was very fond of Caroline, but she knew she was a romantic and saw the good in everyone. She was probably a little bit naive about men like Lawrence. She had lived a sheltered life with the love of her husband and family around her. All Fiona could do was look out for her and make sure she didn't get hurt.

Chapter Eleven

"Fancy some company this morning on your walk?" asked Fiona when she rang Caroline a few days later.

She hadn't been able to shake the nagging doubts she had about Lawrence, and she wanted to spend some time with her friend to try and figure out just how things were really going between them. She had an awful feeling that Caroline was being taken for a ride by the dashing Lawrence. They rarely got a chance to have a proper chat at the gallery. It had been so busy lately, so Fiona thought a nice, long walk on the beach would be just what they needed to catch up properly.

She arrived at Butterfly Cottage, well-wrapped up in a deep-purple wool jacket, a massive, lavender, mohair scarf and bright-red, velvet trousers tucked into sheepskin boots.

When Caroline opened the front door to her, she smiled at the glamourous, colourful vision before her. "Well, you are sight for sore eyes, that's for sure. Come in, good to see you," she said, holding Peggy back from jumping up at her. Peggy had come to stay with Caroline while Bert and Edna had gone to Penzance for the day.

"Hello, Peggy, old girl," said Fiona, making a big fuss of the dog. She knew that there would be no peace from Peggy until she felt she had well and truly welcomed any visitor. Once she was satisfied, she quite happily went off and collapsed like a bear rug in front of the fire.

"She is so gorgeous," said Fiona, taking off her boots as Peggy wandered quietly away and then handed Caroline her jacket and scarf.

"She is. I love having her to stay — she is great company. I missed her when she went back to Bert and Edna after the incident with the intruder. She is such a big softie, but she does look quite intimidating to anyone who doesn't know her. She's great company on my walks too, of course, and I am doubly lucky today to have your company too! Fancy a coffee before we head off?"

"Thank you, that would be lovely. It's a beautiful, crisp morning out there — a nice, hot cuppa will keep us warm," said Fiona, following Caroline into the kitchen.

They chatted about the exhibition and their colleagues, catching up on the mansion gossip. There was always some interesting titbit of news going round the staffroom, particularly with the younger members of staff, who would often dramatically pour out their woes about their love lives to the more mature members of the team, hoping for some pearls of wisdom. Tom and Philip, in particular, were always ready to act as Agony Aunts, but always in a most amusing way. It led to some very interesting lunch-break conversations sometimes.

"It was a shame you didn't get to join us at the beach party — it was a great night," said Fiona, looking across at Caroline.

"I was really sorry to miss it, but by the time Lawrence and I finished our meal, it was getting late, so I just went straight home. I didn't think you would miss me."

"Of course, we missed you, but we guessed Lawrence had detained you," she replied, raising an eyebrow.

"Don't look at me like that. I know it must seem that I just dumped my plans with you guys to fall in with his plans."

"That's exactly what you did, but never mind. I hope he's worth it," she said, patting Peggy who had come over to put her head on Fiona's lap.

An awkward silence fell between them as they sipped their coffee, looking out at the garden, before Fiona picked up the conversation again.

"It's so lovely out here, Caroline, especially on a lovely day like this. Are you OK though, being on your own after that intruder incident?"

"I have the alarm now, and Bert and Edna are just down the lane. But I must admit that when they are away, it would feel lonely if I didn't have Peggy. After that incident, I did feel very vulnerable for a while, but I'm OK now, and Lawrence comes out now and again," she said.

"And how is Lawrence these days? You two all loved up and happy?"

Caroline laughed. "For goodness' sake, Fiona, we are not teenagers. Although he does make me feel young again, when I'm with him. He is such good company and so charming. I'm very fond of him."

"Is there a 'but' coming?" asked Fiona, guardedly.

"This is all so new to me — this dating game. I never thought I would want a relationship again, and then along came this gorgeous man who seemed attracted to me. I really couldn't believe it. He awoke something in me that I thought was long gone. I feel young again when I'm with him, but he is so suave and sophisticated, worldly-wise, and I feel a bit of a prude at times."

"You are no prude! You are one of the most elegant and attractive women I know. You mustn't let him pressurize or manipulate you, Caroline," she said, patting the back of Caroline's hand.

"Funny you should say that. That's exactly what Lawrence said on the phone last night. He rang me at midnight from Miami."

"Miami? What's he doing there, and when did this all happen? Did he forget the time difference? That was a bit thoughtless."

"So many questions! He is at the Miami Art Festival. He went on Saturday; that's why we went out for a meal the night of the beach party. It was a bit out of the blue, as far as I was concerned, and yes, I think he did forget the time difference, but he was very excited about an opportunity that had come his way."

"What sort of opportunity?" asked Fiona, feeling the hairs on the back of her neck stand up.

"Some new and upcoming artist he has come across."

"Really? When did he become a patron? That's a huge festival., I would have thought it was out of his league, but I suppose he knows a lot of the right people."

"Suppose so. Anyway, he has come across a South American artist who is getting 'hot', as Lawrence says, and he wants to invest in one of his paintings. Lawrence says he not that well known in Europe yet, but in six to twelve months' time, that could change, and his work will double in value."

"Really?" said Fiona, raising a dubious eyebrow.

"Yes, apparently so. Lawrence says he has invested in artists like him before and made a small fortune. Anyway, he asked me if I wanted to go fifty-fifty with him on one of his paintings, but he stressed that he didn't want to pressurize me."

"I bet he did. You haven't invested, have you?"

"Not yet. He said he would call me today, after I've had some time to think about it, but I need to decide this afternoon and transfer the money into his account."

"How much are we talking about?"

Twenty-five grand."

"What! That must be some painting!"

"That's just my fifty percent share," Caroline said sheepishly.

"Holy moly! Caroline, I really think you need to check this out a bit more, before you invest, and not just take Lawrence's word for it. Excuse me for asking, but can you afford to risk that sort of money?"

"Absolutely not, but Lawrence says it's a sound investment. I really don't know what to do."

"Please, Caroline, back away from this. You hardly know Lawrence. I'm not saying he's trying to con you or anything, but that's a huge sum of money to risk on something you know nothing about."

"But Lawrence knows his stuff — shouldn't I trust him? He says if I'm not interested, he will ask one of his London investors, but he needs to know today."

"Well, for what's it's worth, I suggest you pass on this one and tell him you might be interested in the future when you know more, but you can't invest just now."

"I suppose that makes sense. It is all a bit of a rush, isn't it? Yeah, I will tell him, when he calls, to count me out of this one."

"I really think that's wise, but please don't tell me if it's sells for a fortune and you've lost out!"

"I won't! We shall see how this one fares. Right, are you ready for that walk? I know Peggy certainly is," she said, laughing at Peggy, who couldn't wait to get out through the back door when she heard the word 'walk'.

They walked along the beach, with Peggy running in front, dashing in and out of the waves. The wind was freezing, but the winter sun was warm on their faces when they stood with their backs to the wind, gazing at the cliffs in the distance.

"It's so beautiful here, isn't it? I could never go back to city life, much as I miss my boy back in the big smoke," said Fiona, taking in deep breaths.

"It is. We are very lucky to have been able to escape down here. I know we are a long way from our loved ones, but I could never leave the sea, now that I have lived beside it these last few years," said Caroline, turning to walk into the wind again.

"It's so exhilarating and blows away all your worries — and your hair!" laughed Fiona, taking a red, woolly hat out of her pocket to tuck her hair up inside.

"So, tell me. How are things with you? We've talked enough about me," said Caroline, linking her arm with Fiona's.

"Oh, I am just fine. I love my job, and I love my pots. They both keep me busy, and no stress!"

"It must have been very stressful for you in your old job. Do you miss the buzz though?"

Fiona shook her head. "Not at all. I had way too much buzz in the Met. I had had enough and was lucky to retire early. The last few years nearly pushed me over the edge. I've never told anyone at work, but I was involved in a very nasty case and suffered PTSD as a result. It took me a couple of years to realise I just couldn't do it any more, and my ex-husband was no damn use, telling me to pull myself together."

"I'm so sorry to hear that. I had no idea that was why you took early retirement," said Caroline.

"I had done my time with the Met — twenty-five long years and the same for my marriage. My ex-husband was a serial philanderer, which I had turned a blind eye to for years for the sake of Henry, but it finally fell apart when I got no support from him at all. Coming down here, though, has really saved my soul. It is a blessing to live in this wonderful county. And before you ask — I'm not lonely, and I don't need a man," she said, laughing.

They reached the bend in the beach, with the view of the harbour across the bay. The tide was coming in, so they could go no further. Peggy came bouncing back to them, knowing it was time to head back home. They walked, the wind on their backs blowing them along the sand, and by the time they got to the cottage, they looked very windswept.

"Fancy some soup?" asked Caroline, as they opened the gate.

"Oooh, lovely. Just what we need," she replied.

After a lunch of soup and bread, Fiona sat back in her chair. "Thank you, that was delicious. And thank you for a lovely morning. I'm so glad I called you."

"I'm glad you called, too. Thank you for coming out and thank you for listening and your advice."

"Just you remember how special you are, and don't get bullied into something you are not comfortable with.

Lawrence is the type who likes to get his own way, and he will do whatever pleases him; just like going off to Miami on his own and not telling you. Take your time with him and be careful. You have been on your own for a long time, which makes you vulnerable and maybe a little too trusting."

"Yeah, you're right. I must have more confidence in myself and my instincts. You are a good friend, Fiona," she said, giving her a big hug, with Peggy muscling in for some attention herself.

Fiona was just putting her coat on when Caroline's phone rang.

"Is that Lawrence?" she asked.

"Yes! Oh dear, I don't know how to tell him."

"Just tell him you can't invest at the moment. He must appreciate that it's a big ask. Do you want me to stay while you talk to him?"

Caroline nodded, as she answered the call and put it on speaker. "Hi, Lawrence."

"Hi, love. You, OK? Have you had a think about our golden opportunity? I'm meeting Javier at ten."

"Yes, I'm fine, and yes, I've had a think, but I'm sorry — I can't invest this time. I need a bit more time to look into it all. Maybe next time."

"Don't you trust my judgement? I wouldn't get you involved in anything risky. You could double your savings in six months. It really is a cracking opportunity. Are you absolutely sure?"

"Yes, I am. It's not that I don't trust your judgement, but I'm just too nervous to potentially risk my savings."

"Fair enough. I have other investors who believe in me. Never mind — your loss. I need to go and get on to them. Bye, Caroline."

"I'm sorry, Lawrence, I hope…" She didn't get to finish her sentence before the line went dead.

"Hmmm, he didn't sound too pleased," said Fiona, coming over to put her arm around Caroline.

"No, he sounded decidedly miffed! You did the right thing. He must realise that was a big ask. If he has other investors, he won't miss out, so don't worry yourself," she said, trying to comfort her.

"That's another test I've failed miserably."

"What do you mean?" asked Fiona, who wasn't pleased when she heard the story of the karaoke bar and how Caroline had felt that he had been testing her in some way. "I don't believe he took you somewhere like that and expected you to throw yourself into the spirit of the thing. I wouldn't have done it for love nor money!"

"Ah, well, maybe I'm not the woman for him. I found it hard to see what a gorgeous man like him saw in someone like me, anyway — a boring, middle-aged widow."

"Don't you dare put yourself down! He is the one who should count himself lucky. Just chill out about him and take him or leave him — that's my advice."

"You're not a fan, then?" laughed Caroline.

"Not hugely — just be careful. Let me know how things go when he gets back. Trust me, you have done the right thing to walk away from that so-called investment. Get me the name of the artist, and I will see what I can find out for you. I still have friends in lots of departments," said Fiona, giving Caroline a hug.

"Thanks, Fiona. Javier something. I can't remember the surname, but if I find out, I will let you know. Thanks for all your support," she said, opening the front door and holding Peggy back from going outside.

"Bye. See you soon. Bye, Peggy," she said, giving Peggy a pat before walking down the path like a brightly coloured rainbow.

"Bye, drive carefully," shouted Caroline from the porch, as Fiona drove off in her little sports car.

She was thankful for her kind words and encouragement, but no matter how hard she tried, it didn't stop her feeling hurt at the way Lawrence had treated her.

Chapter Twelve

It turned out that Lawrence stayed away for nearly a month. He had rung her briefly a week after she turned down the investment opportunity, but he had made no mention of it. He sounded his usual self and told her he was unavoidably detained and missed her terribly but could she do him a huge favour. Caroline wondered what was coming, so when he asked her if she could help Mandy out in the gallery on Saturday, she had been relieved that he wasn't asking her to invest again.

"Thank you so much. My other lady has caught the flu, but Mandy knows the ropes, and it probably won't be busy anyway, until I get back. I've taken all the best pieces to Chelsea — better chance to sell them there before Christmas," he said, when she agreed to help.

Now Caroline had just had one more week to work at the museum until it closed at the end of the season. Christmas was just over a week away, and she still wasn't sure what she was doing. She usually spent the festive season between her two sons and their families, travelling hundreds of miles, but it was worth it to see the excitement on the children's faces and spend time with them all, albeit in two separate households.

Her sister, Elizabeth, had called her to catch up after her time away on the cruise. She was very surprised when Caroline said she didn't know what she was doing for the festive season.

"What do you mean? You always go to the boys," she said, sounding exasperated with her younger sister. "Promise me you won't stay down there on your own?" she said.

"I won't, I promise. I will make my mind up in the next few days. The boys won't mind, hopefully."

"Well, I don't know about that. I really don't know what you're up to. It's nothing to do with that chap you've been seeing. If it is, you are rushing things — you hardly know him. Christmas is the time for family. I will ring you again at the weekend. I have to go, there's someone at the door. Take care. Bye, dear," she said hanging up abruptly.

Caroline knew she was right. Christmas was for families, and she had no idea why she was dithering. Lawrence had told her he usually went to stay with his brother and family on the Austrian/Swiss border, but he hadn't said what he was doing this year. It didn't mean he was staying in St Mawdley; she didn't even know when he was coming back. She needed to get a grip and make up her mind and do what she wanted to do, just like he did when he flew off to Miami. Maybe she was overthinking their relationship, but he was the one who kept saying he was besotted with her.

Now he was back in London, attending his exhibition at his friend, Julien's, upmarket gallery in Chelsea. He had sent Caroline a link to the exhibition, and she was very impressed. She had even posted it on Facebook, so that her friends could see how talented he was.

When he had called her to explain about the delay in getting back, he had sounded very tired, blaming jet lag, although she could hear the clink of glasses and sound of laughter in the background, so he wasn't that tired. He did say that he missed her and looked forward to seeing her very soon.

Caroline certainly missed him, but she felt a little bit taken for granted. It was almost like he was dangling some kind of emotional carrot to keep her hooked, only to snatch it away when it suited him. She was beginning to get annoyed with herself for being so dependent on his company, telling herself to have some self-respect, but she knew that if he came back and took her in his arms, telling her how much she bedazzled him, her resolve would slip away like a fog in the sun.

She needed to toughen up and take her mind of Lawrence, so when the museum asked her to help out for the last day of the Giacometti exhibition, she had been glad to have the extra shift as a distraction to help fill her time until Lawrence came back in a few days' time.

The car park was filling up already, as she arrived on the Saturday morning. It was going to be a very busy day.

Fiona was just parking her little sports car, so Caroline waited for her.

"Hello, dear, ready for action?" she asked, as Fiona joined her on the path.

"Yeah, I am. I love it when it's busy like this. I'm going to miss the buzz of this place when we close down for the duration, but it will give me time to spend on my pots," she said, walking briskly along.

"Did you get that kiln you were after?" asked Caroline.

"Yes, it's all set up in the garage. I can't wait to start firing, but I'm very nervous of it. What are you going to do over the recess? Have you heard from Lawrence? He has been away a long time."

"He rang me from London when he got back from Miami. He is exhibiting at a friend's gallery in Chelsea. I posted a link on Facebook — did you see it?"

"Yes, I did — very fancy. Did he say anything about the 'investment'? she asked, making inverted commas in the air.

"No, he didn't mention it. Anyway, what are you doing at Christmas?"

"Nothing much, but I will go up to London to see Henry and his girlfriend, sometime over the holidays. I miss my boy," she said, just as they reached the staffroom.

The noise was deafening as everybody gathered, ready for the briefing, before they would all go their separate ways to the different galleries.

As they all guessed, it was a very, very busy last day. Hundreds of visitors came for their last chance to see Giacometti before the exhibition closed, who knew when he would be exhibited again in Cornwall.

Caroline was just coming back from her lunch when Octavia on reception called her over. "A very dishy gent was asking for you earlier. I didn't realise you were at lunch and sent him up to Giacometti. Is that OK?"

Caroline was delighted. "That's Lawrence, he must have got back early. Thanks, Tavie, I'll go straight up."

However, she made a detour to the ladies' cloakroom to fix her hair and apply more lipstick. She was so excited to be seeing him and glad he had come out to see her. She hoped he had missed her as much as she missed him.

She arrived up in the gallery which was heaving with people.

Her colleague, Alfie, nodded to her as she came in. "Someone was looking for you. I think he went into Gallery Two."

"Thanks, Alfie, I'll be back in a jiffy," she said, leaving her folder on the chair and hurrying over to the adjacent gallery.

She looked around, trying to pick him out amongst the crowd of visitors, but she couldn't see him anywhere. She had decided to go back and wait by the door when she felt a tap on her shoulder. She spun round with a beaming smile but got the shock of her life when she saw Freddie standing in front of her.

"Hello, Caroline. Were you expecting someone else?" he said, bumping into her as someone pushed past.

"Freddie! What are you doing here?" she exclaimed, her eyes growing wide in disbelief.

"Just passing... Come to see you, of course," he grinned at her.

"How did you know I was here?"

"I put two and two together and tracked you down. Facebook is a wonderful source of information. You posted a link a few weeks ago about this exhibition. I am over to spend the Christmas holidays with Alison and the family, but I thought I would take a trip down to Cornwall for a couple of days. I am sorry if I have shocked you."

"Well, it is a bit of a shock. I don't know what to say," she replied, still looking stunned.

"Are you free for dinner tonight?" He asked, his eyes full of mischief.

"Dinner? I'm not sure. Where are you staying, by the way?" she asked, hardly believing this was happening.

"An Airbnb near St Mawdley — Honeysuckle Cottage," he replied, slightly amused by her reaction.

"Martha and Jack's place? It's just up the road from me. Listen, Freddie, I'm supposed to be working, but I get a break at 3 o'clock. Have a look around the exhibition and meet me in the cafe at three. We can discuss it then, OK?"

"OK, see you there. You look well, by the way," he said, touching her arm gently.

"You, too. See you later. Enjoy…" she said, waving her hand around at the works of art, as she almost ran out of the gallery, eager to escape and regain some composure.

She felt very guilty just leaving him high and dry like that, but she was supposed to be working, and she still hadn't recovered from the shock of seeing him there. If it hadn't been so busy, she would have tried to excuse herself for half an hour, but she couldn't leave Alfie to deal with all these visitors on his own. Freddie would just have to entertain himself for a couple of hours.

Freddie watched her walk away. *She took that better than I thought,* he said to himself. He realised it had been a very impulsive, reckless thing to do, but the idea had come to him on Eurostar, while he was checking something out on the internet — something he felt Caroline should know. He had intended to try and meet up with her sometime over the next couple of weeks anyway, while he was back in England, but he had decided on the train that he needed to see her as soon as possible.

So, when he had arrived in London, instead of heading for CastleAvon, he had boarded the train for Plymouth and picked up a hire car from the station, calling his daughter to tell her he had been delayed. Finding a B & B had been easy, but it was pure luck that it was so close to Caroline.

The long train-journey had also given him time to read the letter that he had stuffed in his pocket as he hurriedly left his apartment that morning. It was from Francois. He hadn't seen her all week, and she hadn't returned his calls. He had intended to go round to see her before he left, but he wasn't sure he could be bothered any more. She knew he was leaving for England, and she could have called him, so he decided to leave her alone. Her mood swings were so unpredictable, he wasn't sure he cared enough to cope with them. He was quite curious, though, as to why she had written to him. As he read it, he was surprised but then also relieved.

'*Mon Cherie Armour,*

Forgive me for writing you like this, but I won't have time to see you before you leave for England.

I have exciting news!!!! The producer who came to opening night has offered me a leading role in his new film to be shot in Marseille next year. I am to play the part of a successful international lawyer in a murder mystery. Is it not wonderful? I am so excited!! It is my dream, as you know. I will be leaving for Marseille after the show finishes in the new year, so I won't be here when you get back.

But my darling Frederic, I think the time has come for us to take different paths. I must follow my dream, and you must follow what your heart tells you. I have loved you, but I know your heart does not belong to me. I will miss you, but the time has come to say au revoir.

Take care of yourself. Find happiness and wish me well.

Francois X'

Freddie felt the letter still in his pocket. He had been quite saddened when he read it. It was always sad when a relationship didn't work out, even if it had been such a volatile relationship as this one had been, but the writing had been on the wall for the last few weeks — it had just taken one of them to make the break. He had always known that she would put her career before him. He was happy for her, but deep down he always knew she was not the woman for him.

He looked around at the crowded gallery, wondering what had brought him here. Were the Fates weaving out their plan for him? He picked up a leaflet from a box on the wall and turned his attention to the story of Giacometti, until it was three o'clock and he could meet with Caroline. He walked back through the gallery, and for some reason, he felt very pleased with himself.

Chapter Thirteen

Caroline came down to the cafe at three o'clock to see Freddie sitting and waiting for her. She had got the shock of her life when she saw him earlier in the gallery — she had been so sure it was Lawrence. But here was Freddie in Cornwall — what was she to do after he had come all this way? She looked across at him, as he stood up and reached forward to kiss her on the cheek.

"I'm sorry to have given you such a shock. I hadn't really planned it until I was on board Eurostar. You know how impulsive I can be," he said, smiling at her.

She sat down opposite him, hardly believing her eyes.

"Shall I get you a cup of hot, sweet tea for the shock?" he asked.

She laughed. "A stiff brandy, more like, but they don't sell alcohol in the café."

Freddie went up to the counter and ordered two teas and some cake. Caroline watched him. He looked very well. His hair was a little longer than it had been in CastleAvon, little silver curls touching the collar of his navy-blue coat. He had shaved off his beard too, looking even more like the Freddie she had known all those years ago, except for the laughter lines around his eyes.

He sat back down and put his coat over the back of the chair, revealing a pale-green sweater underneath, which matched the colour of his eyes. The waitress brought over a pot of tea and cake and set it down on the table. Caroline poured the tea, adding milk. Freddie offered the sugar, smiling mischievously at her.

"No, I don't need the sugar, thank you," she said, smiling. "But I could do with an explanation."

"Well, it's a long story, and I don't think we have time to go into it here. So, will you come out to dinner with me?" he asked with a gentle smile, taking her hand in his.

Caroline looked at him, her heart softening at the closeness of him.

"I don't suppose there is any harm in meeting an old friend for dinner. 'Friends forever' we said in CastleAvon, didn't we?"

"We did indeed," he agreed, smiling at her.

"Why don't you come to my cottage? It will be more private, but don't tell Martha at the B & B where you are going — she is a terrible gossip."

"Thank you. I understand. I will be discreet."

"Discreet? Sitting here in the cafe with you will be the talk of the staffroom by half past three," she laughed. "Anyway, it is nice to see you. I just wish you had messaged me beforehand."

"Yes, I should have done. I will next time," he said, smiling at her.

She glanced over at the clock above the service counter, realising her tea break was nearly over. "Listen, I'm sorry to rush off, but I only get a fifteen-minute break, so I need to get back. I will see you this evening. Here is my address. Just follow the lane off the main road, half a mile down the hill from where you are staying, signposted 'To the Beach'. Butterfly Cottage is the thatched one on the right. See you at seven?" she said, scribbling down the details and handing them to him.

"Perfect. Can I bring anything? A bottle of wine? What do you like?"

"I'm easy, whatever you prefer. I will pick up something from the deli on the way home. You OK with vegetarian?"

"Yeah, that's fine," he said, standing up to kiss her on the cheek. "See you later."

"Bye," she said, giving him a little wave.

Just then, Fiona walked past, doing a double take. Caroline hurried on, back to the gallery, before Fiona could ask any awkward questions.

Fiona was settled in the Chinese Collection when Caroline's mystery man walked in, smiling at her as he picked up an information leaflet and started to look around. The gallery was quiet now. Most of the afternoon visitors had made their way up to Giacometti. He was studying a Chinese, bronze, ancient artefact, referring back to the leaflet and studying again the exquisite detail on the small, bronze wine vessel.

He looked over at Fiona. "This is incredible, isn't it?"

Fiona came over beside him. "Remarkable. It's over three thousand years old and very, very rare. Do you see the little owl face on the front there?" she said, pointing through the glass case.

Freddie bent closer. "Oh my, it's beautiful. It must be worth a fortune!"

Fiona nodded — they never discussed the value of the objects or paintings. "It is, indeed. We are very lucky to have it," she said, standing back.

Freddie carried on browsing. Fiona thought he seemed a lovely man and very good-looking. Nicer than Lawrence. This guy seemed kinder, especially his eyes. He was looking at a small, bronze bird in the display cabinet and called over to Fiona.

"What on earth is this for? I can't seem to find it in the leaflet," he said.

Fiona came back over to him. "Ahh... our little bird. It was a symbol of respect in ancient China, presented to a man when he reached the esteemed age of seventy. It would be placed on the top of his walking stick, and people were expected to bow and pay him respect when they would meet him out walking."

Freddie grinned at her. "I would like one of those when I reach seventy — not enough respect for your elders, these days."

Fiona laughed. "Well, you have a while to go yet."

Freddie carried on looking around, seeming to be fascinated with the collection. As he was leaving the gallery, he turned to her. "Thank you for your input — that was very helpful. It's a wonderful collection. I live in Paris, and I haven't seen as good a collection of Chinese bronzes there," he said, turning to go.

Fiona smiled, and then the penny dropped when he mentioned Paris — he was Caroline's old boyfriend. She walked over to him. "Are you Freddie, Caroline's friend? I saw you in the cafe earlier. I'm Fiona, a good friend of hers."

Freddie broke into a smile that reached to his eyes. "Yes, I'm Freddie. Nice to meet you, Fiona," he said, shaking her hand.

"Lovely to meet you, too. Are you over for the holidays?" she asked.

"Yes, over to spend time with my daughter and her family for Christmas, but I took a little detour down here to catch up with Caroline," he replied.

"Well, she will be finished soon, so not long to wait. Have a nice evening, and enjoy your time with your family," she said.

Freddie smiled that warm smile again. "I hope so. Thank you, Fiona," he said, and left.

Fiona watched him walk over to the lift. He looked a little sad. She wondered what was going on. She remembered Caroline telling her that she had met up with him a couple of months ago, after over forty years. He was really nice, nicer than that Lawrence. Fiona didn't trust him — she knew his type too well. He reminded her too much of her— ex-husband.

She watched Freddie step into the lift before she walked silently on the polished oak floor back through the now-empty gallery. It was the best part of the day when the gallery staff had time and peace to enjoy the beautiful grand space to themselves. She stopped to look out through the tall Georgian windows, down towards the lake, with the sun beginning to set, casting a rosy glow on the rippling water. She caught a glimpse of Freddie walking down the drive towards the car park, his long coat billowing out in the breeze, looking very pensive.

Caroline was hurrying off at the end of her shift, quickly waving goodbye to her colleagues in the staff room and telling them she would see them at the Christmas party. Fiona caught her eye and gave her a wink, but Caroline rushed out the door, blowing her a kiss. She knew Fiona was curious about Freddie, but she needed to get to the delicatessen before it closed.

"Hey! Wait a minute," called Fiona, running down the corridor to catch up with her.

Caroline turned around. "I'm in a rush, Fiona, I need to get to the shop before it closes."

"OK, OK. I won't hold you up. I can walk just as fast as you, and you can tell me all about your mystery visitor as we go," said Fiona, linking arms with her as they reached the main entrance and set off at a very brisk pace towards the car park. "I was talking to him earlier, up in the Chinese collection. He seems very nice. When he said he was from Paris, I put two and two together, after seeing you abandon the poor chap in the café," said Fiona, giving Caroline a playful nudge.

"I didn't abandon him... Well, I suppose I did, but I was on duty up in Giacometti; I couldn't stay and chat. Anyway, he was the one who dropped in out of the blue — he gave me a terrible shock!" she said.

"He seems very nice and very good-looking, too. Got lovely eyes. So, tell me — what's going on?"

"Stop it, Fiona. He's just an old friend. Nothing is going on. He just happens to be in Cornwall and dropped by to say hello," said Caroline, trying to sound casual.

"Well, must be keen if he came all this way. So, why are you rushing to get to the shops? Is he coming to dinner?" she asked, getting frustrated at Caroline for not telling her more.

"He is, actually. I could hardly not ask him round when he came all this way, and he's only staying up the road from me, at Martha's B & B," said Caroline, as they reached the car park.

"That's handy. Well, I think he's very nice. When does Lawrence get back?" she asked, unlocking her car.

"Tomorrow. Listen, it's just dinner with an old friend — it's no big deal," said Caroline, looking at her watch. "But if I don't get a move on, there will be nothing to eat for dinner. Bye, Fiona, see you at the Christmas party," she said, getting into her Mini.

"Have fun! Be good!" shouted Fiona, as Caroline sped off out of the car park.

Caroline arrived home just after five thirty, with a lovely vegetable lasagne, salad and a delicious cheesecake. She went through to tidy up the sitting room and light the fire, before going up to shower and get changed.

She was still in a state of shock. She couldn't believe Freddie Harrison was coming to have dinner with her. A couple of months ago she would have been over the moon at the idea, but now she wasn't so sure. So much had changed in her life since that time in Warwick, and it was all due to Lawrence.

Chapter Fourteen

Caroline was up in her bedroom, getting dressed. She had decided to wear a dress for a change and put on a knee-length, navy-blue, velvet cocktail dress. It had a pretty heart-shaped neckline, and she felt good in it. It would give her the confidence to deal with Freddie. She was sitting at her dressing table, brushing her hair and piling it into a chignon, when her phone rang. She hoped it wasn't Freddie chickening out. She was delighted when she saw it was Lawrence. "Hi, how are you?" she asked.

"Exhausted. It's been a hectic day. Listen, my love, I'm not going to be back tomorrow. Something has come up, and I need to stay on for a few more days, but I'll be back by the end of the week," he said, raising his voice slightly over the background noise.

"Oh, that's disappointing. So, will you make it back in time to go to the Christmas party at the mansion with me? You do remember, don't you?" she asked.

"Oh, sorry, I completely forgot about that. No, I won't be back. It can't be helped, I'm afraid," he said.

Caroline could hear him inhaling smoke from a cigarette. He never smoked in front of her, but she was aware that he did occasionally. He said it relieved stress.

"Oh, that is a shame. I was looking forward to showing you off, but I understand. Business is business," she said, feeling very deflated.

"Absolutely — can't be helped. How are you? Have a good day?" he asked.

"Yes, it was busy — last weekend of Giacometti," she replied.

She was about to tell him about Freddie when he cut in. "Well, you can put your feet up now, for a while. Sorry, dear, but I have to go. I will ring you tomorrow. Take care and have a good rest this evening. Bye, love," he said, hanging up.

Caroline looked at the blank screen on her phone. *'Put your feet up and have a good rest'. I'm not a geriatric,* she thought, chucking her phone onto the bed in a temper, feeling very annoyed with him for forgetting about the Christmas party. She had told everyone she was bringing him. *Damn it. Damn him!*

She put her lipstick on and checked herself in the full-length mirror. *You don't look too bad at all, for a geriatric,* she thought, as she smoothed the hugging-figure dress down over her slim hips and went downstairs.

She had just put the lasagne in the Aga when she heard a knock on the front door. She checked herself in the hall mirror, before opening the door to find Freddie standing there with a huge bunch of flowers, a bottle of wine and her all-time favourite chocolates.

"Good evening," he said, handing her the flowers before kissing her on both cheeks.

"Wow, these are fantastic, thank you so much," she said, noticing the strong perfume of the flowers, mixed with the unmistakable male fragrance of Chanel Bleu coming from Freddie. "Welcome, come in. Let me take your coat. So, you found me without any trouble?" she asked, taking his coat.

"Yes. I must admit that I checked it out in daylight on my way back to the B & B this afternoon, so I knew the way. I walked down so that I could have a drop of this," he said, setting a bottle of Malbec on the hall table, along with the chocolates.

"My favourites, thank you. Come through to the sitting room," she said, hanging up his coat in the hall cupboard and quickly setting the flowers in the kitchen. She thought how smart he looked in a blue, checked shirt, navy cords and a pale-blue, cashmere sweater. He looked very handsome indeed.

The fire was blazing in the grate, warming the sitting room up. Freddie made his way over to it to warm his hands. "Forgot my gloves. It's cold out there," he said, smiling at her. "You look lovely, Caroline. That dress suits you."

Caroline found herself blushing. "Thank you. What can I get you to drink?" she said, going over to the walnut, Art Deco drinks cabinet.

"A scotch would be nice, thanks," he said, sitting down by the fire. "This is a very pretty cottage. How far is it to the sea? I thought I could hear it as I walked down the lane?" he said, accepting a crystal, whisky tumbler with a very generous amount of scotch.

"Not far at all. I discovered the cottage as I was trying to find the beach. In the winter, when the trees have lost their leaves, I can see the cliffs. I will show you later, if there's a good moon," she said, sitting on the sofa, also with a generous scotch.

They chatted comfortably, sipping their drinks. Caroline told him about moving to Cornwall and her work at the gallery and how much she enjoyed it.

"I met your friend Fiona this afternoon. I was looking round the amazing bronze collection after you left. She was very informative. Is that what you do?" he asked.

"Yes, she told me she had met you. And yes, that's what I do too. We are there for guidance and information if requested, not like the old idea of a museum gallery guide that sits in a chair nodding off or bombarding visitors with details they don't want. It's a great job. I started as a volunteer, and now I work two days a week. But we close down now for conservation cleaning, till March, so I am a lady of leisure again," she said, finishing her drink which had helped her relax in this most bizarre situation.

"Good job I came when I did then, or I would have missed it all. More importantly, I would have missed you," he said, smiling over at her and taking a last sip of the whisky.

"Another whisky?"

"No, that was a good Scotch, but I will stick with the wine now, or else I might be like an old museum guide and nod off!"

Caroline laughed and got up to poke the fire with an iron.

Freddie reached forward and took her hand. "I can't believe I am here. It seems the Fates were looking kindly on me. If I had left it till next week to come, I may not have found you."

"I can't believe it, either. You gave me the shock of my life, standing there in the gallery. Anyway, I'm glad you did. It's good to see you again but let me know next time!" she said.

Freddie reached for her hand and kissed the back of it. "I will. It's so good to see you, too," he said, looking up at her.

Caroline bent down and kissed him on the cheek. "Dear Freddie, always impetuous," she said.

He pulled her closer and kissed her tenderly on the lips. "I'm sorry, I shouldn't have done that. It's the Scotch," he said, totally embarrassed and bewildered by his actions.

Caroline stood back, touching his cheek and smiling. "I'm going to check on the lasagne. Why don't you open the wine? There's a corkscrew and glasses in the cabinet. I won't be a minute," she said, going through to the kitchen where she leant on the work bench, taking slow, deep breaths.

Her legs had turned to jelly, and she had butterflies doing somersaults in her tummy. Freddie had always given her those feelings, and he still did. It was a long time since a simple kiss had had that effect on her. Not even Lawrence had made her feel like that. *What is happening to me?* she thought, turning to look at herself in the reflection of the window, feeling very perplexed and needing a few moments to compose herself.

She picked up the already beautifully arranged bouquet of flowers and dropped them into a vase of water, standing back and admiring them on the kitchen table, which she had already laid with an Irish linen tablecloth, silver cutlery and crystal glasses. It all looked lovely and not too romantic. There were no candles. She hadn't wanted to give Freddie the wrong idea, but she wasn't so sure now. Anyway, she was pleased she had made the effort. She checked the lasagne in the oven, judging it would be another fifteen minutes, and composed herself before she went back into Freddie.

Over dinner at the kitchen table, they chatted about their lives.

Freddie told her he was working on an anthology of his poetry. "Some going back decades, I may add."

Caroline raised an eyebrow at that, remembering the poems he had written for her.

"Yes, there is one from our time together, although I have tweaked it quite a bit. I think I have improved over the years, but I have kept nearly everything I have ever written, so this anthology is going to be quite a tome," he said proudly.

"That's very exciting. I'm so glad you are able to concentrate on your writing," she said, pouring some more wine.

"Well, having free accommodation helps. My aunt and uncle wanted to keep the Paris apartment in the family, in case they ever decided to come back from New York. But they love it there — near to their son and daughter and their families — so I doubt they will return. I will cross that bridge if and when I come to it. For the time being, I am happy where I am. I have a house in CastleAvon that I rent out, so that gives me some income to fall back on if my writing doesn't pay the bills. So far, so good."

"And what about your lady friend?" she asked.

"Francois and I have decided to go our separate ways. Well, actually she decided, but it's for the best. We were really not suited to each other. I was very fond of her but not in love with her. I wish her well and have no doubt she will be a movie star one day, even though the opportunity came late in her career."

"That's life, isn't it? It can be a bit of a rollercoaster, and you never know what's coming round the bend. Can I help you to some more lasagne?" she asked, seeing his empty plate.

"No thank you, that was delicious."

"I can't take the credit — it was from the local deli. Would you like some cheesecake?" she asked, clearing the plates and stacking them by the dishwasher.

"Yes, I have a very sweet tooth, if you remember," he said.

"I do. Still take loads of sugar in your coffee?" she asked, setting the cheesecake on the table.

"Afraid so. That looks superb. Is that the deli too?" he asked, as Caroline nodded, handing him a piece on a plate.

"So, that's enough about me. What about you and this chap I saw you with in a Facebook post?"

"Lawrence? We have just been seeing each other for a few weeks, but we became very close when I sprained my ankle and was laid up for a week. He was a real trooper, so very kind and attentive. We have become more than friends recently. He is good fun to be with and always planning things to do. He is just back from the Miami Art Festival, and now he is in London this week, exhibiting at a friend's gallery."

"So, you didn't go to Miami with him? Or London? If you were my woman, I wouldn't have left you behind," he said seriously.

"No, not really my scene. I love art, but not that side of it. More cheesecake?" she asked, smarting slightly at his remark.

"No thank you, that was delicious. I saw the link to the London Gallery on your Facebook newsfeed. One can learn a lot from Facebook. It can be useful or very damaging — you always need to be careful," he said, looking directly at her.

Caroline wondered what he meant by that. Had she posted something on Facebook that she shouldn't have? "What do you mean? By the way, you still haven't told me why you needed to see me again?"

"A couple of reasons. One: after we met in CastleAvon, I couldn't stop thinking about you. I guess I needed to know if it was just nostalgia for an innocent first love, or was it something more than that?"

"So, what do you think now?" she asked.

"Too early to say," he said, grinning that cheeky grin that she remembered so well.

Chapter Fifteen

Caroline cleared the plates and got up to make coffee. "What's the other reason?" she asked, her back to him. When he didn't answer, she turned round.

He looked very serious. "Sit down; leave the coffee for now. There is something I need to tell you, perhaps I shouldn't have done what I did but I was worried about you."

Caroline sat back down, feeling nervous.

"What have you done Freddie/" she asked, her heart pounding.

"It is to do with Facebook. Remember I said one needs to be careful what is listed on there? I had my suspicions about your Mr Wainwright."

Caroline nodded.

"When I looked at the link you had posted on Facebook, about his exhibition in London, I saw some photographs that I may have misinterpreted, but I'm not so sure I did."

"What photographs?"

"On another link attached to that Chelsea Gallery Facebook page, there was a photograph of a preview party. I thought I recognized your friend from the selfie you had posted. I am quite sure it was him." He hesitated.

"Can you show me?" she asked nervously.

Freddie took his phone out of his pocket. "Maybe I am wrong. You tell me," he said, handing her his phone showing a picture of a packed nightclub, scantily-clothed girls pole dancing in the background, men sitting at tables, girls sitting on their laps, and there, in the corner of the photograph, just in shot, was Lawrence with a young, Asian girl on his lap, her arms around his neck, kissing him, one of his hands discreetly resting on her thigh.

Caroline set the phone on the table as though it had scorched her. "When was this taken? Can you tell?" she asked, her voice breaking.

"Two weeks ago, at a Soho nightclub. I'm sorry, Caroline," he said, putting his phone back in his pocket.

"That can't be right. He was in Miami two weeks ago. There must be some explanation. Maybe it's someone who looks like him?" she asked, desperately hoping it was true.

"Does he have a twin brother?

"He has a brother, but he lives in Switzerland. I think he's a politician, and he's not a twin. I've seen pictures of him — he looks nothing like Lawrence."

"It's a bit of a coincidence that someone who is the spitting image of your chap is also at a gallery staff-party," said Freddie, raising an eyebrow.

"So he was in London, not Miami! He told me a downright lie — why? What a fool I've been," she said, feeling devastated and betrayed, as a tear rolled down her cheek.

Freddie got up and came round beside her, taking her in his arms as she sobbed her heart out. "I am so sorry you had to find out like this and that it was me who had to tell you. You do not deserve this. If I get my hands on him, I will punch those perfect, white teeth of his to the back of his long, elegant throat," he said, holding her tightly.

"I'm glad it was you who told me. You are one of my oldest, dearest friends. I just can't believe how gullible I have been. I very nearly invested a large sum of money with him!" she said when she stopped crying, but she was still shaking as she told him about the art-investment opportunity.

"What? Oh, Caroline, thank God you didn't! If you ask me, he is not only a philanderer but possibly a conman too, and you deserve better than that. You were very vulnerable to men like him, with their suave and sophistication. I bet he drives a flashy car?"

Caroline looked up into his sweet, kind face, nodding her head. "Yeah, a very expensive, vintage Jag, which I admit impressed me, I'm ashamed to say."

"You have nothing to be ashamed of. He is the one who took advantage of you," he said, kissing her on the forehead.

A little later, sitting side by side on the sofa and clutching glasses of brandy, Caroline began to calm down and was no longer shaking.

"Oh, Freddie, what am I going to do? Do you really think he could be a conman? Why did he make up a story about staying on in Miami?"

"I don't know the answer to that. Maybe he was genuine about the painting — I don't know," he said, shrugging his shoulders. "But it's not unusual for conmen to create this sort of jet-set lifestyle, offering an investment opportunity to vulnerable women they have only just met. At least you didn't meet him online, so you know where to find him and have it out with him. Or you can just take yourself off to your family for Christmas, enjoy your time with them and deal with him when you get back. He doesn't deserve any explanation from you. He will probably guess he has been rumbled anyway, if you don't take his calls, and then he will move on to his next victim," he said, as Caroline burst into tears.

"Oh, I'm sorry, I shouldn't have said that. I'm just so enraged by him. Come on, take another sip of brandy," he said, hugging her tighter.

"I came this close to falling for that investment," she said, pinching her fingers together. "It was Fiona who told me to back away. Thank God she did!"

"She sounds like a good friend. I liked her when I met her. Come on now, no more tears — he's not worth it," he said, wiping a tear away with his thumb.

They sat together until the fire began to die and Caroline's tears had dried. Freddie tilted her head up towards him and kissed her on the forehead. "You said you would show me the cliffs from your garden. It's a full moon — shall we go and take a look?"

"OK. We will need our coats," she said, standing up and going out to the hall cupboard.

When they were wrapped up, she led Freddie out though the stable door, from the kitchen onto the patio. They could hear the waves crashing as the tide came in. An owl hooted in the woods, just as a cloud cleared the biggest, brightest moon, it's light beaming onto the garden as though they had switched on a light.

"Wow!" said Freddie, looking through the trees, towards the cliffs. "What a view, and just look at those stars! I don't get night skies like this in Paris. It takes your breath away!"

"I know. I often come out here and stare up at the heavens. I used to be quite content to do things like that."

"The stars are always there when you need them," he said, putting his arm around her and holding her tight, as they stood in silence in awe, the sky turned red with flames of colour.

"Thank you, Freddie, for being so kind," she said, looking up at him, as he lowered his lips to hers and tenderly kissed her.

"That wasn't the whisky, this time. I have wanted to do that again, all evening," he said, kissing her again, and this time she kissed him back. She remembered how he had kissed her all those years ago — it was exactly the same.

When they went back inside, Caroline put some music on and sat down beside Freddie on the sofa, leaning up against him, his arm around her, watching the flames in the fire, the way they used to do as teenagers. When the music ended and the fire died out, Freddie got up to leave. He had offered to stay and sleep on the sofa, but Caroline insisted she was OK and needed to be alone to try and sort her head out.

"I will call you in the morning, and maybe we can go for a walk on that beach of yours," he said, as he put his coat on.

"That would be lovely. Let's talk in the morning. I hope you sleep well. Thank you, Freddie," she said, as he kissed her cheek.

"Try and get a good night's sleep, and you will feel stronger in the morning. Goodnight, Caroline," he said, as he set off down the path, the moonlight guiding his way.

Caroline did her best to sleep, but her mind just wouldn't switch off. She tossed and turned in her bed. *How could I have been such a fool to think Lawrence seriously cared for me?* she asked herself. The feeling of betrayal was sickening.

She wondered what he was doing at this very moment. Was he with that girl from the nightclub, or maybe with a different escort in his bed tonight? She wondered how many women in St Mawdley had fallen victim to his charms and his 'investment opportunities'. Maybe she was a laughingstock.

Freddie had said that Lawrence sounded like a serial philanderer. Lawrence had admitted to her that he had had many affairs when he was married, but he had implied that it was payback for his wife cheating. She would like to hear his ex-wife's version of that story.

She stared out of her window at the stars. Freddie was right — they always seemed to appear when you really needed them.

Her thoughts turned to Freddie. It had been a lovely evening until he broke that awful news. She was so comfortable with him — their values were so similar. They had history, and he was a genuinely kind man.

When he had kissed her, the decades had fallen away, and she had felt like a teenager again, but then she remembered that Lawrence had made her feel young again. She knew now that it wasn't the same. There was no deep feeling of love. It was infatuation on her part, and entertainment and possible financial gain for him.

Chapter Sixteen

She woke early the next morning, the sun just beginning to rise. It was going to be a nice day, she thought, and then she remembered about Lawrence, and tears sprung to her eyes. Last night she had laid awake, her mind awash with a million thoughts. She had been shocked and numb when she found out. Now she felt crushed by what he had done and sick in the pit of her stomach, wondering who he was waking up besides, torturing herself with wondering what they were doing. She lay there, just looking out of the window, the branches of the trees swaying gently across the brightening sky.

Thank God Freddie had seen that Soho photograph and warned her. Imagine if she had told her family about Lawrence, introduced him to her sons or invested in that 'painting', which probably didn't exist.

It was bad enough that her Facebook friends had seen her with him, smiling and happy, laughing together at the camera. She reached for her phone and opened up Facebook. She looked at that photograph taken outside the Tate Gallery, one last time, and she quickly deleted it.

If only it was as easy to delete him from her mind, which is what she knew she had to do.

She was shaken from her thoughts by her phone ringing. *Oh lord, what am I going to say to him?* Then she saw it wasn't Lawrence. She sighed with relief and answered the call.

"Good morning, Caroline, it's Freddie. How are you? How did you sleep?"

"Oh, hello, Freddie. Not too bad. I drifted off eventually."

"Good, I'm glad to hear that. It's a lovely day. Do you fancy a walk on the beach?"

"Yes, that would be nice; blow the cobwebs away."

"Great. I'll be round in an hour — is that OK?"

"That's fine, come when you're ready."

Freddie set the phone down on the table after he hung up. He thought she sounded OK. A bit subdued, but no wonder after the shock of seeing that photograph and trying to process the awful betrayal. He wished he could take the pain away for her, but it would take time. He thanked the gods that he had done his detective work on that bastard, while he was on the train. He had been curious. There had just been something about him that he didn't like when he had seen the selfie of him with Caroline, and it hadn't just been jealously. He knew his type, and he knew he wasn't Caroline's type, but he had also been shocked when he had stumbled on the Soho picture.

"Everything all right, Dr Harrison?" asked Martha, coming over to his table. "More toast, coffee?"

"No, thank you. That was a lovely breakfast," he said, patting his stomach, as Martha cleared his plate away.

"My pleasure. Lovely day. Off somewhere nice later?"

"A good walk to blow away the cobwebs, and then I'm not quite sure."

"Well, your room is available if you decide to stay — just let me know."

"Thank you. I'll settle up for last night and give you a call if my plans change."

"That's absolutely fine. Not busy at this time of year," she said, going back through to her kitchen.

What a lovely man, she thought, wondering what his story was. She knew he wasn't a medical doctor; he had told her he was a writer. Maybe he was here doing research for a book. She got a few novelists staying here when they needed inspiration from the Cornish coast. She hoped he would come back for another night.

A little later, he packed his stuff in the hire car and drove round to Caroline's cottage. It really was a lovely spot, and he looked forward to getting down to the beach and the sea.

Caroline opened the door, looking bright and fresh. Her hair was hanging loosely in soft curls, touching her shoulders, just like it always had, except now it was streaked with silver, from the passing years. She looked lovely, and he could feel his heart beat a little faster.

"You look properly attired for the beach," she said, noticing his wellies and wax jacket.

"My 'grandpapa' gear — never come over without it," he said, kicking off his boots to step inside.

"Coffee? Have you had breakfast?" she asked, going through to the kitchen.

"Coffee would be great. I've just had a very tasty, enormous full English, but her coffee was not so good."

"Oh God, no pressure on me then. Hope mine is up to scratch," she said, filling a battered, old percolator with ground coffee.

"Perfect! Those make the best coffee," he said, when he saw the old aluminium pot. He sat down at the table, looking out of the window. "What a gorgeous garden. Didn't appreciate last night how long it is."

"It's what made me buy the cottage. I'm not really a gardener, so I keep it simple. It's my contribution to the wildlife — well, that's my excuse for the untidy borders."

"It's perfect. I sometimes miss a garden to relax in, much as I love my balcony. So, how are you this morning?" he asked, as she sat down opposite him, waiting for the coffee.

"Battered, foolish and feeling like an idiot," she said, shrugging her shoulders.

"Battered I understand, but you are no idiot. Men like him leave a trail of misery behind them and just carry on with their lives. So, you have to put him out of your mind and carry on with your life," he said, reaching out to touch her hand and squeezing it gently.

"I know. I woke up feeling sick the moment I thought of him. I'm not going to do that again."

"Good girl. Give yourself time and space, and don't give him another thought."

"Easier said than done, but I will give it a damn good try," she said, getting up to lift the coffee off the hob and grabbing a couple of mugs from the shelf.

"Smells good. I can't function without a decent coffee, first thing."

"Me too. Oh, I nearly forgot the sugar for you!" she said, getting up again, to fetch the sugar bowl from the cupboard.

"So, what are your plans for Christmas?" he asked, scooping two big spoonsful of brown sugar into his cup.

"I will ring the boys today and check their arrangements and then spend the week travelling between them. I enjoy dipping in and out of their lives — a bit like Mary Poppins," she laughed.

"Nice to see you laugh. That sounds like a good plan. I'm no Mary Poppins, but I am enjoying spoiling the grandkids when I see them."

They sat contentedly, talking about their grandchildren and sharing pictures from their phones. Caroline began to relax and enjoy his company again, but she couldn't help seeing images of Lawrence in her mind.

She knew she needed to get out and let the sea and the beach work their magic.

"Are you ready for that walk?" she asked when she saw he had finished his coffee.

"Can't wait; dying to see your beach," he said, getting up and going through to the hall to grab his coat and wellies.

Caroline took her old coat down from the rack by the back door and pulled on her boots. "We will go out this way," she said, opening the stable door.

Freddie zipped up his coat. "Right-ho, I'm ready — let's go."

They walked down through the garden to a rickety gate at the bottom, which opened into the woods. A path led through the trees. A little robin was hopping about, looking for a snack. It cocked its head at them, looking at them with its clear, bright, beady little eye, as if to say, 'How dare you disturb me?' Caroline remembered her mother quoting an old saying: 'Robins appear when a loved one is near.'

Minutes later they came to the golden sands of St Mawdley Bay, the waves crashing onto the shore.

"Oh my God, this is breathtaking," said Freddie, climbing down the sand dune and holding his face up to the sky and the wind.

Caroline watched him, knowing he was feeling the way she had the first time she had run down onto the hard, firm sand.

"You are so lucky to have this at the bottom of your garden. I bet you never tire of stepping out here," he said, taking deep breaths of the fresh sea air.

"Never. It always lifts my spirits, no matter how low I get. This place has been my saviour many times. Bert and Edna fought to save the wood for years, from a holiday developer who wanted to turn it into a caravan park. Thank God they won in the end, and now it's a nature reserve in the care of the Woodland Trust," she said, smiling at him.

"Well done to Bert and Edna. It takes real determination to stand up to big developers and thank goodness they did — it must be a real haven for wildlife. Come on, take my hand. Let's walk, and you can show me more of this secret bay," he said, as she came over to him, putting her hand in his.

They walked for miles along the sand. If the tide had not been fully in, they could have walked into St Mawdley. When they reached the bend in the bay, they stood together, looking over at the harbour in the distance. With Freddie's arm around her, Caroline relaxed, the wind blowing in her hair, and all her troubles seemed to fade away.

After a while, they headed back to the cottage, meeting Bert and Edna on the way. When Caroline saw them in the distance, her heart sank. How was she going to explain Freddie?

"What's the matter?" he asked when he felt her slow her pace. "Don't you like anyone else on your beach?"

He grinned when he saw a huge dog bounding towards them.

"They're my neighbours. They are going to wonder what I'm up to, holding hands with another man," she said, just as Peggy came crashing into them, skidding on the sand, her whole-body wriggling in delight at seeing Caroline. "And this is Peggy," she said, bending down and ruffling her thick black-and-tan coat.

"What a gorgeous girl you are," said Freddie, kneeling down beside the adorable dog and patting her, just as Bert and Edna came up to them.

"Peggy! Come here, girl. Sorry about that, Caroline. She saw you and took off — you know how much she loves you," said Bert, stroking Peggy when she came and sat obediently at his side.

"No problem, Bert, I love her too. By the way, this is Freddie, one of my oldest, dearest friends from way back. Freddie, this is Bert and Edna, my newest, dearest friends and neighbours," she said, introducing them, as Freddie shook their hands.

"Pleased to meet you, Freddie. Are you here for a few days?" asked Bert.

"Not sure yet," he answered cautiously.

"Well, if you stay on, come round to us for an early Christmas tipple. We would love to hear what Caroline got up to in the old days," said Edna, looking at Caroline and giving her a wink.

"Thank you," said Freddie, calling Peggy over to him. "She really is a magnificent dog, and so strong!" he said, as Peggy leant all her weight against him, in order to get an even better rubdown and cuddle.

"Aye, she's a grand dog. Keeps us active, that's for sure. Mind you, she's as much at home at Caroline's — it's her second home now," said Edna, grinning at Caroline.

"You know I love to have her — she's great company," said Caroline, stroking Peggy.

"Well, come on, girl, let's get on with our walk and let these folk get back," said Bert, calling Peggy over as he linked arms with Edna.

"Bye, hope to see you again, Freddie," said Edna, hugging in close to her husband as they strode off, following Peggy who had taken off to run into the waves.

"He looks a nice chap — more Caroline's type, I would say," said Edna, speaking into Bert's good ear as they walked away.

"They're old friends, Edna, for goodness' sake. Stop your matchmaking."

Edna gave Bert a playful nudge. "Old friends I have no doubt, but more like old loves. Did you notice the way he held her hand? Fingers intertwined — that's the way we used to walk before we had to link arms to prop each other up," she laughed. "Oh, I hope he stays on for a bit; give that Lawrence fella a run for his money. I'm not keen on him — too bloody suave, for my liking."

Bert looked over at his wife, raising his eyes to the skies. "You are incorrigible, Edna Butterworth!" he said, picking up the pace just as Peggy ran over to them, shaking her coat dry and covering them in wet sand. "Oh, Peggy!" said Bert, laughing, picking up a stick and throwing it as far as he could for Peggy to fetch.

By the time they got back to the cottage, Freddie and Caroline were both tired and hungry.

"I haven't walked that far on a beach for years. Anytime I go to the beach with the grandkids, it's buckets, spades and sandcastles. I enjoyed that, but I'm hungry. May I take you out to lunch?" asked Freddie, flopping down on the kitchen chair as Caroline hung up their coats.

"I enjoyed it too. Nice to have company. The pubs will all be busy with Sunday lunches. I have some of my homemade soup in the fridge — would you like that?" She asked.

"Homemade, eh? Not from the deli? Well, I will have to try that," he said, leaning back in the chair, watching her as she got the soup from the fridge and poured it into a pan on the hob. "Can I help?" he asked.

"You can get the bread from the cupboard and some bowls," she said, stirring the soup and pointing to the appropriate cupboards.

The two of them busied themselves getting lunch, constantly apologising as they bumped into each other in the small kitchen. Freddie set the bowls and spoons on the table, as well as a couple of glasses of water.

"These are lovely bowls," he said, looking at the vibrant colours and swirling design.

"My friend Fiona made those — you met her in the gallery. It's a hobby of hers, which is fast becoming a little business. Lots of the craft shops stock her pots and bowls," she said, pouring the soup, the steam rising.

"They are gorgeous — very Cornish. This soup smells wonderful," he said, testing the temperature with a small sip. "Tastes good too!"

Caroline cut some bread from the large granary cobb loaf, leaving a pile stacked on the breadboard. "Help yourself to bread. This is very much my staple diet in the winter. I hate cooking for myself, so this is easy for a couple of nights' suppers," she said, just as her phone rang. "Damn thing, excuse me a minute," she said, going over to the coat rack to get her phone out of her coat pocket. "Oh no!" she said, looking at the screen. "Lawrence!"

Freddie looked up at her, as she stood ashen faced by the edge of the table. "Don't answer it. Ignore it and sit down to your soup," he said, taking her hand.

Caroline did as he said, setting the phone on the table and looking at it.

"You can block his calls it you want to," said Freddie, when he saw the look of worry on her face.

"I will have to speak to him sometime, but not yet," she said, picking up her spoon.

They enjoyed their lunch together, feeling warm and replete after it.

"Let's go through to the sitting room and light the fire. I'm exhausted," Caroline said.

"I really should be getting on my way — it's a long drive up to Warwickshire."

Caroline turned to him. "You are very welcome to stay. I do have a spare room, in case you're wondering, and we have Bert and Edna's consent," she said, grinning.

Freddie smiled and pulled her in close for a hug. "Thank you. I would love to stay, but only if you let me take you out to dinner."

Caroline looked up at him. "That's a deal," she said, as he kissed her softly on the lips.

After a lovely, lazy afternoon by the fire, watching an old movie, and quick phone calls to their families to tell them their plans, they drove out to a gastropub owned by a celebrity chef, in the neighbouring village. Caroline didn't want to go to the Harbour Inn. The memories of dining there with Lawrence were too raw. Freddie had phoned ahead and booked a table, which was lucky, because when they arrived, the small car park was almost full.

"Looks busy," he said, taking her hand as they walked into the crowded restaurant.

"I don't know where all the people come from, but he does have a good reputation. We were probably lucky to get a table," she said, as the head waiter showed them to the last vacant table in the corner by the kitchen doors.

"Will you be all right there, sir, madam?" he said, handing them the menu and taking their coats.

"This is fine, thank you," said Freddie. "I think they have squeezed this table in for us. Are you OK there?" he said, grinning at her sitting under a stag's head hanging from the wall behind her.

Caroline looked up from the menu and smiled. "I am more than OK, love. Looks like we have company," she said, nodding her head towards the stag.

She looked across the table at him, his eyes twinkling in the candlelight. It was almost as if neither of them could believe they were here together. The low hum of conversation all around them, the clinking of glasses, the sound of laughter now and again — it seemed surreal.

They relaxed and chatted about everything and anything, mostly about their families and their work, enjoying the ambience of the charming 16th-century pub. The food was exquisite. Freddie had ordered boeuf bourguignon, the scent of herbs and red wine drifting across to her. She had the scallops which were incredible, simply cooked with no fussy overpowering sauces, and they both enjoyed the creme brûlée, which was divine. The celebrity chef even made an appearance at the end of the evening, wandering round the tables, hoping his guests enjoyed their meal.

By the time they got back to the cottage, they were beautifully tired, soporific, and ready to relax in front of the fire with a brandy nightcap.

Freddie pulled her close to him, as they listened to some classical guitar music. "How are you doing?" he asked, kissing the top of her head as she leaned on his shoulder.

"I'm OK, thanks to you. I don't know how I would have coped if you had not been here."

"Well, I'm glad I was, but I'm sorry I was the one to tell you."

"Thank God you did. It could so easily have gone on for months or until he got bored with me, or God forbid, drained me financially! Maybe he was already bored, and the trip to Miami and London were just excuses to get away and back to city life for a while. It was no great romance with him when I think about it. For him, I was a bit of fun, an accessory on his arm, a challenge perhaps, a soft financial touch, maybe. For me, I think it was a kind of escapism, but I can't believe how easy it was for him to manipulate and make me believe in him. After I saw you in CastleAvon, I realised how empty my life here was, and I realised how lonely it was, too. He just came along at a time when I really needed company and a bit of attention. I'm not sad. I'm hurt that I was used by a man like him, and I'm angry at myself for being such a stupid fool."

"You're no fool. Men like him think they are the centre of the universe. You need to try and forget him," he said, pulling her in for a hug.

They sat quietly, the fire embers glowing red. She lay with her head nestled in the curve of his neck, and she could feel the warmth of his skin. He shifted slightly and pulled her in closer. The music stopped, and the only sound was the crackling in the fire grate and the ticking of the mantle clock. She lifted her head and looked at him. His expression was serious.

"This reminds me of when we were teenagers in your parents' sitting room on a Saturday night after we came back from the cinema. The coal fire burning brightly, an LP on the radiogram. No brandy though, just a couple of mugs of cocoa," he said, giving her a squeeze.

"Those were the days," she said, snuggling up to him.

"They could be again, if you wanted it to," he said quietly.

Caroline straightened up. Looking into his eyes, she saw love. This man that she knew so well; he had given her comfort and reassurance in a way that only true friends could. Really knowing someone like she had really known Robert, didn't happen very often — if at all, for some people. She was lucky to have found that again in Freddie.

"I think I would like that," she said, as he cupped her face in his hands, kissing her lightly on the lips.

They lay quietly in each other's arm, the only sound the ticking of the clock. The fire had died down, and the room was getting chilly.

"I think it's time for bed," he whispered.

Caroline looked up at him and started to speak.

He put his fingers to her lips to silence her. "You need a good night's sleep, so finish off your brandy and show me where the spare room is," he said, kissing her on the forehead.

The next morning, Caroline's phone woke her from a lovely, deep sleep. She reached for it, squinting at the screen, seeing it was Lawrence. *Blimey, he's early this morning,* she thought and wondered cynically if he set a reminder to call her every morning. She disconnected the call and lay back on her pillows. Her emotions were all over the place — anger, sadness and regret; especially regret that she had fallen for his charm so easily.

It was only just dawn, the winter sun brightening the sky, with a touch of frost on the windowpane. She heard a gentle tap on her bedroom door just before Freddie's face appeared, peeping round. He was wearing a cashmere sweater over his pyjamas.

"I heard your phone ringing — was that him? Are you OK?"

Caroline sat further up in the bed and waved him over, patting the edge of the bed for him to sit on. "Yes, I didn't answer it," she said.

Just then, a text message pinged. She opened it.

'Are you OK? Been trying to ring you. X'

She showed it to Freddie.

"Hmmph! Are you going to answer that?" he asked.

"I'm going to have to speak to him one of these days," she said, setting the phone on the bed beside her, facedown.

"How are you feeling this morning?" he asked her, reaching over to give her a kiss on the cheek.

"I feel OK. A bit better, a bit stronger and a helluva lot angrier."

Freddie patted her hand. "Angrier is good, because I discovered something last night. I couldn't sleep, so I googled him. Have you never done that?"

"I hate the internet. Facebook, WhatsApp and texting are my limits. I never browse. Anyway, what did you find?" she asked, not sure she really wanted to know but knowing she needed to.

"I checked out the website for his business — he sells stuff online. Did you know he did nudes?"

"No, he told me he did mostly seascapes, rarely did portraits."

"Well, they're not portraits as such, mostly reclining nudes." Freddie wasn't sure he should have told her; she looked stunned. "I'm sorry, but you needed to know what sort of man he really is. He's not just someone who needs women in his life all the time. I would say he's obsessed with women."

"My God. Show me the pictures. You're right, I need to see what I'm dealing with."

Freddie got up and went to fetch his phone. "Are you sure? You can just take my word for it," he said, when he came back and sat down on the bed.

Caroline nodded, as he opened his phone and showed her a screenful of pictures. Scrolling down, he came to the nudes reclining on the red, velvet sofa she remembered seeing in his studio. She wasn't that shocked by the art. Artists paint nudes all the time, and she thought they were quite well painted until she saw a face, she thought she recognized.

"My God, it's little Mandy!" she said, as she zoomed in on the face. "It really is her. I can't believe it — she's only sixteen. She works in the gallery for him on Saturdays. She's such a sweet girl. The b*****d! Taking advantage of a lovely, young girl like that." Caroline felt as though a wrecking ball had hit her. She handed the phone back to Freddie, as tears welled up in her eyes.

He looked at the picture of the young girl and sadly shook his head. Caroline buried her head in her hands and sobbed. Freddie took her in his arms, holding her tightly, rocking her back and forth. After a while, she wiped away her tears and sniffed, sitting up.

"I'm going to need some tech help from you," she said, picking up her phone. She had a stronger sense of herself and more self-confidence than she had had for a long time.

"Sure, what do you want me to do?" he asked, pleased to see she had moved into a more fighting spirit.

"I'm going to send him a WhatsApp with a couple of photos — the Soho one and the one of Mandy, but only her face! I doubt they will need any explanation. The only message will be that I know he lied to me about staying in Miami and the painting of Mandy must be destroyed, or I shall go to the police, and he must never contact me again!"

Freddie kissed her on the cheek. "Good girl, that's the spirit. He will get the message loud and clear, but I'm not sure he shouldn't be reported for underage soliciting. Some of those other girls might be only kids too."

"Well, let's start with this. I will speak to Mandy this week before he comes back. The gallery is closed, but I have her home number. Right, let's do this," she said, wriggling herself into a better position.

After they had sent the message with the photographs, they lay back against the pillows, wondering how long it would take him to respond. Freddie had his arm around her, looking out of the window. A few minutes later, Caroline's phone pinged with a message.

'I can explain. I will be back on Thursday. Let's do dinner at Tommy's. X'

Caroline could not believe it. "What on earth does he take me for? Does he think a fancy dinner in a fancy restaurant can smooth this over? He is unbelievable."

She texted him back: 'Don't even try to explain. The photos speak for themselves. I want nothing to do with you, and I'm speaking to Mandy's mother, so you better start looking for another assistant.'

Freddie pulled her back down, and they lay in each other's arms. A few minutes later, the phone pinged again.

'For God's sake, Caroline, don't be so uptight, and do *not* do anything you will regret. I will see you and deal with this when I get back.'

They were sitting in the kitchen a little later, clutching mugs of coffee and staring out at the garden, when they heard a knock on the front door.

"Hello, dear," said Edna, when Caroline opened the door, standing back for her to come in. "I won't come in, dear, my boots are muddy. We saw Freddie's car was still here, so would you like to come over for a sherry this evening, about six o'clock?"

"That would be lovely. He's going up to his daughter in the morning. Thank you, we will see you later," she said, as Edna waved goodbye and went down the path.

"Did you hear that, Freddie? I accepted for us — is that OK?" she asked, going into the kitchen where he was starting to make scrambled eggs.

"Fine, that will be nice. They seem a lovely couple. This is nearly ready. Will you butter the toast while I serve up?"

Their last day together flew by. Another long walk on the beach in the afternoon and then drinks with Bert and Edna. Caroline told them that she wouldn't be seeing Lawrence any more, and if they could keep an eye on the house while she was away, in case he came out, she would appreciate it.

Bert was concerned for her. "Nothing to worry about, Bert, but he just wasn't the man I thought he was. He didn't take me ending it in a very gentlemanly way. I doubt he will show his face here again, but I'm just letting you know that he is not welcome."

Edna was sitting beside her and patted her on the knee. "I didn't think he was right for you, my dear, but Bert and I were just so pleased to see you getting out and having fun. Anyway, you have lovely Freddie now," she said, smiling.

Freddie got on famously with them. Bert in particular was interested in Freddie's poetry. Bert had been Head of English at the local grammar school and was passionate about books and poetry, so he took great pride in showing off his collection of the classics. Freddie was impressed by some of his first editions.

Edna insisted they stay on for dinner. "I have a big pot of stew, so there's plenty to go round. Anyway, I want to hear more about your life in Paris, Freddie — a city I love. Bert and I had our honeymoon there; a wonderful city — so romantic," she said, giving Bert a cheeky wink.

It was late by the time they got back, feeling slightly tipsy after having gotten through a couple of bottles of wine, followed by very strong Irish coffee. The fire had gone out in the sitting room.

"It's chilly in here; I didn't think we would be away so long. Shall I light it again, or are you tired?" she asked.

Freddie took her in his arms to warm her up. "I'm quite tired, and I have a long drive tomorrow. I should probably go to bed, but I don't want to be apart from you," he said, hugging her tight.

Caroline looked up at him, shivering. "Well, we either light the fire or go to bed. It's too cold down here — the heating has gone off. Let's get a couple of large brandies and take them up to bed."

A little later, Freddie knocked on her bedroom door and came in wearing his pyjamas. "Room service," he said, holding two large, crystal, brandy goblets and the bottle of brandy. "Not sure what you meant by large ones," he said, setting the bottle and glasses on the bedside table and sitting on the edge of the bed beside her. He leaned over and kissed her gently. "I don't think we need the brandy to keep us warm," he said, holding her tightly as he pulled back the duvet and climbed in beside her. He reached over and switched off the lamp, just as a moonbeam shone brightly through the window onto the bed.

They woke up early the next morning, grinning at each other. Freddie stroked her face with his finger. "Morning, my love. I love waking up next to you."

A small tear trickled down her cheek. He wiped it away. "Don't cry. I know why you are sad. I'm sad too. We have only just found each other again, and now we have to part."

Caroline moved closer to him, resting her head on his chest. "I know. We can't let our families down, but I don't want you to go."

Freddie stroked her back, running his finger slowly up and down her spine, thinking. "Maybe it's time we did what we want to do. Is there any reason why we could not do a road trip and visit them all — together? It would be a bit of a surprise for them, but I think it would be a happy surprise."

Caroline leaned on her elbow, looking up at him. "Really? I suppose our kids have surprised us in a multitude of ways down the years. Maybe it is our turn now. But are you sure? We can't go blasting our way into their homes if we aren't sure about us," she said, wondering if they could really do it.

Freddie took her face in his hands. "I'm sure, are you?"

Caroline reached up and kissed him. "I'm sure, too. Let's be brave together and see if we can get it right this time," she said, as he rolled over, taking her in his arms and kissing her tenderly.

Chapter Seventeen

The next couple of days flew by in a flash. Freddie had helped her get the outdoor Christmas lights down from the loft and took great delight in draping them along the bare branches of the cherry tree by the driveway. Bert usually did it for her, but after the burglary, she hadn't felt in the mood and hadn't asked him this year. But Freddie had commented on the lack of festive decorations, apart from the holly wreath and the potted Norway spruce at the front door. She had told him then about the outdoor lights, and before she knew it, he was getting the stepladder to go up into the loft.

Bert and Edna were delighted when they walked past that evening, and Peggy barked loudly when she saw the coloured bulbs hanging from the cherry tree.

"We thought you weren't going to bother this year — so glad to see you did," said Edna, when she saw Freddie and Caroline standing on the porch beside the brightly lit Norway spruce, admiring Freddie's handiwork.

"It's thanks to Freddie. Even though we won't be here, it will be nice to have them welcome us back when we return," said Caroline, snuggling into Freddie.

"They look lovely, dear. We must be on our way now, but we will see you before you go," smiled Edna, waving as they carried on with their walk.

"Did you hear that, Bert? They must be going away together for Christmas. Isn't that wonderful?" said Edna quietly, when they were further down the lane.

"It is indeed, but let's not jump to conclusions. Caroline will tell us when she's ready."

Later that evening, Freddie and Caroline rang their families and explained they would each be bringing a plus one for Christmas. The initial reaction was surprise, naturally, but also curiosity. Caroline explained to her sons that Freddie was a very old friend that she had reconnected with and that he would be staying in a nearby hotel, while she stayed with them as usual, so there was no need for them to worry about accommodating him. Freddie told his daughter the same thing, which greatly allayed their worries about sleeping arrangements. Both Freddie and Caroline felt that that was the best way for everyone, especially the grandchildren, to get used to the idea and for them all to get to know each other. It had cost them a small fortune to get hotel accommodation over Christmas, but both agreed it was worth it.

Caroline was anxious to get away before Lawrence got back, but she didn't want to miss the Christmas party/dinner dance at the mansion and hoped Freddie would be happy to go with her.

"Of course, I would love to come and meet all your friends, but I have only casual clothes with me. Is it a black-tie event?" he asked when she mentioned it the next morning over breakfast.

"It will be very mixed. I imagine some of the directors will be formal, but my colleagues usually go smart-casual, although the girls like to take the opportunity to dress up."

"That's OK then. I look forward to it," he said, reaching across the table to take her hand in his.

"Great! I will ring Fiona and tell her that you are coming with me. She can let the others know. I don't want any confusion when we arrive."

"Good idea, and after you call her, let's go for a nice, long walk. Maybe we can pick up Peggy on the way?"

"My idea of a perfect day!" she said, taking his hand to her lips to kiss.

The next evening, they arrived by taxi at the mansion, which was bedecked with a row of small, twinkling Christmas trees standing along the pillared portico at the entrance to the grand salon, where the party was being held. Dazzling chandeliers, an enormous Christmas tree and tables laid with crisp, white linen, sparkling glasses and shining silverware created an atmosphere of a bygone era. There was a string quartet playing quietly in front of a dance floor, which was where many of the staff were currently mingling.

As Caroline and Freddie walked in, Fiona came over to greet them, wearing incredibly high heels and looking absolutely stunning in a Chinese-style, red, silk, fitted dress with a Mandarin collar and her long, blonde hair tied back in a huge, black, velvet bow.

"Hi, you two, I saw you coming up the drive. We have a table over in the back corner. It's a bit quieter there, so we can have a bit of a chat," she said, kissing Caroline on the cheek. "You look lovely, Caroline. What a fabulous colour — very retro fifties — I love it!" she said, admiring Caroline's electric-blue, knee-length dress with a heart-shaped halter neck, a belted waist and a full swing skirt.

"Thank you, you are too! Fiona, I know you have already met Freddie, but allow me to properly introduce him."

"Hi, Freddie, lovely to see you again," she said, as Freddie reached over to kiss her on both cheeks.

"Hello again, Fiona, lovely to see you," said Freddie, as he took Caroline's hand and followed Fiona over to the table where Tom, his wife Harriet, and Philip and his wife Patricia, were in conversation with a very refined, distinguished, older-looking gentleman.

"Caroline, Freddie, let me introduce you to Charles. He's my plus one," said Fiona, winking at Caroline and taking Charles by the arm to introduce him.

"Good evening, pleasure to meet you. I've heard a lot about you, Caroline," he said, in a deep, velvety voice, taking her hand to kiss it and then turning to Freddie to shake his hand firmly.

"Lovely to meet you, Charles. I must say, though, that Fiona has kept you a bit of a secret."

"Oh, she takes me out and dusts me off every now and again. We live next door to one another," he said, looking fondly at Fiona.

When all the introductions were over, they settled themselves at the table. Everyone got on very well and the interest in Freddie was high, but Caroline was delighted to see her best friends taking so warmly to him. Tom and Philip gave her a discreet thumbs up from the other side of the table, which meant a lot to her.

After the exquisite meal and amusing speeches from their principal patron and the chief executive, to thank them all for their hard work over the last successful year, it was time for the sixties' band to start playing and get everyone up on the dance floor. Tom and Philip were quick off the mark to take their wives onto the floor for the first of many jives, which was great entertainment, especially for the younger staff members who watched in awe at their expert moves. It wasn't long before they had everyone doing their best to join in, and as usual, they were the life and soul of the party.

Caroline watched Fiona dancing with Charles and looked forward to hearing more about her mystery man, when they had a chance to get together in the new year. It was obvious that Charles was absolutely besotted with her, but all Fiona had said when they went to the cloakroom earlier was that he was a very dear friend. Caroline thought they made a very attractive couple. He was tall and well built, with a thick head of collar-length, wavy, silver hair swept back off his handsome face. He had a real twinkle in his eye and was so very charming. He had told Freddie earlier that he was a retired sea captain. He was definitely the most dashing Captain Birdseye that Caroline had ever met.

But Caroline only had eyes for Freddie as they danced the night away, and at the end of the splendid evening, it was time for the last dance which got everyone onto the floor. Freddie took Caroline in his arms as the band started the famous intro to Neil Diamond's hit 'Sweet Caroline'.

"You didn't request that, did you?" she asked him, as he grinned at her.

"I might have done," he laughed, as the music played, building into the iconic crescendo.

"Oh, Freddie!" she said, just as he took her hands in his and pulled her in close, while everyone joined in the chorus with the loudest 'Bah, bah, bah!'

Chapter Eighteen

New Year's Eve

Cornwall

Caroline and Freddie arrived back at Butterfly Cottage after their whistle-stop tour of England and their families. The outdoor festive lights hanging from the cherry tree and the dazzling, white lights on the little potted Christmas tree on the porch welcomed them back, as they pulled into the driveway.

They had spent a couple of days with each family, and although they were only flying visits, it had given them all the chance to get to know each other. It had snowed just enough for them to have fun with the grandchildren, but not enough to disrupt their travelling. They had built snowmen, had snowball fights and even went ice skating. Caroline's grandchildren had loved Freddie, and Freddie's grandchildren had loved Caroline, so it was a great success and a Christmas to remember. As they left, they had promised to return for longer after the New Year.

Now they were back, just the two of them, totally exhausted. They had a few days to relax before travelling over to Paris. Freddie wanted to show her the Paris he knew so well, the Paris that the tourists never saw.

Freddie brought their luggage in while Caroline put the kettle on for a cuppa.

"What about dinner? Shall I pop into St Mawdley and pick up a takeaway?" she asked, pouring the hot water into the teapot.

"Let me go," said Freddie, sitting down at the kitchen table.

"No, you have done all the driving this week. Sit down, have a cuppa, and then you can light the fire. And when I come back, we can snuggle down on the sofa, with a pizza and a bottle of wine."

Freddie pulled her onto his lap. "Are you always this bossy? Not sure I signed up for that," he said, nuzzling her neck.

"Freddie Harrison, I am not bossy. Now drink your tea and get the fire lit!" she laughed, as he started tickling her.

"Do you give in and promise no more bossy boots?" he said, tickling her even harder.

Caroline squealed, tears rolling down her cheeks. "OK, OK, no more bossy boots."

He stopped tickling and kissed her. "I love you, Caroline. Take care, drive safely. I will have a nice, roaring fire waiting for you."

Caroline eased herself off his lap, took a slurp of tea and grabbed her car keys. "OK, won't be long. Love you," she said, grabbing her coat.

St Mawdley was heaving with people gathering for the fireworks. She managed to park in a side street and walk down towards the Italian takeaway. She foolishly hadn't rung ahead, so she had to wait for her order. She decided to walk down to the harbour to see what was going on with the New Year's celebrations, rather than hanging around outside the takeaway.

She wasn't surprised when she saw hundreds of people crowded on the front. It was popular event, attracting folks from far and wide. It was such a pretty harbour, lending itself so well to a firework display. The last time she had been was her first year in Cornwall. The crowds were bad then, but even worse tonight. She planned to surprise Freddie later, with a walk down to the beach at midnight and watch from there. The display would be tame compared to Paris celebrations but a lot more romantic to watch from the beach, just the two of them with only the stars for company.

She loved him so much. The last week had been truly special. She had been very nervous introducing him to her sons and their families, but they had taken to him immediately, especially the children. Freddie's family also had been very welcoming of her. Alison had told her she was so pleased to see her dad so happy.

Caroline couldn't believe how her life had changed so much in such a short time. Perhaps Freddie was right when he said the Fates had it all planned out and it was meant to be.

The pubs were all busy, people spilling out onto the terraces. She was getting jostled about and hugged by merry strangers wishing her a happy New Year. It was all too much, so she decided to walk back and wait at the takeaway.

She had just turned the corner by the bookstore, waving to Sophia and her husband, who were hanging out of their upstairs window and watching the merriment in the street below, when she felt a hand on her elbow.

"Well, well, well. Good evening, Caroline. What are you doing in town? Looking for me?" asked Lawrence, smiling down at her.

"Lawrence! No, I'm in to pick up a takeaway, actually," she said, trying to shake her arm free.

"You still mad at me? Don't be like that. I told you I could explain those photographs. They weren't what they seemed, honestly, especially that one in the nightclub," he said, attempting to kiss her.

Caroline pushed him away. "Don't take me for a complete fool. You lied to me! Lord knows I was stupid enough to trust you in the first place. Let go of my arm, please," she shouted, trying to compete with the noise from the crowd.

"Awh, Caroline, come on. Come and have a drink with me. We are having a party in the Harbour Inn. It's New Year's Eve, for Christ's sake. Don't be such an old stick in the mud," he said, steering her up the quiet lane that led to his studio, pushing her up against the wall and kissing her hard on the mouth.

Caroline could taste the alcohol on his lips, and she could see the glazed look in his eyes. She pushed him back and he staggered. "You're drunk, Lawrence. Leave me alone. I never want to see you again," she shouted, turning to go back to the harbour, but he blocked her way.

"Caroline, my dear, don't go getting all upset. Come here. Let's go up to my house and have a quiet drink if you don't want to join the party. I've missed you — let me explain. By the way, where did you go at Christmas? I came out to see you when I got back from London, but you had disappeared. That old guy Bert told me you had gone away; the silly old fart didn't look pleased to see me. What did you tell them about me?" he said, coming close to her and grabbing her hand, pulling her in to him.

Caroline was scared. She had never seen him drunk like this, and he was very strong, holding her very tight against him.

"Let me go! Or I will scream blue murder!" she shouted.

"Shut up, Caroline, for God's sake. Come on, let's go inside," he scowled, dragging her up the lane and fumbling in his pockets for his keys, as they got close to his cottage.

He opened the door while she struggled with him, but he was too strong for her to break free and he pushed her in, throwing her down on the old leather settee and locking the front door.

"Sorry, Caroline, I didn't mean to hurt you, but you were making such a bloody awful racket. Now, let's get something to drink, and you can calm down and tell me what you've been up to," he said, getting a couple of beers from his fridge and handing one to her.

"I don't drink beer. Now unlock the door and let me go, please," she said, standing up.

He pushed her back down again. "I hear you spoke to Mandy's mother about that painting. You shouldn't have done that. She's been spreading all sorts of gossip about me — even accused me of being a paedophile, for God's sake! Mandy was a very willing model — she loved it. Her mother didn't like it when I told her that," he said, smiling nastily and leaning over her, his breath stinking of beer and cigarettes.

"How could you do that — take advantage of that lovely, young girl?" she said, biting her lip.

"Don't interrupt me! I didn't take advantage of her or anyone; my models enjoy posing for me," he shouted, his face just inches from hers. "I would still like to paint you," he said more quietly, stroking her hair.

"Never!" she cried, flicking his hand away from her face.

He raised his hand as if to strike her but changed his mind. Caroline looked into his eyes, the eyes that she had found so beguiling and had captivated her for the last couple of months, but now all she saw was a cold, steely stare and a look of contempt.

"Anyway, it doesn't matter now. I'm going back to London to get away from all this provincial tittle-tattle," he said, collapsing down beside her just as her mobile rang.

She reached into her bag to retrieve it, but Lawrence took it from her and cut off the call. "We don't want to be bothered with that now, do we?" he said, talking slowly, emphasising every word and setting his beer bottle on the floor at his feet and taking her in his arms.

"Let me go, Lawrence," she said, trying to break free of him, as he grabbed her breast and started kissing her.

Her phone rang again, and this time he picked it up and threw it across the room.

"Why did you lie to me about staying in Miami, when you were actually back in London?" she asked, trying to engage him. She felt frightened by his darkening mood.

He shrugged his shoulders. "I didn't lie. If you remember, I didn't say where I was. But Caroline, dear, you are not my keeper. I don't have to tell you where I am or what I do. Being clingy is not a particularly attractive trait in a woman."

"How dare you! You were the one who made all the moves."

"Oh, Caroline, dear, you can be very naive at times. I know you led a sheltered life up in the sticks in the

Cotswolds, but you honestly didn't really think it was love, did you?"

Caroline slapped him hard across the face. He looked shocked and rubbed his cheek. Caroline could see the track of her hand.

"So, you have got a bit of spunk in you, after all. Well, in that case, come on. Let's go upstairs, or shall we just make ourselves comfortable here?" he laughed, throwing her back and holding her down. "You have teased me long enough, Caroline, I won't wait any longer," he said, leaning over her and kissing her roughly, holding her arms above her head, as she did her best to break free.

Freddie was now frantically worried, thinking Caroline had had an accident. She wasn't answering her phone. He was even more worried when he called the takeaway to see if she had been in and was told she had but that she hadn't come back for the pizza. He tried phoning her again but was cut off, and when he tried again, he heard a bang and then just muffled sounds in the background. Something was seriously wrong; he could feel it in his bones. He grabbed his car keys, running out in panic, screeching the tyres as he drove off towards town. He kept his phone line open, trying to figure out what was going on.

When he arrived on the outskirts of St Mawdley, he abandoned the car on the roadside where other cars were casually strewn about — New Year's Eve revellers, no doubt. He ran down the hill towards the harbour, where he saw the crowds gathering. The place was heaving, and he had no idea where to look for her. He asked for directions to the Italian takeaway, from a reserve policeman who was trying to control the flow of pedestrians, and when he found it, he pushed past the queue of people towards the pickup area.

The young lad behind the counter handed him the pizza. The pickup time on the ticket was over an hour ago. He left it on the counter and ran out to the street.

"Hey, you forgot your pizza!" shouted the young lad.

"You have it!" he shouted back and ran on towards the harbour.

The noise was deafening with the amount of people and street entertainers. He kept trying to listen to his phone and figure out where she could be. He was starting to panic, fearing she had been attacked in the street and couldn't reach her phone. A group of very merry young lads grabbed him by the arm, leading him into the crowd towards the bonfire on the beach.

"Happy New Year, mate!" they shouted, as he broke away.

He ran up towards the shops, shouting her name.

A young girl approached him. "You all right, mate?" she asked.

"I'm trying to find my partner — she's not answering her phone," he said, looking frantically around.

"Maybe she doesn't want to talk to you, mate — get a life!" she laughed, going back to join her rowdy friends.

Freddie ran through the crowd, knowing it would be pure luck if he spotted her. He went back up towards the shops, shouting her name.

"Hey there, you, OK?" shouted a young woman from a window over the bookstore.

"I'm looking for my partner, Caroline Reynolds. Do you know her?" he called up to her.

"Yeah, we saw her earlier on her way back up Gillimot Street," said Sophia, looking confused. She thought Caroline was going out with that Wainwright chap.

Freddie thanked her and ran towards the street she had pointed to, but he couldn't find it. It was then that the penny dropped. He thought Guillemot Street was where the Wainwright Gallery was. She must have bumped into Lawrence.

He ran back to the bookstore to ask again where Gillimot Street was, but the young couple had gone. He tried listening to his phone again, but all he could hear were muffled sounds. He looked around for someone in a hi-vis vest, to ask for directions, and spotted a woman with a collection bucket.

"Excuse me, do you know where the Wainwright Art Studio is?"

The woman looked puzzled. "Sorry, can't hear you?" she said.

Freddie repeated what he said, shouting this time.

"OK, I'm not deaf. It's up by the post-box, a little, narrow, cobbled street. Careful, or you'll miss it."

Freddie thanked her and ran off, looking for the post-box. It was quieter when he reached it, so he tried to listen again. He was getting so frustrated at not being able to hear.

He shouted into the phone, "Caroline!" He listened, and then he thought he heard her.

"Oh, bugger this, I'm too old for this caper," said Lawrence, trying to hold Caroline down as he wrestled with her on the sofa. "Come on, upstairs with you," he said, dragging her by the arm into the kitchen, as she kicked and screamed.

She tried her best to fight him off, but he was just too strong for her, and she cried in vain for Freddie.

"Whose Freddie?" he asked when he got her to the bottom of the stairs.

"A better man than you!" she screamed, just as she heard banging on the front door. "Freddie!" she shouted.

"Shut up!" he said, striking her hard across the face.

She fell backwards hitting her head on the hard flagstone floor. Lawrence stood in shock, sobering up very quickly, looking at her lifeless form, as a trickle of blood oozed from the back of her head.

Freddie had run up the cobbled street and found the gallery which was all locked up and dark. He remembered Caroline telling him that Lawrence lived next door. He went over to the half-glazed front door of the cottage beside the gallery and banged on the door. He tried to peer in, but it was dark-stained glass, and he couldn't see a thing. He banged again on the door, shouting her name, and then he heard her. He banged again before wrapping his fist in his coat and smashing the stained glass.

"Open up, or I'll break this bloody door down!" he shouted, when he saw Lawrence standing in a doorway at the back of the dark room.

A moment later, he saw Caroline lying on the floor. He stood back, lifted his foot, and with all his strength, he kicked in the door, the old frame giving way.

"What the hell do you think you are doing, breaking down my door? Who the hell are you, anyway?" shouted Lawrence. The vein in his neck was throbbing. He looked stunned as he stood beside Caroline.

Freddie saw red when he realised, she was hurt. "You are a b*****d of the first degree!" he said, storming over and landing a hard punch on Lawrence's jaw, sending him flying back and landing in his egg chair.

"What the hell…" he said, spitting his two front teeth out into his hand.

Freddie ran over to Caroline, kneeling down beside her. "What have you done?" he said, glancing back at Lawrence.

"Nothing, she just fell," he said, lying back in his chair and trying to stem the blood from his mouth.

"Ring for an ambulance, you idiot, and fetch me a rug — she's freezing cold!" shouted Freddie, as he desperately tried to feel for a pulse. "Caroline, my darling, wake up. Please, God, wake up!"

"She's not dead, is she?" asked Lawrence, as he handed him the rug from the sofa.

"Get a bloody ambulance, for God's sake!" shouted Freddie.

Lawrence looked around for his phone.

"Forget it, I'll do it!" said Freddie, as he dialled 999.

Fortunately, there was an ambulance on standby at the bottom of the town, in case of any accidents or incidents with the crowds of New Year's revellers, so it wasn't long until they heard the siren and saw the flashing lights.

"Good Lord, what happened here?" asked the paramedic, as he clambered over the broken glass from the smashed-in doorway.

"She fell and hit her head; there's blood oozing from the back of her head. I haven't moved her," said Freddie.

"What's her name?"

"Caroline," he replied quietly.

The paramedic kneeled down, feeling for a pulse, and then shouted to his mate who had just appeared at the door, with the community policeman beside him.

"Caroline, can you hear me, love?" said the paramedic, leaning close to her ear. "We will need to intubate her and get her moved as soon as we can," he said to his colleague, who had joined him in the kitchen.

Freddie looked on in horror as they worked on her. Lawrence sat in shock, as the policeman asked him his name and some details about what had happened.

"She just fell — I didn't touch her!"

"What is your relationship to her, may I ask?" said the policeman, turning to Freddie.

"She is my partner. I was going to ask her to marry me, tonight," said Freddie sombrely, just as the paramedics got her onto the stretcher to carry her out to the ambulance.

"I need to go with her," said Freddie to the policeman.

"Not before I have tried to establish what happened here. We have a critically injured woman on the floor, Mr Wainwright here has lost a couple of teeth, the house has been broken into and you look unscathed. So, name, address and occupation, please."

"Please, can't that be done at the hospital? I need to go with her," said Freddie, just as he noticed Caroline's phone lying on the floor by the fire. "That's her phone. It's been on for the last half hour. You will find out exactly what happened if you could listen to that!" said Freddie, picking up the mobile, handing it to the police officer and glaring at Lawrence.

"Let him go with her, I will tell you what happened," said Lawrence, standing up, not sure what the police could establish from the phone.

Just then, another officer appeared at the front door.

"Ahh, Paul, will you go with Dr Harrison to the hospital and take his statement? I will stay here with Mr Wainwright. Off you go, Dr Harrison, but we want a full statement," said the policeman to Freddie, just as the ambulance doors were closing.

"Thank you, Officer," he said, running out to get in the back of the ambulance beside Caroline.

"I will follow," said the second officer to the paramedic, as lights and sirens were switched on and the ambulance and police car set off for the hospital in Penzance.

The next couple of days were harrowing for Freddie. Caroline had been rushed straight to theatre as soon as she arrived at the hospital. The doctors said she had a subdural haematoma, which they needed to drain if they were to save her from serious brain damage. They told Freddie to contact her family, as the next forty-eight hours were critical.

The phone calls to Caroline's sons had been the most difficult he had ever had to make, and when David and James arrived the next afternoon, they were ashen faced. David had flown down from Manchester to Exeter, where James had picked him up as he drove the hundred and fifty miles from his home in Surrey, and with another hundred miles to go, it was no wonder they were exhausted when they arrived.

The three of them had taken turns to sit by her bedside in intensive care for the next three days, talking to her constantly, hoping she could hear them. The doctors warned them that they wouldn't know, until they woke her from the induced coma, if she would be brain damaged or if she would even survive off the ventilator.

On the fourth day, the doctors felt confident to try and rouse her. Freddie, David and James sat out in the family room next to the intensive care unit, and for the first time in his life, Freddie prayed. David and James saw the anguish on his face and knew that he truly loved their mother.

"She will make it, Freddie. She's a stubborn woman — she won't give up," said James, putting his arm across Freddie's shoulder.

Freddie patted James' hand and bowed his head. The three of them sat in silence, as they nervously waited to hear from the medical team. It was over an hour later before a doctor came out to speak to them. He looked very grave, as he brought a chair over to sit down opposite them.

"She is off the ventilator and breathing on her own, so that's a good sign."

"Thank God," said Freddie.

"But we still won't know, until she wakes up, just how much damage has been done. I'm sorry, but it's still a waiting game," he said, reaching out to pat Freddie on the knee.

"Thank you, Doctor, for everything you and the team have done. When can we go back in to see her?" asked David.

"Just one of you at a time. Why don't you take it in turns, and two of you get some sleep," he suggested.

"I'm not leaving her. You boys go back to your mother's place and get some rest. I promise I will call you the moment she shows signs of waking up."

"All right, but can we just go in together for a minute before we go?" asked David, who looked exhausted.

"Just for a minute," said the doctor, as he stood up to go back into the ward.

The three men in Caroline's life walked slowly over towards her bed. They were relieved to see there was no longer a ventilator connected to her, although there was still a drip attached to the back of her hand, but she looked peaceful as she lay between the crisp, white sheets.

David and James bent over and kissed their mother on the forehead, as tears stung their eyes. Freddie stood back and watched the two handsome, young men tower over their mother, who looked so small and frail next to them.

"Promise to ring as soon as she shows any signs of coming round. We will get some sleep and be back later," said David, pulling Freddie in close for a hug.

"I promise. Off you go," said Freddie, as he pulled up a chair and sat down beside the bed, taking Caroline's hand in his and kissing it softly.

Freddie kept the vigil up for the next two days, sharing the time with David and James. He kept talking to her, hoping she could hear him, telling her how much he loved her. Nurse Simpson stopped to check her blood pressure and change the IV fluid bag.

"Keep talking to her Dr Harrison. Patients often tell us they could remember hearing things and wondered if they had dreamt it."

Freddie smiled at the Nurse as she left to attend to another patient. He felt completely drained sitting there in this eerily quiet ward with only the sounds of machines bleeping and whirring, keeping people alive.

Finally, on the third day Freddie felt movement from Caroline's fingers as he held her hand. It was very slight, but she responded by moving her fingers again, when he spoke to her. He cried at the simple gesture and called the nurse over.

"That's a good sign — she's coming back to us," she said, as she went over to the nurses' station to report to Sister.

When the rest of the medical team came over to do some tests on her, Freddie went out to find the boys, who were sitting in the family room.

"She moved her fingers when I spoke to her. The nurse said that's a good sign that she's coming back."

"Thank God," said the boys in unison, as the three of them stood in the middle of the room, embraced in a group hug.

Chapter Nineteen

Three Weeks Later

"Are you sure you can manage, dear?" asked Edna, as she stood watching Freddie get Caroline out of the car.

"I'm fine, Edna, don't worry. All I want to do is get into my own home again," said Caroline, smiling up at her dear old friend.

"Come away, Edna, and give Freddie some room," said Bert, who was standing back and holding Peggy, who was desperate to say hello to Caroline.

"Oh, Peggy, you gorgeous girl. Bring her over, Bert. I'm steady, really, I am," said Caroline, as Bert allowed Peggy to get close for a gentle pat.

"You look well, dear, but you must continue to rest," said Edna, as Freddie took Caroline's arm to help her up the path.

"I will make sure of that, Edna, but it's not going to be easy," laughed Freddie, helping her through the front door.

"Oh, it's so good to be home," said Caroline, as she walked slowly down the hall and into the kitchen to get a look at the garden.

Bert, Edna and Freddie watched her as she touched all her familiar things, and they all felt incredibly grateful and relieved to have her back. Edna wiped away a tear when she saw the shaven gap of hair and nasty scar on the back of Caroline's head, and she silently cursed Lawrence for what he had done to her. Bert put his arm around his wife, knowing what she was thinking.

"Right-ho, we shall leave you to it. There's a nice Victoria sponge and some scones in the cupboard and clotted cream in the fridge, so you can have a nice afternoon tea when you are ready," said Edna, casting aside her dark thoughts of Lawrence.

"Oh, thank you so much. That will be lovely. I can hardly wait for a decent cup of tea," said Caroline, sitting down at the kitchen table.

"Well, I had better get the kettle on," said Freddie, as Bert and Edna left, quietly closing the door behind them.

After a fabulous cream tea in the sitting room, Caroline and Freddie rested back on the sofa, feeling very soporific. The fire was blazing away, and before long, they had both dozed off. It was Caroline who stirred first and looked over at Freddie, who was snoring softly, with his head back on the cushion. *Dear Freddie,* she thought. *He has hardly left my side for the last three weeks.* She knew he hadn't even left her bedside for the first few days. The boys had told her that they had tried to get him to come back to the cottage for some rest, but he had refused.

It had been such a difficult time for them, and she was glad that she had eventually been able to encourage David and James to get back to their families. They had been away far too long, but it was so lovely to have them with her during those days after she had woken from the coma.

She shuddered when she thought of the whole awful tale, rubbing the back of her head where the stubble itched, but at least her hair was beginning to grow again, and thankfully the rest of her thick hair managed to conceal the evidence of surgery.

She didn't really remember that much about what had happened, only what she had been told. Lawrence had admitted that they had been arguing and that he had hit her while under the influence of alcohol. She never thought for a moment that he had deliberately tried to seriously injure her. She was sure it was an accident when she fell back and hit her head on the hard flagstone floor.

The police had done a thorough investigation, and Lawrence was held in custody while she was in an induced coma. Apparently, the police tech-wizards had been able to retrieve the forty-minute phone call between her mobile and Freddie's, so that clarified exactly what Freddie had told them about trying to find her, and

Sophia at the bookshop could corroborate that she had seen him frantically searching. She had also told the police that she had seen Caroline walking in the direction of Gillimot Street.

The case against Lawrence was dropped when Caroline said she didn't want to press charges. She didn't want to get caught up in a court case and drag the whole awful saga on for months. She wanted him out of her life as soon as possible, even though everyone else thought he should do time for what he had done. But she thought that a week in custody, plus a hefty bail fee, not to mention the loss of his two perfect front teeth, had been enough to teach him a lesson. However, Fiona told her that he better not ever put a foot wrong again, or she would see to it that they lock him up and throw away the key. She had mentioned to one of her old colleagues at the Met to take a look at his website and check out his online activities, just in case.

Caroline was just grateful that Freddie had found her when he did and that the medical team had acted swiftly. She had received the very best care and rehabilitation, and she couldn't sing the praises of the NHS enough. All she had to do now was get her strength and fitness back and then get on with her life.

She reached over and kissed Freddie softly on the cheek.

"Sorry, my love, did I drop off?" he asked, sitting up and shaking his head.

"We both did — it was a lovely snooze. It's dark outside now and sounds a bit of a wild night."

"I shall go and get some more logs in and batten down the hatches. How are you feeling?" he asked, rubbing the sleep from his eyes.

"Feeling good, sitting here with you. All lovely and cosy. It's so good to be home, and I can't wait to get down to the beach."

"A few more days rest before we venture down there. Lots of rest and lots of physio — that's what the medics said, remember?"

"I remember. I really hate all those exercises, though. A good walk would do me far more good," she said, as Freddie looked at her askance. "I know, I know. I will do the damned exercises, but I still can't wait to get down the garden," she said, grinning.

"Maybe in a couple of days. I can't wait, either, to go with you."

It was the weather that kept Caroline from getting out to the beach, not Freddie. It was a wild, windy and wet start to February, so she had to content herself with looking out of the window at the garden. A week later, the stormy weather abated, and all was calm again, as a brilliant full moon shone in through the kitchen window as they ate their dinner.

"Would you like to go out for a stroll under the stars?" asked Freddie, as he cleared the plates away.

"Where's my coat? You really don't need to ask!" she said, getting up from the table before he could change his mind.

They walked down the garden towards the woods and onto the beach. The waves were crashing in, the white surf dazzling in the moonlight, the stars twinkling in the dark, midnight-blue sky. Hand in hand, they walked along the edge of the water, looking up at the stars.

"Nothing beats this. Oh, how I have missed the smell and the sound of the sea," she said, cuddling in close.

"I couldn't agree more. I am standing on a beautiful beach with the woman I love, under the stars. I love you, Caroline," he said, getting down on one knee in front of her on the sand, holding a small, red, velvet box up to her. "Will you do me the honour of becoming my wife?" he asked, opening the box to reveal an antique platinum ring set with a beautiful, single diamond sparkling in the moonlight.

"Oh, Freddie, you really are full of surprises," she said, clasping her hands together in delight and excitement. "I would love to be your wife," she said, as he took hold of her left hand, slipping the ring on her finger.

They kissed gently, tenderly and lovingly, as the heavens above them were filled with shooting stars.

THE END

EPILOGUE

A few weeks later, when Caroline felt stronger, they travelled over to Paris to spend a couple of months to decide where they wanted to set up home together. Caroline had been enraptured by the Paris that Freddie took such a delight in showing her. Everyone seemed elegant and glamourous. The women were exquisitely dressed, the men suave and sophisticated, with that famous '*je ne sais quoi*'. People-watching from the cafes on the streets of Paris was way more exciting than St Mawdley.

The Champs-Elysees, the grandeur of the Arc de Triumph, the splendour of the Place de la Concorde with the magnificent fountains and gardens, had all taken her breath away, and she understood why Freddie loved living there. She had fallen in love with the Rodin Museum and the Louvre, getting up very early to avoid the queues and crowds. She loved strolling around the antique shops on the Left Bank, admiring the work of the pavement artists. She marvelled at the exquisite gems in the elegant jewellery shops around the square at the Place Vendome.

Michelle took her shopping at places the tourists didn't go, and she found some amazing vintage designer dresses to wear when she and Freddie went out to dine in some of the fancy restaurants. But mostly they ate in the apartment, cooking together and creating wonderful meals from the fresh produce they bought every day in the local markets. They were comfortable in each other's company and respected one another profoundly.

At night, when Paris became the 'City of Lights', they wandered hand in hand along the Seine, like lovers had done for centuries, watching the reflections of the buildings on the banks shimmering in the water. They enjoyed a romantic dinner on a Batteau-Mouche, marvelling at the sparkling Eiffel Tower against the dark, night sky.

The whole city was so vibrant and alive, but they eventually decided that England was where they needed to be, near their families. Freddie knew his time as a citizen of Paris had reached its final days, but they would come back again many times in the future, for holidays. His aunt and uncle had agreed to rent the apartment to a young family that Freddie knew, who desperately needed a home, and Uncle Claude was pleased to accommodate them, setting the rent considerably under market value, to allow a young family to enjoy it and look after it.

Freddie's friends had thrown a party for them at Michelle's bar. Michelle had stretched out her hands to Caroline in welcome when Freddie introduced her, kissing her on both cheeks. Alain had made a fabulous cake in the shape of the Eiffel Tower. They were all sad to see him go, but also very happy to see him so in love with his English rose.

Francois had also arrived with Henri, the film producer. She was looking very glamorous, every inch the rising movie star. She and Henri seemed very close. She looked happy, thought Freddie, and he was pleased for her. She even managed to give Caroline a frosty kiss, but just on one cheek, Freddie noticed with amusement.

Michelle and Alain were particularly sad to see them go but promised to visit them in Cornwall. Freddie had become very fond of Alain and felt confident leaving Michelle in his loving care.

They arrived back in England as the daffodils were covering the borders of Butterfly Cottage Garden and a carpet of bluebells were covering the woodland floor. They had decided to make Cornwall their home. Freddie knew he could work there, and he planned to build a timber-framed writer's retreat at the bottom of the garden, where he could hear the sea as he worked. He had decided to keep renting out his Warwickshire home as an additional income for them, and along with his income from his writing, he felt they were both on an even financial footing.

Caroline intended to return to The Mansion Gallery as soon as she felt up to it. She knew it was important for them to have their own interests and pursuits. The honeymoon period couldn't last forever, although Freddie had questioned this. Normal life would have to resume one day, and over the last couple of months, their relationship had been tested to the hilt, but they had found a strength in each other, and they were best friends as well as lovers.

Lawrence had moved back to London, much to their relief. They had heard from Bert that after the police investigation, he had very quickly sold his studio and cottage to a developer for an exorbitant sum, and they were now being converted into a luxury holiday let. Caroline never heard from him again and wanted to put that episode with him in the back of her mind in a locked box. The hurt from the mental scars would take longer to heal than the physical scar on the back of her head. She knew she had been vulnerable, but she still berated herself for falling for his charm so easily.

Fiona's pottery business was going from strength to strength now that she had her own kiln. She supplied the gift shop at the mansion, as well as many more craft shops in the Southwest, which kept her very busy. She was considering renting a proper studio in a local Artisan Community Centre, very much encouraged by Charles, who, Caroline was pleased to hear, was becoming a bigger part in Fiona's life. But she said she would never give up her time at the mansion with her friends and colleagues. She and Charles had presented Caroline and Freddie with a beautiful, large, porcelain fruit bowl as a wedding present., The coastal, vibrant colours of blue, white and yellow was a centrepiece on the kitchen table and much admired.

They married in the Summer in the tiny, tenth-century church near St Mawdley. It was so small that it only just held their immediate families and their closest friends, but that was all Caroline and Freddie wanted.

She wore a Chanel, pale-blue, silk dress with a three-quarter-length lace coat over it. Michelle had helped her find it in a vintage haute-couture shop in Paris. Her hair was piled high on her head, with pale-blue, silk ribbons and flowers threaded through it. She wore her diamond-and-sapphire pendant and earrings, with Robert's ring now on her right hand, and Freddie's antique diamond now took its place on her left hand She felt wonderful as she walked down the aisle with her two sons on either side and all seven of their grandchildren following behind. the girls were all in ivory, organza dresses, with blue, silk flowers in their hair, the little boys laughing and giggling in sailor suits.

Freddie and his son-in-law, Ben, stood at the altar, looking very handsome in dark-blue, linen suits, white shirts and pale-blue, silk ties. Peggy sat obediently beside them, with the wedding rings tied round her neck in a blue, silk purse. Bert and Edna nervously watched, hoping she wouldn't get too excited, but they were ready to step in if she did.

The reception afterwards was in Bert and Edna's garden, which was wider than the one at Butterfly Cottage and could easily accommodate the marquee. The buffet food, supplied by the local delicatessen, was superb, and the champagne flowed as everyone relaxed and mingled. The tables were covered in white linen tablecloths decorated with the blue, red and white of the French flag and the black and white of the cross of St Piran, the Cornish flag. Michelle had supplied the champagne, and Alain had made a spectacular cake, adorned with a bride and groom, which they had brought over in their car.

It was a low-key affair, but it was perfect. Everyone was very happy, including Peggy, who was beside herself with excitement at all the people in her garden, not to mention all the tasty titbits of food that no one could resist giving her.

Caroline and Freddie stood together and watched them all. They knew how lucky they had been to be given a second chance, and they didn't intend to waste a moment of their remaining years together. They felt blessed. They wanted to seize the gift of love with both hands. It was a grown-up love they had this time, but a love that made them feel young again.

The Fates had woven their future, as they had their past. Their lives had been lived as they had meant to be. Each of them had families they adored, created in a different time, from a different love.

But now a new time had come for Caroline and Freddie, and what was left of their lifetime, they would cherish as long as they lived. Freddie took Caroline in his arms and kissed his teenage sweetheart, as their families and friends looked on. None of them could ever have imagined how this had come to be. It was amazing how destiny intervened, and life turned out as planned. It could be so very unpredictable, but love can endure and find its way, with the hand of Fate and the help of the gods.